FRAYSER

JUN 27 2013

A BRIDGE TO JUSTICE

Carol AuClair

A Bridge to Justice
Copyright © 2013 Carol AuClair
All rights reserved

Published by Next Century Publishing
www.nextcenturypublishing.com

No part of this publication may be reproduced, stored in a retrieval system, or transmitted in any form or by any means—for example, electronic, photocopy, or recording—without the prior written permission of the publisher. The only exception is brief quotations in printed reviews.

Credits: Taylor Sherrill, Photograph of Author
Original cover watercolor by Carol AuClair, Copyright © 2011

Third Edition
ISBN 978-1939268-174 (paperback)

Printed in the United States of America

To reach the author:

www.carolauclair.com

For my children, Sharon Ashenbrener and Erik Fernandez, with appreciation and love.

Acknowledgments

All creative efforts are helped immensely by the encouragement of those who appreciate the work. I want to thank my husband, Mick, for being the "first eyes" for each one of my chapters as they were written. His support and constructive comments were invaluable. The second eyes belong to my daughter, Sharon Ashenbrener, an avid reader with a keen eye for detail and a talented writer. I truly appreciate her "young thirty-something" viewpoint as well as her enthusiasm for my work.

Jon Heiden, former Tucson Police Department detective and longtime friend, was a trusted resource for parts of this book.

For his encouragement along the way I thank my son, Erik Fernandez. Among the many who offered support in special ways, I am especially grateful to Minda Burr, Chris Chesser, and Fran Parella.

Chapter 1

It had been a very long drive. Miles and miles of tall evergreens had passed Kate's car window. The overcast October sky dulled the greens somewhat but they held their beauty. A sign read "Lake Pendant 5 Miles." She was almost there. She knew that a long bridge crossed over Lake Pendant before entering the town of the same name. A restaurant and bar sat on the right side of the highway just before the bridge. She turned off the highway and pulled into the parking lot, her heart pounding. It was her thirtieth birthday and she was starting a brand new life. But first she must cross the bridge.

As she rested her head upon the steering wheel, her wavy auburn hair fell loosely around her face enclosing her in a momentary cocoon. Her panic subsided for a moment. She could begin again. She would begin again. But she was just so very tired.

After a few minutes she pulled back onto the highway and headed onto the bridge. The muscles in the back of her neck were taut; her fingers tightened on the wheel. She ignored the vast panorama of lake water that stretched out in both directions, keeping her gaze locked on the back of the car in front of her. Her breathing was shallow and rapid. "Just look at the road, not at the water," she kept reminding herself. Small beads of perspiration collected on her upper lip and her shoulders ached. Finally, she saw the brake lights of the car in front of her come on and dared to look to the side and confirm that she had reached the other shore. She was able to draw a deep breath once again.

Lake Pendant was a small lumber mill town built along the lakefront and the west bank of the Pearl River that flowed out of

Lake Pendant. The main north-south highway ran through the middle of the downtown. A mix of old businesses, restaurants, real estate offices, and specialty boutiques shared space in the century-old brick buildings that lined Main Street. Kate turned off into the residential area just south of downtown. In just a few moments she pulled into the driveway of the modest cream-colored house that had been the home of her Aunt Belle and before that, the home in which her mother and her aunt had spent their childhood. It was her home now. Belle, her mother's only sister, had recently died after a short and sudden illness. Kate was the last surviving member of the family, having lost both of her parents before she was twenty-six. This house, newly bequeathed to her, was old but had been well-cared for. A small ranch style, it would do just fine for the beginning of her new life.

Inside there was a stale, closed-up smell that seemed to mirror her heart and mind. "We will be compatible," she mused wryly to the little house. A large tea kettle sat on the stove and she filled it with fresh water and set it to boil, searching for a mug and some tea bags. She turned the thermostat to a reasonable temperature, but kept her coat on. Cold, she decided, was like loneliness, seeping into your bones and constantly reminding you of its presence. The furnace began its ticking sound and the fan came on. She welcomed the noise — a sure promise of the coming warmth.

She had put over two thousand miles between herself and her former life. She wondered if it would be enough. It had to be. Aunt Belle's death was an untimely one in all aspects but one. Kate felt guilty just thinking how well the timing of her Aunt's death had served to meet her needs. "Thanks, Aunt Belle," she said out loud as if she were still there, "I owe you one."

A night's sleep and the reappearance of the sun brought new energy to Kate. Armed with the Classifieds and a cup of strong coffee she began making calls in the hope of securing a job. With her background in nursing, she looked for openings at the hospital first but was disappointed to learn that the only position open was in pediatrics. Not an option. There didn't seem to be any private physicians looking for new employees, either. Down at the bottom of the page she noticed a small advertisement for an in-home care nurse. She frowned but circled the ad anyway. She was not interested in in-home care. It was usually very tiring work and the environment could be very bleak and unpleasant. The plain truth was she really didn't have much of a choice. The pay was not what she could make in a hospital, but she reasoned that without a rent payment she would do all right if she watched her expenses carefully. At least she could get by until a better job came along. And there was an added benefit. She wouldn't have any nosy coworkers asking her questions about where she came from. She made the call.

Beulah Wright was an eighty-five-year-old confined to a wheelchair after a stroke. Her speech was fine and her mind was sharp, but she could do little for herself as there was not much strength in her limbs, and she couldn't move her left arm and leg at all. This was all Kate knew about her new patient when she left for work the following Monday. As she followed the directions scribbled on a small piece of paper, she saw that the neighborhood was old but the homes were stately. When she found the right mail box, she turned down a long driveway winding through tall, mature, long-needled pine trees. Finally, the house came into view, large and painted white with a wrap-around porch. The doorbell was answered by the night nurse, Violet Hanes, a plump and friendly middle-aged woman.

Kate followed Violet through the foyer to the large living room and stopped abruptly with an almost audible intake of breath. A long bank of windows revealed a stunning view of Lake Pendant. She winced and turned her face away instinctively. She had not realized the house was on lakefront property.

A small and gentle voice spoke, "Is something wrong?" Quickly, Kate composed herself. She noticed the small-boned, delicate, white-haired woman sitting in a chair near the fireplace.

"No — uh sorry," Kate answered, but her face was flushed. "It's — it's just that the view is so beautiful!" She walked across the room, bent down, and extended her hand, "I'm Kate Reed. It's nice to meet you, Mrs. Wright."

"Thank you, dear, but the pleasure is mine," Beulah said. She smiled warmly at Kate. "You're tall and slim, but you have a look of strength about you. Tell me, do you think you would have trouble hoisting me in and out of this ugly wheel chair?"

"Oh, no, certainly not. I've been trained for these kinds of tasks," Kate assured her.

"Well, that's good to hear," Beulah replied. "Why don't you spend some time with Violet, so she can get on home? She will show you around and then you and I can get better acquainted." Kate followed Violet into the kitchen and Beulah turned her gaze back to the lake.

An hour later, Violet, satisfied that she had given Kate a thorough briefing, said goodbye and left, but not before she had placed the requested tray holding two porcelain cups, milk and sugar, a steaming pot of Earl Grey tea and a plate of Scotch shortbread on the coffee table in front of the fireplace.

"Now dear," Beulah said. "Tell me about yourself."

Well, there it was, Kate thought — the inevitable question. She busied herself pouring a cup of tea for Beulah. "There's not much to tell," she responded. She went on to explain about the passing of her aunt and inheriting her home. Beulah's hand shook as she took the cup but she was determined to hold it herself.

"Where did you come from then?" asked Beulah.

"East of here," Kate answered hoping that her answer would be enough.

"I see," said Beulah. There was a slight pause during which Kate felt Beulah's gaze upon her, suggesting she somehow knew there was so much more to tell.

"You won't find this job too taxing," Beulah remarked. "My family insists that I need someone here round the clock, but it seems like a lot of fuss, if you ask me." Kate could see that Beulah was still an independent woman at heart, even though her body was failing her in ways that couldn't be ignored.

"Mrs. Wright, I want you to tell me just how much you want me to do for you. I will take my cues from you."

"Well, the first thing you can do is call me Beulah," she said with a smile. "If we are going to be around each other all day, every day we might as well become friends and enjoy it!" It was hard for Kate not to respond to the warmth that this woman was exuding.

She found herself relaxing just a bit for the first time in a long while. Looking around she decided it wasn't just Beulah, but the feel of the house as well. The room where they sat was richly paneled in a warm wood. There were built-ins everywhere that one could conceivably put them; window seats with worn but cozy cushions and bookcases filled to overflowing gave an overall cozy feeling. The fire place was large and faced in brick, an intricately carved mantle framing it. It seemed that every shelf and surface that didn't have books, had framed family pictures of all sizes. This was clearly a room where families had lived, laughed and loved.

Kate noticed that a worn Bible sat on the table next to Beulah's wheelchair and she frowned. On the mantle a golden cross stood reflecting the sunlight from the windows.

Kate realized that Mrs. Wright must have noticed her staring at when she said, "That cross was purchased on a trip to Rome. It always takes me back to a very special time with my late husband. He passed away shortly after our return. It was his last gift to me."

"I'm sorry," muttered Kate. Beulah was certainly not any confused old lady, Kate realized. She was sharp as a knife's edge and didn't miss a thing.

"Oh, don't be sorry, Kate. The Lord knew when it was time for Bert to go home as he does with all of us."

Kate was silent but inside she screamed, "No! He does not know! You are so wrong about that!" The shine of the cross dimmed as a cloud passed in front of the sun. It was as if the same cloud had simultaneously passed across Kate's face.

Beulah leaned forward, "My dear, are you all right?" Kate placed her cup back upon the tray. She did not look up.

"I'm fine," she announced abruptly. "I'm going to go clear away the breakfast dishes." She got up and walked into the kitchen.

The kitchen was a large bright room done in yellow and white. White cupboards lined the walls and a wide window stood over the sink bringing the lake into this room as well. She wondered how long she could keep this job if she had to look at the lake everywhere she turned. A large, rectangular table made of oak occupied a corner of the room. The six captain's chairs surrounding it were sturdy and scuffed. She could picture them filled with children all talking at once. Yes, there had been some good living in this house. You could feel it just standing there. But the house was very quiet now, and the laughter of childhood and the voices were long gone. She didn't realize that there were tears coursing down her cheeks until she tasted the salt in her mouth. Quickly, she wiped them away with the heels of her hands. "Get a grip, Kate!" she sternly admonished herself. With an effort that was beginning to feel routine, she pushed away all thoughts and merged back into that stream where there was no feeling at all.

Chapter 2

It was Saturday morning, Kate's first day off after a week at her new job. She opened her eyes lazily and luxuriated in the knowledge that she had no place she had to be. Early morning had always been her favorite time to think. That's when her thoughts were clearest, and she let her mind wander without restraint. She wasn't particularly eager to get out from under the warm quilt and she could tell by the chill on her nose that the room was colder than she would like it. Might as well just stay put for a while.

The week had gone well and she found the job to be just as Beulah had described it — not too taxing and a lot of chit chat. She liked the old woman and found her to be a very warm person. She was not the least demanding as a patient and Kate found herself looking for things to do for her, but she seemed to make it a goal not be fussed over. Her only challenge had been getting Beulah to do the therapy for her lifeless limbs. Kate had to move Beulah's arm and leg in a pattern of different exercises, and Beulah had little patience for that. It was a daily battle but so far Kate was proving to be the winner.

It had been such a relief to have found a good job so soon. She had been more nervous about that than she cared to admit, for she knew that Lake Pendant was not a large town. She was eager to explore it a little bit today, but first she needed to pay some attention to the house. Though in good order, it needed a fresh cleaning and the pantry needed to be restocked. She had been eating her meals at Beulah's all week, and she knew there wasn't much in Aunt Belle's pantry other than flour, cake mixes, spices and cold cereal.

When she could afford it, she was going to buy a new mattress, too. Every night as she crawled into bed she immediately rolled into a depression in the center and stayed there all night. She might as well be sleeping in a hammock. Like the proverbial frog in the slow-to-boil water, Aunt Belle must have gradually gotten used to that over time.

The bedroom had nice wallpaper with a small blue floral pattern, and the furniture was a good quality maple. Small pictures hung here and there on the walls, some with little poems, the kind you might see at garage sales. They certainly weren't anything she would have chosen for herself, but at the same time, she decided that she would leave them be for now. This house and the things in it were the only connections she had left to her family, and she found unexpected comfort in them.

There wasn't much in the way of unpacking to do. All she had brought with her were her clothes, some file boxes, her high school yearbooks and a stack of photo albums. And of course, the precious box with the dog-eared Winnie-the-Pooh blanket and the one-eyed teddy bear. It was amazing to her that she had so little to call her own. But what would she have wanted to keep from her old life? When faced with that question before the drive west, only a small pile of things had earned a place in the "keep" pile.

Kate's reverie was interrupted by the doorbell. She looked at the bedside clock and was startled to see that it was already ten o'clock! Fumbling with the belt on her chenille robe, she ran to the front door, feeling the chill of the cold floor on her bare feet. Peeking through the small diamond-shaped window in the door she saw a woman about her age standing on the porch with a covered plate in her hands. "Oh great," she sighed. She hadn't planned on this. She opened the door a few inches, her hair falling wildly around her face.

A huge, way-too-cheery-for-morning smile spread across the woman's face. "Hi," she said. "I'm Dee! I live next door." She gestured to the right. "I brought you some zucchini bread and wanted to say 'Welcome'!" There didn't seem to be a choice here. Kate opened the door and Dee walked in, "Gosh, I'm sorry! I thought you'd be up by now."

Kate took the plate with the bread wrapped in colored plastic wrap and tied with a matching crinkle ribbon. "Thank you," she murmured. "I'm Kate."

"Oh, I know who you are!" Dee beamed. Kate froze for a second. She said nothing. Dee went on, "Your aunt told me about you. She always said that if anything ever happened to her, that her niece, Kate, would have her home. So, I just put two and two together. I'm real sorry about your loss. Belle was a great lady and a real good neighbor. This town is worse off without her."

"Sit down, Dee," Kate motioned toward the kitchen. "I'll put some coffee on." The truth of it was that she was grateful for the freshly baked bread. She had not been looking forward to another morning eating the same cold cereal that she didn't even like. "I look a mess," she apologized, running one hand through her hair as she turned the coffee maker on and grabbed two mugs.

"You look," said Dee, "like people *should* look on a Saturday morning!" Dee was wearing an oversized red flannel plaid shirt over a white long sleeved turtle neck shirt. She had on blue jeans and a pair of fur-lined Ugg boots. "I don't think I'd win any prizes in this outfit," she laughed as she looked down at herself.

Kate had to admit that there was something very refreshing about this surprise visitor with her short, curly blonde hair and engaging smile. She seemed very down to earth and real — qualities that had become very important to Kate. Of course that didn't necessarily mean she was. "Have you lived in this neighborhood for a long time?" she asked.

"About two years now," she said. "We kind of have something in common." Again, Kate tensed. What did this woman know about her? "Yeah," Dee continued, "That was my Grandpa's house next door and when he passed away, it came to my folks, but they have a place over in Washington, so Randy and I moved in. Randy's my husband. My mom was going to sell it at first, but when I asked if we could live in it, she said yes, if we kept up everything and took care of the utilities and paid the taxes. So it works out pretty good for us. It's a great neighborhood and so close to town we can walk it easily."

Kate relaxed a little. "I was planning to do some exploring in town today. Maybe I'll just walk then."

"Randy is over there now with our boy, Kevin. Kevin loves to go to the Farmer's Market. It's every Saturday at the park. There's a man there who sells these wonderful gooey cinnamon rolls and Kevin just loves them. He comes home all sticky every time and I have to clean him up, but what can I do? He looks forward to that all week long! I don't ever go because I would be tempted to eat them, and I don't need any extra pounds." Dee grinned.

"How old is Kevin?" Kate asked quietly.

"He's four and full of vinegar! You'll meet him soon enough. He loves people."

Kate sipped her coffee and sliced some pieces of the zucchini bread, offering them to Dee. "No thanks," Dee said. "It's for you. I made one for us too." Kate bit into a piece and found it to be delicious. One thing was for sure — Dee knew her way around a kitchen. "Well, I should really go home and let you get on with your day. I just wanted to say hi and tell you that I'm right next door, and if you need anything, I'm there."

"Thank you, Dee. I really appreciate it." She walked her to the door and waved goodbye. *I guess I'll spend the rest of my life wondering who I can and can't trust,* Kate thought.

She ended up driving after all, knowing that she would be bringing home bags of groceries. She parked in front of the bank and set off in no particular direction. It was fun to browse through the gift shops and the book store. She discovered a very nice woman's clothing store and made a mental note of a couple of things that she would come back for when she received her first pay check.

Olsen's, a department store, occupied one corner. It looked as if it catered to farming families. They offered a very large selection of blue jeans, overalls, flannel shirts and lace-up work boots. She didn't spend much time in there.

Particularly enjoyable to her was a feeling of anonymity. Alone with her thoughts, she was free to roam the streets without fear that she would run into anyone she knew. It was very freeing and she felt lighter than she had in a very long time. People smiled at her as she passed them on the street, and she found that almost intoxicating. Funny, she thought, how some things could seem so unimportant and be taken so much for granted until they suddenly disappeared from your life.

When Kate finally found Miller Park, the vendors were dismantling the Farmer's Market. The cinnamon roll man was already gone. Just as well, she thought, I don't need it any more than Dee does. There was one table still selling lettuce, and she bought a large head of it, reminding herself to come earlier next week.

Later, when she had put away her groceries, she sat down and put her feet up on the coffee table. All in all, it had been a very enjoyable day. Maybe, just maybe, she would make it here.

Chapter 3

On Sunday morning Kate walked into town. The house had seemed so quiet and she needed to hear voices, even if they were strange ones. Louisa's Café seemed like a busy enough place and Kate bought a newspaper from the box out front and went in. The place was full but she managed to find a seat at a small table for two. The clatter of cups on saucers and the hum of conversation combined with the aroma of bacon and coffee made Kate glad that she had ventured out on this blustery day.

As she looked around, she couldn't help but compare the difference between Lake Pendant and Careytown, the city in Maryland she had called home for a good part of the last five years. They seemed to be separated by more than miles. Here, there appeared to be one style of dress: relaxed. Flannel shirts, boots, and fleece jackets looked to be the norm. Careytown was definitely more sophisticated. Instead of work boots, there were Nike's. Instead of polar fleece, there was Cutter and Buck and Ralph Lauren. She had to admit that Lake Pendant wasn't devoid of style; it just had its own. She was a little surprised that she found it so appealing. No one seemed to be much interested in putting on airs here. And if they did, she doubted if anyone would care.

The waitress put her plate of eggs and ham down on the vinyl tablecloth in front of her. "Can I get you anything else?" she asked.

"No thanks," Kate said, "I'm fine for now." She stretched the front page of the Pendant Post out beside her plate and slowly ate her breakfast. She was almost done when she heard a familiar enthusiastic voice cry, "Hey, Kate!"

She looked up and saw Dee, a man, and a little boy walking toward her. What were the odds of running into one of the two people in the entire town that she knew? "Hi," she managed with a polite smile.

"Great to see you!" Dee exclaimed. "I'd like you to meet my husband, Randy, and this is our son, Kevin." Kate shook Randy's hand and was surprised to see that little Kevin held his hand up to her too. She placed her hand around Kevin's small one and shook it dutifully. He was a very handsome little fellow with dark brown hair like his father's and large brown eyes and a smile as wide as his mother's.

"Nice to meet you," she said.

"We're just back from church, and Sunday's my break from the kitchen," Dee said. "Why don't you move over and sit with us?"

"Oh, I'm pretty much done here, but thanks anyway," Kate said.

"Nonsense," Dee said. "No one needs to be sitting alone on Sunday morning! Come on and join us!" Kate watched helplessly as Dee picked up her plate and set it down at the table for four nearby. Randy pulled out the chair for her and there wasn't any other option but to sit down.

"Thank you," she murmured.

"You live next door to us!" Kevin announced.

"Yes, I do," she answered.

"I know 'cause I saw you through my window!" he said, then asked eagerly, "Do you have any boys?"

She wasn't ready for the question. Innocent as it was, it came at her like a bullet, and she sat there silently realizing with horror that tears were stinging in her eyes. She wondered if she could keep them from falling. Dee watched her for a second then said quickly, "Kevin, Kate lives by herself and I think that's enough questions. Now, do you want pancakes again or waffles today?" Kevin was easily distracted and the moment passed, but Kate felt embarrassed by her involuntary reaction. If Randy noticed he didn't let on. He was a good-looking man with a rugged outdoors feel about him and seemed pleasant but rather shy. He appeared content to let Dee do most of the talking.

Kate finished her coffee and stood up. "It was so nice to meet you Randy and Kevin" she said, "I'm sorry, but I need to go. I have lots of things to do today. Thanks again for the delicious bread, Dee." She put a ten dollar bill down next to her plate and walked toward the door.

Once outside she thought about what she had just said. She didn't have a lot of things to do today. In fact she had done all of her chores yesterday. She hated lies. It wasn't in her nature to lie, and she was dismayed to find that it came so easily. How long could she pretend that she would be able to just reinvent herself? It didn't help that she was the kind of person who wore her emotions on her face. Her mom and dad had always teased her, saying, "Don't ever play poker!"

She pulled her jacket more closely around her and walked slowly back to her house — yes, she was thinking of it finally as *her* house, not Aunt Belle's. That was progress, at least. But the ache in her heart that had sprung up again with no warning was not going away. And she knew of no way to get rid of it. It felt like a heavy stone in her pocket. If only she could just get her hands around it and throw it far away! But she had tried and always, it came back, triggered by any number of innocuous things.

Kate was relieved when Monday came and she could get back to Beulah's and have the distraction of her duties. She found that she was growing very fond of Beulah in just a short time. This gracious lady was as full of life as anyone she had seen in a wheelchair, young or old. Her limbs might not work well, but her mind was as sharp as could be, and she didn't miss much.

It was time for the dreaded exercises, and Kate prepared to move Beulah. As usual, she balked. "Now, come on Beulah. You know we have to do this," Kate said patiently.

"I don't believe in a useless expense of energy!" Beulah retorted. "This arm and this leg are not going to work again, and I seem to be the only person willing to accept that!"

"You don't know that for sure. And if you're wrong, you will have eliminated the chance to have it happen. It only makes sense to give it a chance," Kate argued, not for the first time.

"Bah humbug!" Beulah sputtered, her one good arm folded firmly across her chest. "You know, Kate, a good part of living life is accepting the truth about things and getting on with it."

Kate lifted Beulah gently and laid her down on her mattress. She held her leg and began the slow routine bending of her knee. The joint was stiff and she knew that this caused Beulah discomfort, but to her credit, she did not complain about the pain — only about the uselessness of the exercise. "You know, if the doctor didn't think it would do you good, he wouldn't be requiring this," Kate said.

"I was already forty years old when that doctor was in diapers! What does he know?" Beulah retorted. Kate chuckled in spite of trying not to. One of the things she enjoyed so much about Beulah was her feistiness.

With the unpleasantness of the exercises out of the way, and Beulah back at her favorite spot by the fireplace, Kate brought in a tray with two sandwiches and two mugs of steaming hot tea. This was her favorite time of the day as the two women from two completely different generations could sit and talk. Though she had been careful not to say much about herself, she had learned quite a bit about Beulah. For one thing, she had four grown children and ten grandchildren. None of her children lived in Lake Pendant anymore. In fact, all of them had tried unsuccessfully to get Beulah to move to their respective cities, but she had made up her mind that this was the house that she was going to live in until God saw fit to take her home.

"Why don't you want to try living in another city?" asked Kate. "It could be fun and you would have family around you."

"Because this is my home," she said, as if it was so obvious that it didn't need to be said. "Bert built this house for our family in 1953. It's a fine house and it's seen a lot of good times. There isn't a piece of it that doesn't conjure up some kind of memory. When you get to be my age, memories are important, especially the good ones, and I'm happy to say that I've been blessed with more than my share of those. When my kin want to see me, they come and are always welcome." Here she winked at Kate and said with a grin,

"That way, I'm always sure that they want me around because it's their idea!"

"Fair enough," said Kate with a chuckle.

"Speaking of," said Beulah, "My grandson, Mark, is coming tomorrow from Spokane. You'll like him. Everybody does." Hearing the word grandson, Kate envisioned a boy. "How old is he?" she asked.

"Thirty-two, not much older than you," she answered. Kate was surprised, but when she thought about Beulah's age, she realized that it only made sense. "He's Laura's boy. She's my firstborn," Beulah added. "I'm not much into favoritism, but I'd have to say that if I had them, he'd be one."

"Why is that?" Kate asked.

"Well, he's straight as a rod, for one thing. He'll look you in the eye and tell you the truth sure as the sun comes up. He's the most dependable of all of them, and he's kind, too. I keep praying that he'll find a good woman, this time one that appreciates him."

"Uh-oh, sounds like he had some bad luck," Kate said. Didn't she know all about that?

"He had just finished college down in Boise when he met a very pretty girl. Fell real hard for her. No one could talk him out of marrying Vicki even though we tried. They were married for two years, and she just about sent him to the poor house. He was just starting out and wasn't making much back then."

"What happened?"

"Mark told her she was going to have to quit spending money they didn't have, or she was going to have to get a job. So, she got a job all right. She went to work for a hotshot lawyer. Pretty soon she was working late all the time. To make a long, tawdry story short, she wanted a divorce so she could go off and marry her boss. Mark was pretty torn up, but we had all seen it coming. It was just a matter of when. She's living in a pretty fine house now and drives a fancy car, so I guess she finally got what she was truly after."

"That's really sad."

"Well, yes and no. You can't judge a book by its cover — and there it was — the hard lesson Mark needed to learn, but he learned it. He was always one to see only the good in people.

Unfortunately not everyone you meet is a good person. The only trouble is, he's gone too far the other way, and now he has a hard time trusting anyone."

Kate wanted to shout, I know exactly how he feels! but she stopped herself just in time. Just how many "walking wounded" were there anyway? No one would ever know because who went around bragging about being taken for a fool?

Chapter 4

A chilly wind blew through the tree tops in Careytown, Maryland. What few leaves that were still left on the trees gave up their tenuous hold and zigzagged to the ground. On the corner of State Street and Calhoun, one could hear strains of a hymn emanating from within the New Eden Community Church. Inside, Pastor Brent Reed stood and made his way to the pulpit as the choir finished the last verse of *Just a Closer Walk with Thee*. Nervously, he pushed his wire-rimmed glasses farther up the bridge of his nose and straightened his tie. He had been rehearsing this morning's announcement in several different ways for days and still had not come up with anything that had sounded right. But the moment was here and he had run out of time.

After delivering a short sermon, he paused and gripped the edges of the pulpit, his arms straight. He looked out and his eyes met Angie's and he relaxed a little when he saw her smile. "Dear Friends," he began, "I have some important news that I wish to share with you today. You know that the past year has been one of great difficulty for me in many ways. I appreciate so much all the support that you have so generously provided to me. But there has been one person who has helped me beyond measure." Here it was — the jumping off point, the point of no return. He hesitated and looked down for a moment, as if unsure how to proceed. The room was hushed as people waited expectantly for what he would say next.

"My secretary, Miss Angie LeCompte, is someone that has made it possible for me to continue on through some of my darkest hours. She ran things in the office when I couldn't think about anything but what I had lost. Gradually, she came to mean much more to me than a trusted employee and friend. Over time, we have forged a deeper relationship that ultimately has grown into love. Today I am happy to announce that I have asked her to be my wife."

An immediate buzz erupted in the room as the congregation reacted to the announcement. It was difficult for Brent to tell if it was a negative or positive reaction. He assumed that it might be a combination. "We plan to be married next month, right here in our church, for I consider you to be my family, and each and every one of you is welcome to attend. I hope that you are happy for us and for what God has done by bringing us together." He stepped down and the choir stood for the closing hymn. Brent took out his handkerchief and wiped his brow, relieved that this hurdle was crossed. Now he could finally consider it all behind him.

He stood at the door and the congregation filed out past him as they did every Sunday at the close of the service. But this time, Angie stood at his side. Many people shook the hands of both of them and offered congratulations, but there were several he noted that slipped past and did not make eye contact at all. He made a mental note of who they were. Maybe, it wasn't all behind him after all, he thought.

When the last person had gone, the two of them went inside. Brent said to Angie, "Well, I think that went pretty well, don't you?"

"I guess we'll never really know," she replied. "It's hard to believe that in a town this size that someone hasn't seen something. As careful as we were, you just never know."

Brent grabbed her upper arm firmly. "Shhh!" he whispered quickly. Angie pulled her arm free with a look of surprise on her face. "Brent, that hurt," she said rubbing her arm with her other hand.

"Sorry," he whispered. "But we can't say things like that around here…ever."

"Look around," she said waving her arm around the room, "There's nobody here Brent."

"Angie, I'll catch up with you later. I've got some things to put away in my office."

"Fine," she said, still smarting from his reaction. A gust of wind tossed her shoulder length blonde hair back from her face as she left through the front door. Brent continued in the other direction past the pulpit and into the hallway leading to his office. Neither one of them noticed Archie Dean, the church maintenance man, quietly emerge from the small, dark custodial room.

Angie got into her car parked in front of the church. As she pulled out and drove past the parking lot, she saw two or three little groups of people still lingering, so deep in conversation they didn't even notice her go by.

CHAPTER 5

When Kate walked into the living room after putting a batch of Brownies in the oven, she found Beulah nodding off in her wheelchair. She quietly tiptoed to the shelves next to the fireplace and studied the small frames holding family pictures. There was one that was comprised of a group that seemed to be close in age to her. She surmised that they would be some of the grandchildren. There were three men and five women, their arms comfortably around each other's shoulders, dressed in jeans and sweatshirts, smiling at the camera. She wondered which one of these, if any, was Mark, who was due to arrive any minute. It was a good-looking group she thought, though the tallest one was the most striking by far with his thick, wavy, dark brown hair and deep-set blue eyes.

The doorbell rang and Beulah sat up with a start. "Is it one o'clock already?" she asked.

"Yes, you've had a little nap," replied Kate as she made her way to the front door. She peeked through the small peephole in the door. Aha, she thought to herself. So he *was* the tall one after all.

"Hello," she greeted him as she opened the door. "I'm Kate Reed, your grandmother's care nurse."

"And I'm Mark Matson," he said as he reached forward to shake her hand. "I hear that you're doing a great job for Gram."

"She makes that very easy to do, actually."

"Yes," he replied, "She's a great lady. But nonetheless, thanks. She's got a special place in the hearts of this family."

"Come over here and give me a big hug," Beulah ordered with mock sternness. Mark crossed the room and willingly did as he was told, a big smile on his face. It was clear that he was genuinely glad to see her, not like some of the family members of patients that she had cared for, who were paying purely obligatory visits.

"What have you been up to?" Beulah asked.

"Well, I've just wrapped up a pretty lengthy case. It was tough but we managed to get the evidence that the DA needed to take it to trial."

"Good for you, Mark." Beulah looked over at Kate and said, "Mark is a detective and a darn good one, too!"

Mark shrugged his shoulders and said, "She's always been my biggest fan." Just then a timer sounded in the kitchen.

"That's the brownies," announced Kate, and she went in to pull them out of the oven.

"So, Gram," Mark said quietly, "Where did this gal come from?"

"She moved here from somewhere in the east just recently. Her aunt died and left her a house."

"What else do you know about her?" Mark asked.

"Oh, Mark, there you go again. Stop being the detective! She's a fine young woman."

"It's a crazy world out there, Gram. You can't be too careful when you give people complete access to your home."

"I haven't lived this long without developing some sort of intuition. I'm a pretty good judge of people and I know this gal comes from good stock."

"You know, Gram, there are plenty of people out there that go to a lot of trouble to make sure that people think that way about them. It's an art and they are called con artists. It doesn't hurt to do a little checking."

"Well, you'll be wasting your time, but it's yours to waste, I guess," Beulah chuckled.

Just then Kate came in with a plate of warm brownies. "I never knew a man that didn't like brownies," she said stopping in front of Mark and offering him one.

"Thanks," he said, helping himself. "So, Kate, Gram says that you just moved here. Where did you live before?"

"Back east," she said, offering Beulah a brownie.

"Where back east?" he asked.

"Oh, about a hundred miles from the ocean," she answered carefully.

"The Atlantic Ocean is pretty good-sized. What state?"

Kate was beginning to feel uncomfortable. Why did she feel like Mark was pressing her? Or maybe she reasoned, she was just becoming paranoid. "Maryland," she finally answered.

"I've done some casework in Maryland," he said. "What city?"

Kate shoved a brownie into her mouth to give herself time to think. Try as she might, she couldn't figure out a way to dodge such an obvious question.

"Careytown," she mumbled quickly.

"I do know that town," Mark exclaimed. "It's near Fisher. I had to drive through there chasing a witness down several years ago. It's really pretty country. What made you decide to move?"

Kate set the plate down on the coffee table. "Oh, enough about me," she said with a forced cheerfulness. "I'm going to let you two visit. I've got some things to wash up in the kitchen." With that she disappeared through the doorway. She leaned back against the counter with both hands resting behind her on the edge and let out a long sigh. Was this the way it was always going to be? Would she ever be allowed to have a life here without dragging the old one along with it? Angrily she filled the sink with hot sudsy water and scrubbed the bowls and the baking pan as if they were the enemy, scouring them long after they were clean.

Mark was quiet. A large part of his job was noticing the little things that most people didn't see. It was obvious to him that Kate did not want to talk about life before Lake Pendant, but why? He decided that he was going to put some effort into finding out.

"Where did you go, Mark?" Beulah asked, interrupting his thoughts.

"Oh, sorry, Gram." Mark smiled and then continued, "So tell me — what's new around Lake Pendant?"

"Not going to tell me, huh?" she teased him.

"Nothing important to tell," he said and changed the subject yet again. "What do you want for your birthday?"

"What does a woman turning 86 need anyway?" she asked. "I certainly don't need any more knickknacks! I think on every birthday all you kids should come in here and each take at least one thing out. By the time I reach one hundred the place ought to look decent again!"

Mark and Beulah sat and visited for a good long while. He always enjoyed his grandmother's wisdom and insight and the way that she could see things from her own unique point of view. Many times, she had provided him with the impetus to find new ways to solve case problems that had eluded him, and she didn't even realize that she was able to do that. It was just a very clear way of thinking that she had.

About three o'clock, Mark rose to leave. Kate had never returned. Mark thought it possible that she might have been trying to be sensitive to his time with Beulah, but his gut instinct told him otherwise. He had some work to do. He gave Beulah a warm hug. "Goodbye Gram. I'll be back soon. Stay healthy," he said as he let himself out.

Chapter 6

After she was sure that Mark had gone, Kate emerged from the kitchen. "Can I get you anything Beulah?" she asked.

"No, dear. I'm just fine. Why don't you sit down for a spell and take a little break?" Beulah enjoyed her time with Kate and she could understand why this young woman had become a nurse. It was easy to see that it was in her nature to be caring. "You know, I am very thankful that you've come my way," she said to Kate.

Kate blushed. It had been a long time since anyone had affirmed her. It felt very good, wonderful in fact, and she savored it for a moment and then said, "Thank you, Beulah. That was a kind thing to say."

"Nothing but pure truth dear; it's my language of choice," she said with a twinkle in her eye. "By the way, what did you think of my grandson?"

"Well, he's undeniably handsome," she replied. "And he seems to genuinely love you."

"Yes, he surely does. When he was just a little fellow he spent a lot of time here with Bert and me. We took him on fishing and camping trips, and there were lots of overnight visits, too. He seemed to fit right in with the two of us in a special way right from the start. And of course, he loved the lake. That's where he would always be, down there skipping rocks across the water, or jumping off the dock — anything to do with the water was fine with him. Bert took a lot of pride in how well Mark learned to sail and handle a boat, too."

Kate didn't answer. In her mind she was picturing what a cute little boy he must have been. His dark wavy hair and big blue eyes, coupled with that shy grin, was a powerful combination. These mental images brought forth sad memories. Abruptly she realized where her thoughts were going, and she shut them down immediately. She was getting better at doing that. Life seemed so much bleaker and one dimensional with this new form of discipline, but it was decidedly safer.

Beulah broke into her thoughts, asking, "Do you enjoy the water?"

"No," she answered solemnly.

"Did you not learn to swim?" she asked.

"Yes, I can swim," she answered, thinking how much she used to love it. Every summer growing up, she had collected a box full of medals in almost all of her swim team's events. She remembered how the water had been her friend, her refuge but now it was the enemy — ugly, deep, and dark. Tears formed in her eyes

Beulah leaned toward her and searched her eyes. "What happened, dear?" she asked softly.

Kate looked at her and she knew that Beulah could read the deep sadness within her. What was it about this kindly old lady that disarmed her so? The desire to let it all out was so strong, and she fought it. Beulah waited a moment and when there was no answer, she continued. "You know a burden isn't quite so heavy if you let someone else help to carry it." Beulah sat back and waited, allowing her words to find their way past the sadness.

Finally, in just above a whisper, her head down, Kate said, "There was an accident."

Beulah barely was able to hear it, but she managed. Silently she prayed that Kate would have the courage to share this burden. She said, "It's all right, dear. You can tell me."

"I…I uh," she started to speak then stopped. She found that she could not form the words. There was too much pain in them. She felt that if she uttered them that she would fall into a dark hole and never find her way out. She was gripped by what she knew had to be an irrational fear, but its grip on her was too real for any kind of reasoning to defeat it. "I'm sorry, Beulah, but I can't talk about it," she finally managed.

"I understand," Beulah said gently. "Sometimes the weight of things can get to be so heavy that they frighten us. Of course, the longer we keep them locked up in the dark, the heavier they become until we can barely move." Kate felt the heat of Beulah's truth piercing her. That's exactly what was happening to her. She was weighed down and so far removed from the carefree Kate that she had always been that she no longer recognized herself. But still, to step across that chasm and revisit that pain did not seem possible.

She looked up at Beulah and said, "I'm trying very hard to move on with my life. I can't do that if I live in the past."

"Ah, my dear," Beulah answered. "That is the catch! You can't move on with your life until you have truly dealt with the past. Pretending that the past has not happened is like living a lie. Everything that you try to build upon that false foundation will crumble eventually."

"What do you mean by 'deal with the past'?"

"I mean that when bad things happen to us, there are, inevitably, feelings attached to them — feelings of regret, fear, loss, resentment, anger, betrayal, even hatred sometimes, just to name a few. Those are the things that stay alive within us long after the events have passed, and they are also the things that do the most harm, to us and to the people we love."

If that was true, Kate thought, then she was a mess because she carried every one of those feelings that Beulah named. She looked around the room at all the smiling pictures of happy family members. She couldn't imagine how this woman could possibly understand her feelings. They were worlds apart. This woman was surrounded by love, where Kate had no one. She was completely alone.

As if she could read Kate's mind, Beulah went on, "You probably think that I couldn't know what it is to walk in your shoes or imagine what you might have been through, and that may be true. But what is also true is that those things I said apply to every man, woman, or child, no matter what their story is. 'There is nothing new under the sun' — and those aren't my words," she added, firmly patting the Bible next to her chair. "I haven't gotten to this age without being challenged a time or two with adversity, and I've had a chance to learn some important things along the way."

Beulah's words sounded so right to Kate, yet she could not grasp them in such a way that she could fit them to her own life. She felt disconnected, as if Beulah and everyone else were on the mainland while she floated on an island of her own just off shore.

She sat for a moment in the silence that lay between them. They heard the front door open, and Violet came in with a cheerful greeting. Kate looked down at her watch, "Wow, I didn't realize what time it was!" she said, unable to hide the hint of relief in her voice. "I'd better get going." She got up and took her jacket from the closet as Violet was hanging hers. She glanced back at Beulah and saw that her steady, thoughtful gaze was still upon her. "Thanks," she said. "I'll think about what you said." She closed the front door behind her and felt the wind on her face. It was cold, she thought, just like her heart.

Chapter 7

After she had loaded the last of the supper dishes in the dishwasher, Kate opened the freezer and pulled out the small carton of Pralines and Cream ice-cream that she had treated herself to on the way home from work. Grabbing a spoon, she went into the living room and plopped down on the couch, tucking her legs up under her. Picking up the remote, she surfed through the channels for a movie to watch. All she could find were action movies with people being gunned down and lots of blood flowing. She just wasn't in the mood for that. Her last resort was the classic movie channel. *The Bishop's Wife* was just starting, a 1947 black and white comedy starring Cary Grant and Loretta Young. Perfectly harmless and great with ice-cream — a perfect antidote to her day.

As the movie began, she learned that David Niven is an Episcopal bishop planning to build a new cathedral. He has a lovely wife, played by Loretta Young. And they are a happy couple. Of course, why wouldn't they be? He is a man of God, after all. That is what you would expect. She dug fiercely into the carton, scooping out big spoonfuls of the ice-cream and swallowing them as fast as she could. Suddenly, a cold headache throbbed in her forehead, breaking her momentum. What was she doing? She had planned to savor it slowly. And then she recognized it: the anger. Beulah had named it earlier in the day with a long list of other emotions.

Seeing the scenes unfold before her of the happy clergyman and his happy wife had led her thoughts directly back to Brent. She actually remembered feeling like Loretta Young's character, the Bishop's wife, being so proud of her new husband, Brent, the pastor of the New Eden Community Church. Her memories of those days began to play in her mind like a movie of her own...

She hadn't known Brent very long before they became engaged, but looking back now, she realized that the death of her father just two months before had almost catapulted her into his arms. Brent's show of concern and affection were like a balm to her wounded spirit, and she went willingly into a union with someone that she hardly knew. Kate remembered her mother asking her, "Are you sure this is right for you?" And she batted away any of her mother's doubts as if they were annoying gnats.

The first months had been full of excitement as they both adjusted to their new roles, not just as husband and wife, but as pastor and pastor's wife. This was Brent's first church assignment, and he had taken quickly to the attention he was receiving in his new position. Kate, on the other hand, was by nature a private person and was repelled by the scrutiny that she found herself under and the demands placed upon her by her new husband. Instead of jumping into the role, she actually found herself withdrawing.

Added to that was the problem that none of the women felt comfortable opening up to her either, as they did not want any of their personal issues to find their way to the pastor's ear. She found that the young women that she wanted to make friends with were polite but held her at arm's length. When it was time to have a girls' night out and let their hair down, she was never included. She remembered the night that Brent had asked, "Kate, why don't you lead the women's Bible study? It will be a great way to get to know the women."

"Brent, I'm only twenty-five! Some of these women are twice my age! How am I supposed to impart wisdom to them?"

"The same way that I preach to a congregation of people older than me!" he had responded. "You just jump in there and do it. You can't be afraid of everything, Kate."

That was when he had first started tacking on those little judgments to his comments. It wasn't long before they both felt the strain. "You're letting me down." he had said angrily one day.

"You're supposed to be supporting my ministry. Instead you're doing nothing!"

"You're not accepting me for who I am!" she had hotly contested. "You're not even trying to understand why I'm struggling." Instead of bringing them closer to an understanding, their disagreements only seemed to drive them farther apart. When she became pregnant late in that first year of marriage, she welcomed the news with joy, hoping that this would be the catalyst that would draw them back together.

Her newfound joy was short-lived however, as she soon learned that her mother had been diagnosed with ovarian cancer. Battling unstable hormones and frequent nausea, she spent her entire pregnancy driving back and forth to be with her mother in Baltimore. Helplessly, she watched as her mother's life ebbed away before her eyes.

By the time Jackson was born, her mother was in hospice. Two weeks later, she died. Kate remembered feeling terribly guilty about the joy of his birth. How could she feel such joy when her own mother lay dying? But she found that she could. Every time she looked at his little face with his blue eyes, dark hair, and perfect little features, she was overcome with a surge of powerful love. Tiny as he was, he was her little island oasis in a sea of grief.

The time spent away from home and the exhaustion she felt from the frequent trips to Baltimore had further eroded her relationship with Brent. He seemed to view things only in how they affected *his* life. But Kate was encouraged by one thing. Brent was devoted to Jackson. Whatever affection he was not giving to her was going to their little son, and this actually gave her a kind of peace. It was the one thing they were still able to share.

With the passing of her mother, Kate had lost her one and only confidante. It would have been unthinkable to share anything of her marital woes with a member of the congregation. And Brent worked hard at constructing a façade of marital bliss. She found it so difficult to pretend that they were a happy couple when they were out together because as soon as they walked back into the privacy of their home, the wall of silence descended and the smiles evaporated. Sometimes, while out at a church function, she found herself actually believing that things were fine only to be rudely reminded when they returned home and Brent went right back out again without her, staying away for hours.

Living a double life was contrary to Kate's nature, and she was not very good at it. She was amazed, however, at how easy it was for Brent. He could turn it off and on just like a light switch. While in public, he never dropped his guard, never stopped smiling and playing the devoted husband. Kate, on the other hand, struggled to keep up her end and steadily lost ground. The pressures of a new baby, the grief over the loss of her mother, the absence of true friends, and the emotional roller coaster of the double life she was living forced her deeper and deeper within herself.

The one and only reprieve in her church life where she could still be her true self had been singing in the choir. From girlhood she had loved music and loved to sing. When she sang she lost herself in the words of the hymns and in the sweetness of the melodies, and they comforted her in ways she didn't understand. Though being in the choir meant that she was a part of a group, she experienced a feeling of anonymity while she sang, and her sadness lifted. She had looked forward to singing in the service on Sundays and she had never missed a practice.

The words of a familiar and favorite hymn being sung startled her, suddenly breaking her free from her memories. She opened her eyes and sat upright to find that it was coming from the television. She looked at her watch and frowned. The movie was almost over and she hadn't seen any of it! The ice cream in the carton was melted. Where had she been?

She realized that she had taken a mental trip back in time. And for the first time in a long, long time, she had actually *felt* something. Even if it was anger or sadness, it was better than the test-pattern existence that she had been living for so long. Maybe Beulah was right. Maybe the only way to go forward *was* to go back.

She left the soggy ice-cream carton on the coffee table, turned off the TV and the lights, and went to her bedroom. It was enough for one day.

Chapter 8

Angie LeCompte could not have been happier that the news was out about her engagement. Sitting at her desk, she found it hard to concentrate on the work in front of her. After such a long time of keeping their relationship under wraps, it was exhilarating to finally feel like any other bride-to-be. Working here at the church as secretary to Brent had been a lifesaver. She didn't think that she could have endured the long time of secrecy without being able to see him everyday in the office.

She was equally glad that her job had afforded her close proximity to Brent in the aftermath of that tragic night. It was such a shock about Kate but believable, too when you considered what she had been through. It certainly wasn't something she enjoyed thinking about. She quickly put it out of her mind.

There were other things to think about — happier things, like the cake, the honeymoon, her dress. She just wished there wasn't such a cloud hanging over the whole wedding. She knew people were talking. They didn't really know anything, but they talked anyway. She could tell by the way conversations abruptly stopped as she walked by. Some people were noticeably cool toward her, others polite but distant. Well, she reasoned, you couldn't please everyone. If they couldn't be happy for her, then she wasn't going to lose any sleep over it.

More troublesome, however, was Archie Dean. Since he handled church maintenance, she was forced to deal with him almost daily. He did not try to hide his disdain for her. When asked to do certain tasks, he rarely spoke to her, just nodded his head, frowned, and grudgingly carried out her request. When she mentioned his attitude to Brent, he had shrugged it off, saying, "He's just a janitor, Angie, what do you care what he thinks?"

"Aren't you going to say something to him?" she had asked, indignant.

"Archie has been working at this church for twenty years, Angie. I don't need to be creating any more drama right now than I already have to deal with." So, that had been that, and it appeared that somehow Archie seemed to understand his attitude would go unchallenged. She didn't want to admit that Archie made her feel guilty.

With the wedding just days away, she put those thoughts behind her and wondered how many people would actually attend. Her family members were driving from Pennsylvania and some of her old friends, but they didn't really have a count from the congregation as theirs was a blanket invitation. The hospitality committee was planning a reception in the church basement that would follow the ceremony. She had wanted a fancier reception at a hotel, but Brent had insisted that it was important to make it a total church function because of his position as pastor — so punch, finger sandwiches, and cake was all that it would amount to. She resigned herself to the belief that the most important thing was that in just a few days she would be Mrs. Brent Reed, wife of a pastor! She could move out of her cramped apartment and into Brent's home, and the gossipers would have to give her the respect due a pastor's wife. That more than made up for a boring reception.

Three days passed swiftly. And much to Angie's relief, on the appointed day the church was full for the wedding ceremony. Reverend Newcomb, from Hatfield, had agreed to officiate, and before him and the congregation, Brent and Angie exchanged their vows. For Brent, it was more than a marriage ceremony; it was also an official new beginning of his life. He felt a lightness not experienced for over a year. Now he could do the things he wanted to do and not waste so much energy dealing with what-ifs. Angie, he was sure, would be very capable of supporting him in all of his plans to grow the church. Together they would make it what he envisioned it to be, and it would be noticed. Bigger churches awaited him. He was on his way once again.

After the ceremony, guests mingled downstairs in small groups, balancing cups of punch and small plates of finger food in their hands. A happy din of conversation blended with the soft music playing over the speakers. Many well-wishers greeted Brent and Angie and made the customary remarks about how lovely she looked. There was no doubt that it was true; she made a very attractive bride. With her small waist, ample bosom and five-foot-four-inch frame she did not disappoint.

Sgt. Dave Davenport walked up to the happy couple and shook Brent's hand. "Congratulations," he said.

Brent smiled, "Thanks very much and thank you for coming."

"You've been through quite a bit, and I'm real happy to see that you are able to move on," he said.

Brent smiled, turned toward his bride and said, "I'd like you to meet Angie. She's been working for me for a couple of years now. Angie, this is Sgt. Davenport."

"Nice to meet you, pretty lady," Dave said, shaking her hand.

She smiled and said, "You too." Just then someone came up to her and she turned away.

Before he walked off, Dave said to Brent," I'm sorry we weren't able to get that conviction. Sometimes it just works out that way."

"Right," Brent said, a small frown forming. He certainly did not want to be reminded of all that unpleasantness on his wedding day. When Dave moved away, Brent had a view of the punch table and noticed Archie Dean standing there staring at him. When their eyes met, Archie put his cup down and walked out of the room. Brent was momentarily unnerved, but before he could give it another thought the next person had already stepped up to congratulate him.

Chapter 9

It was an unusually warm day for mid-November in northern Idaho. The sun was bright and inviting. The leafless trees gave the only hint that winter had come. Kate went to the closet and grabbed her coat and Beulah's. "This is too nice a day to sit inside. Let's go out and get some Vitamin D from that sunshine!" she said as she walked over to Beulah. "You spend too much time in this house."

"You're probably right, Kate," she answered. "It's so much less bother to just sit here."

"Well, it's no bother to me, Beulah. I'd rather be outside anyway. Besides, you need some fresh air, and we won't get many days like this one for months to come." She helped Beulah on with her coat and then put her own on. Carefully, she guided the wheelchair through the front door and down the ramp next to the porch stairs.

"It does feel lovely out here," Beulah admitted. They headed out on the winding driveway. It was a little chillier in the shade of the tall pines, but when they reached the road they were once again in the sun. "So tell me, Kate, how do you like living in Lake Pendant? Is my little town starting to grow on you?"

"I still don't know anyone but my next-door neighbors," Kate admitted. "When I get home, I just want to curl up with a good book. But I walk whenever I can, and I have to say that the people I see along the way have been very friendly, even if they are strangers. I like the fact that it's a 'walking' town."

"Yes, that's something that we are proud of here. With the rest of the country going to strip malls and shopping centers, it is nice to still have that 'town' feeling, and we've all worked to keep it that way."

They continued along without talking for a ways, both enjoying the unseasonable warmth. Kate finally broke the silence. "I know it sounds weird to say because I haven't been here that long, but this town feels like home to me somehow. When I came here I didn't know much about it, but it's starting to feel like a good fit."

Beulah grinned. "I am delighted to hear you say that! I've always loved Lake Pendant and I'm tickled when someone else takes to it like I did. It's got some rough edges, but the town has heart. Just you wait until the Fourth of July parade! When you see the turnout and all the little ones sitting along the curb with their families waving their flags, it almost makes you tear up." Kate couldn't help but smile at the scene Beulah described. But then she quickly realized that it would bring tears to her eyes for an entirely different reason. Knowing that her own family was gone would make it a painful event for her. Better to stay away.

When they came to the stop sign at the main road, Kate turned the chair around and headed back. She was lost in her thoughts for a long while until she heard Beulah say, "A penny for your thoughts!"

"I was just remembering some things," she said somberly.

"Care to share them?" Beulah asked.

Kate didn't answer right away. Beulah seemed content to give her time to think about it. Finally, she answered, "I've been thinking a lot about what you said a while back."

"You'll have to be a little more specific," Beulah chuckled. "I have trouble remembering what I said ten minutes ago."

"You said that you had to deal with the past in order to move on."

"Ah, yes. There are no exceptions to *that* truth."

"Well, how do you do that? Just remembering painful things doesn't seem to do anything but bring the pain back. So why do it?"

"Because when you feel the pain you also feel the emotions that go with it. Then you can do what you need to do with those emotions."

"I guess I don't understand what you mean, Beulah."

"Well, usually when we have a painful memory, it's because someone has hurt us or let us down in some way. We need to forgive that person so we can heal."

It was a good thing Beulah couldn't see her face right now, Kate thought as she gripped the handles of the wheelchair tighter. She was surprised by the sudden flush of anger that rose within her. Without realizing, she picked up speed in her stride.

"What's the rush?" Beulah asked.

"Oh, sorry," Kate murmured as she slowed down.

"You see," Beulah said, "That's just my point. If you don't take charge of those feelings, they'll take charge of you. Why don't you tell me who you're mad at and why. It might just make you feel better."

"Let me think about it," Kate answered.

"Fair enough," said Beulah. They were soon at the ramp to the porch, and Kate guided her inside and set her chair by her favorite spot near the fireplace. She hung up their coats and disappeared into the kitchen.

While she prepared the grilled cheese sandwiches for their lunch, she was fighting an inner battle. Part of her wanted desperately to tell all. She had come to trust Beulah. Right now she was the only person in the whole world she felt remotely close to. But she could lose that in an instant by letting her into the pages of her past. What if she didn't believe her? Why should she believe her? She felt like a fly suspended in a spider's web, just waiting for the inevitable.

The yellow kitchen was so cheery that she decided to set the table in there. When she had it all arranged, she wheeled Beulah to the table. "Mmm...smells good," Beulah said. "I can't exactly work up an appetite sitting in this chair, but somehow you manage to make me feel hungry!" Kate smiled and sat close to her so she could help her if she needed it.

"When I was little," Kate said, "My favorite lunch was grilled cheese sandwiches. My mom buttered both sides of each piece of bread before she put the sandwiches together. They were so yummy!"

"She taught you well," Beulah said, "because this is the best grilled cheese sandwich I've ever had!"

"Thanks," Kate said, "not just for saying that, but for being so nice to me."

"I could say the same to you," Beulah answered. "You always make me feel like I'm having a friend over for a visit instead of having a nurse watch my every move."

"The truth is Beulah, right now you are my only friend." Beulah looked at her softly, and with her good arm she reached over and put her hand on Kate's.

"Well," she said. "It's a privilege and an honor to be called a friend." She turned her gaze toward the window for a moment before she continued, "I've had a lot of very dear friends in this town over the years. One by one they have all passed on. The last one was Elsie and she died last March. You and I have more in common than you think."

Kate had never thought about what it might be like for Beulah. She had been too busy thinking about herself. She was at a loss for words. What was there to say — sorry I've been such a self-centered jerk? She hung her head, ashamed.

Beulah interrupted Kate's thoughts, "One of the true blessings of those friendships was the way we were able to help each other out over the rough patches. Having someone to talk to was always such a help. It didn't necessarily fix anything, but at the same time, it lightened the load just knowing that you weren't alone. Somebody cared. It made all the difference." Beulah looked earnestly into Kate's eyes and said, "I care, Kate."

Tears began to slide down Kate's cheeks. She couldn't stop them this time. All the months of holding it in gave way like a sudden breach in a levee. As her shoulders shook from the weight of her sobs, she could feel Beulah's one good arm encircle her shoulders. For the first time in a long time she felt safe.

Chapter 10

When Kate arrived for work the following morning, she felt fatigued after a restless night spent tossing and turning. With the arrival of the dawn had come her decision. She would tell Beulah what had happened. If she didn't believe her, so be it. She was past the point of caring about that. Yesterday's meltdown over lunch told her all she needed to know about the cost of bottling things up. She hadn't realized how tired she had become from holding it all in. What had made her think that would work for very long?

Beulah's expression of concern for her had been like a key opening a rusty lock. For just a moment, she had felt as if she was crying on her own mother's shoulder. That had brought even more tears. How she had missed her mother! Her last heart-to-heart talk had been with her mother the month before she died. No wonder she felt like an island.

After the physical therapy exercises were finished, she settled Beulah by the fireplace and brought in a tray with a fresh pot of tea and two cups. She sat in the chair facing her and filled each cup, adding sugar and lemon.

"I'm glad you made some tea," Beulah said. "We can sit for a spell. It will do you good. You look a little tired."

"It was a long night," Kate admitted as she handed Beulah her tea.

"I'm not surprised," Beulah answered, "I've sensed for a while that you're carrying a heavy load. I'm not much use to anyone trapped in this wheelchair, but I can still be a good listener. Why don't you tell me what sent you running clear across the country in search of a new life?"

Kate took a long sip of the brisk tea and began by telling of her marriage to Brent. She described her giddy excitement about the wedding and mentioned the shadow of her mother's doubts. "I wish I had listened to her. She was right, but I just couldn't, or wouldn't, see it."

"That's one of the great frustrations of parenting," Beulah noted.

"It was partly my fault at first," Kate went on. "I didn't understand what was expected of me as a pastor's wife. I felt so uncomfortable about some of the things that he wanted me to do. The more I disappointed him, the more distant he became."

"Couldn't you talk about it with him?" Beulah asked, "Pastors are supposed to be good at that."

"That's what I thought, too, but when I tried talking about it, he just got angry and said that I didn't care about him or his church."

"Hmm," Beulah murmured with a frown.

"When I got pregnant, I thought it might bring us back together, but then my mom got cancer, and I spent the rest of my pregnancy going back and forth to Baltimore to be with her. Brent didn't like that. He said my mom was well cared for and I should be home more, that 'it didn't look good' for me to be away so much."

"Did your mother live to see her grandbaby?"

"Yes, but she was so ill by then that she couldn't even hold him. I laid him next to her on the bed and she managed a weak smile. A little tear ran down the side of her face, but I knew she was so happy to have him next to her. He was only two weeks old then." Kate paused for a moment. Her heart filled up with an odd mixture of sadness and joy to think of that moment. She continued, "It's almost like she was just waiting to see Jackson because that same night she passed away."

"I'm so *very* sorry Kate," Beulah said, a deep note of concern in her voice. "Was your husband with you?"

"No. He had meetings, he said."

"Had he ever gone with you to see your mother?"

"No. He was always so busy."

"Well, how about the funeral? Did he go with you then?"

"Yes, but after the service we had to leave right away. I wanted to stay and talk to some of her friends, but Brent was impatient to get back. I still feel badly about leaving so soon. I was her only child, and my father was gone. Aunt Belle wasn't well enough to make the trip."

"Tell me about your son," Beulah said.

Kate's eyes were teary as she answered, "His name was Jackson. He was the most beautiful little boy you've ever seen. He had my hair and my eyes. And he was very sweet-natured. As long as he was fed and dry, he was a happy camper."

Beulah hesitated for a moment and said softly, "You said, 'was'…"

Kate let her head drop and fixed her gaze on the cup in her hands. She could not bring herself to look at Beulah. The surface of her tea shimmied from her trembling hands. Beulah waited. Finally Kate said almost in a whisper, "He drowned — just before his second birthday." Tears fell silently down her face but she didn't even try to wipe them away.

"Oh, Kate," said Beulah, "there is no pain like the loss of a child. I know."

"You do?"

"Yes. Bert and I lost our first, a son, when he was just a year. There was a terrible influenza going around that winter and little Bertie came down with it. Penicillin was still pretty new then and in short supply. The doctor was waiting for another shipment when Bertie got sick. By the time we got it, it was too late."

Kate reached over and squeezed Beulah's hand. "You were right yesterday when you said that we have more in common than I think."

Beulah smiled and nodded in agreement. "Losing a child is something that you can't possibly understand until you have endured it. To know the desolate ache of empty arms, and the loss of your little one's entire future, and your part in that future — you have to have walked that road yourself."

They sat quietly for a few moments, reflecting on their parallel memories. The tea was getting cold but it seemed unimportant. Beulah was the first to speak. "After Bertie died, I was blessed to have a lot of understanding from my husband, but I am guessing that might not have been the case for you."

"You have *no* idea," said Kate.

"What do you mean?"

"It's a long story," she said, sighing.

"I have nothing but time," Beulah said as she leaned back in her chair. "I think it's about time you told your story."

Chapter 11

Angie and Brent had been back from their honeymoon for a week. As she unpacked the last of her boxes, Angie sighed with relief at finally being settled into Brent's house — now *their* home. She didn't really like the idea that he had shared this house with Kate, but there was nothing that could be done about that. The church owned the house and it was where they had to live.

With a box cutter she slit the tape on the bottom of the last empty box and folded it flat. As she carried it down the hall, she passed the closed door of the nursery. Something was going to have to be done about that, she thought. She had noticed that Brent kept the door closed at all times and never entered that room when she was around.

As she passed through the kitchen on her way out to the trash can, she saw Brent sitting at the small table munching on an apple. He was totally engrossed in a book. She carried the box out and shoved it in the can trying to make it fit, but the can was just too full, so she took it out and leaned it against the can. She went back into the kitchen. Brent still didn't look up.

"Well, hey," she teased, "What does a girl have to do to get noticed around here?" Brent looked up absentmindedly and smiled, returning his gaze to his book.

"I guess the honeymoon's over," she said with a grin.

"Sorry, Angie, it's a good book," he said as he closed it.

"Oh, I'm just teasing," she said, then continued. "I just finished putting away the last of my things. Now I can think about fixing up the place a little bit."

"What's wrong with it?" he asked, frowning.

"Oh, you know, it just needs some more color, maybe some new pillows on the couch. And the kitchen curtains *definitely* have to go — way too 'froufrou'." She rolled her eyes as she looked at the blue gingham with the white ruffles. "But what I really want to do is turn the nursery into a sewing room. It would be perfect because it gets so much light."

"Forget it, Angie," Brent said.

"But Brent, you never go in there, and I could really use that space," she explained.

"You can figure something else out," he answered.

Now she was piqued. If there was anything that frustrated her, it was impracticality and this surely qualified. To waste an entire room in a house that already was too small made no sense. "Brent, you can't just close that room up like it doesn't exist."

"Angie," he said, his voice cool, "This doesn't concern you. Leave it be."

"I believe in dealing with things, Brent, and you're not dealing with this. And you're wrong — it does concern me. This is my home now, too, and you can't just make part of it 'off limits'!"

Brent suddenly pushed his chair back and stood up. He dropped the apple to the floor. The look in his eyes was almost frightening. Angrily he slammed the book down on the table and said coldly, "Nobody touches that room."

Angie backed up a bit and stared at Brent, amazed at how he was talking to her. "What in the world is the matter with you?" she asked angrily. "That is a perfectly good room, and there is no good reason why I shouldn't be able to use it."

He looked at her with a piercing gaze and raised his voice, "I don't think you heard me. Nobody touches that room!"

"Brent, that's just crazy!" Angie shouted. "Jackson's been gone for over a year. He's not coming back. You have to accept that." Before she knew what was happening, Brent closed the gap between them, and with a full swing of his arm, slapped her hard across the face. She lost her balance from the sheer momentum of the blow and fell to the kitchen floor, a look of total surprise and horror in her eyes. Brent stepped over her and went out the back door, slamming the screen door behind him.

Angie sat up and put her hand to her cheek in disbelief. She could feel her jaw begin to throb. Tears filled her eyes as she sat on the floor, and her shoulders began to shake from the sobs that racked her body. What had just happened? Who was that man? It surely wasn't the Brent she knew.

Finally, her tears subsided and she got up off the floor. She walked into the bathroom and looked in the mirror. Her tear streaked face was bright red on the side where he had hit her. Already she could see it beginning to swell. She rushed back into the kitchen and opened the freezer, grabbing a bag of corn. With shaking hands she held it to her cheek. Her heart was pounding. In the span of five minutes, her whole life had turned upside down.

Not sure what to do, Angie laid down on the living room couch, resting the freezing bag of corn on her face. She certainly couldn't go out looking like this. She played the conversation over and over in her mind trying to figure out what had gone wrong. Maybe she had been too harsh in her statement about Jackson. That was probably it. Brent was still grieving over the loss of his son and she had touched a nerve. But still, why would he attack her like that? It didn't make sense. He was a pastor!

She laid there for several minutes feeling the exhaustion from the whole experience. Then she got up, went into the kitchen, and threw the corn back into the freezer. She fumbled in the cupboard, found the bottle of aspirin, and swallowed two of them. She returned to the couch and within twenty minutes she was asleep.

The sound of a car door slamming woke her. She looked at her watch. It was five thirty. She had been asleep for over two hours! As she heard the back door open, she realized it was Brent and sat up quickly, not sure whether to run and hide or stay put. Her face ached, and when she felt it with her hand, she knew it was pretty swollen.

Brent walked into the living room holding a huge bouquet of flowers, half of them the brightly colored gerbera daisies he knew she loved. Gone was the monster that had fled earlier. The Brent she knew came over to the couch and sat down meekly beside her.

"Angie, I am so sorry," he said, placing the flowers in her lap. "I don't know what came over me." He hung his head. "All I can say is that I know it shouldn't have happened, and I hope that you can forgive me. When you mentioned Jackson, I just lost it. The thought of changing his room into a sewing room was like wiping away his very existence."

Angie didn't know what to think. How could this be the same man who had struck her down just a couple of hours before? But sitting beside her was her husband, the man she loved, and she needed his comfort right now more than anything.

"But Brent, how could you have done that to me?" she asked solemnly.

"When you said what you did about Jackson, I just reacted without thinking."

"How do I know it won't happen again?" she asked warily.

"Because, it won't. I've never done anything like that before, and I never will again. The last thing I would ever want to do is hurt you." He gently stroked her swollen cheek, and she did not pull away.

"I want to believe you but I don't know if I can," she answered.

Brent put his arms around Angie and pulled her close to him. She let herself relax into his embrace. She couldn't help it. It felt so good to have his arms around her. "You can," he whispered, his mouth against her ear. "Trust me. Everything will be all right. I forgive you; say that you will forgive me." She was silent as he held her. "Say it, Angie," he whispered again, "Please — say it."

She was crying softly now. "I forgive you, Brent," she said, her head nestled alongside his neck. "I'm sorry that I said that about Jackson."

"It's okay, Angie. I'm sure that you won't do it again."

Just for a second, Angie stiffened at his response. It sounded odd to her, the way that he had phrased it, but she decided to leave it alone. She'd had enough drama for one day. Brent released her from their embrace and stood up. He laid the flowers on the coffee table, held out his hand to her, and pulled her up. Slowly he led her down the hall to the bedroom. She went willingly, wanting to forget the pain of the day and to lose herself in the familiarity of their love.

CHAPTER 12

Kate had prepared and served lunch for herself and Beulah. She knew she needed energy to wade through the chaos that her life had been before coming to Lake Pendant. When everything was put away, she went into the living room and settled into the large upholstered chair opposite Beulah. And she sighed.

"I said a little prayer for you while you were washing up in there," Beulah said with a twinkle in her eye. "For courage and for strength and that God would help me to help you."

Kate looked up and raised one eyebrow, "That was sweet, Beulah, but to be quite frank, I think we're pretty much on our own in this world."

"Maybe when you tell me what's happened to you, I will understand why you feel that way," Beulah said gently. Kate sat quietly, trying to figure out how to begin. Her eyes were moist as she fixed her gaze on a potted plant on the mantle. The ticking of the anniversary clock that sat next to it was the only sound in the room. Beulah waited and said nothing.

Finally Kate began, speaking slowly, her voice low, "It was on a Wednesday night, my night for choir practice. It had been a bad week with Brent. We'd had some terrible arguments, and I was really looking forward to getting to the church and just singing. I was almost out the door with Jackson to take him to Hannah's; she was the one who babysat for him on Wednesday nights. Just then the phone rang and it was Hannah. She told me that one of her kids had just gotten sick, and it probably wasn't a good idea to bring Jackson over." Kate paused for a moment and winced, "Right then I made the decision that cost my baby his life. Instead of just staying home, I gathered up the Pac 'N Play and some toys and took him with me. I just needed to get out of the house so badly."

Beulah listened thoughtfully, never taking her eyes off Kate as she continued her story. "After practice, I put Jackson into his car seat and loaded up the Pac 'N Play. He was fussy because he was tired. I was in a hurry to get him home, and I pulled away from the curb and headed down the road toward the bridge that crossed Lake Barrego. Our house was just on the other side of the lake." Kate looked down at her lap and rubbed her forehead with both hands. "I'm not sure what happened next. I've tried and tried, but I just can't remember this part. I must have seen something or hit something — I don't know. But the next thing I do remember is waking up and feeling the cold water gushing in through the open window and surrounding me. It was so dark, and I didn't know where I was. I didn't even know how I'd gotten into the water. By the time I was fully conscious, the water was over my head. I managed to get my seatbelt undone, and I felt my way over the seat to get to Jackson. I was so scared. I couldn't see anything. I felt around until I touched one of his shoes and then I had to find his car seat buckles. I tried to get his buckles undone, but I knew I was running out of air. I had to get some more or I'd pass out and I'd never get him out. I pulled myself through the window, and pushed off from the top of the car, and swam to the surface. I took a quick breath of air and dove back down. I could see the beams of the headlights faintly, and I swam toward them but all of a sudden the water got really hard to see through and the light beams were disappearing as I was swimming toward them. I knew then that the car was falling much farther down. I kept swimming, but I was running out of air again. I barely made it back up to the surface."

Kate began to cry. She couldn't stop the tears. "I couldn't save him," she cried, her eyes full of pain and torment. "He was too far down!" Sobs shook her body as she relived the horror of that night, knowing how terrified Jackson must have been, feeling totally helpless to save the one person in her life that she loved beyond all reason.

Beulah used her one good arm to propel her chair toward Kate. She pulled a handkerchief from her pocket and placed it in Kate's hands. "My dear Kate," she said, "dear, dear child." She placed her hand on Kate's shoulder and kept it there until the tears ceased. "What an unspeakable tragedy," she said as she took Kate's hand in her hand. "But you must know that you did everything you possibly could to save him."

"Did I?" she asked in anguish. "If I had just kept trying longer I might have been able to get his buckles undone! What if I could have? I'll never know now."

"You are a mother, Kate," Beulah said emphatically. "And you are an experienced swimmer. You would not have left your son until you knew that to stay one more second would have been too late." Fresh tears rolled down Kate's face at Beulah's words.

"I — I don't know how to thank you for the kindness that you show me," stammered Kate.

"Nonsense. It's nothing but the honest truth!" Beulah retorted.

"You don't understand, Beulah. You're the only one who believes that."

"What are you talking about?" she asked, leaning forward intently.

"The next day, I was taken down to the police department, and for fourteen grueling hours, I was questioned about why I had decided to kill my son."

"Why in the world would anyone have thought that?" Beulah asked, incredulously.

"Because my husband told them that is what I had done."

"Surely they wouldn't just take his word," Beulah said.

"He is a pastor — a 'man of God'," Kate said with derision. "And the detective in charge of homicide attends our church. No one knows the Brent that I know. They all think he is beyond reproach."

"But Kate, why would he do such a heinous thing?"

"That's just it. I don't know. All I know is that he was so angry with me that I was actually scared of what he might do."

"Back up a bit and tell me what happened when you realized that you couldn't dive down the second time," Beulah asked.

"I swam to shore as quickly as I could. The bank was steep and I climbed up by grabbing on to the tall grass and the brush and pulling myself up until I could finally get on my feet. Then I ran to the road, but there was no traffic in either direction. I turned away from the bridge and ran back the way I had come, and finally I saw a long driveway. I felt dizzy, but I just told myself 'keep running, don't stop!' There were lights on when I reached the house, and I was yelling 'Help me!' A man came out and I tried to explain what had just happened, but I was crying so hard and shaking so badly that he was having trouble understanding me. His wife came out, and they helped me inside and she put a blanket around me. He must have called 911 because an ambulance came. I think I was in shock. I must have looked pretty bad. I was all wet, so I didn't realize that the side of my head was bleeding.

"When I got to the hospital I was frantic. I kept telling people that my son was in the lake. Finally, a policeman came into the ER and asked me what had happened, and where and when, and I told him. He said that they would get divers out right away, and he left.

"I must have fallen asleep. I don't remember, but when I woke up I was all stitched up, and I was lying in a private room. I saw Brent standing by the door just watching me. As difficult as things had been between us, I was so glad to see him. I said, 'Brent, I'm so glad that you're here!' I held out my arms to him, but he just slowly walked toward me and stopped at the foot of the bed. I will never forget his next words."

Beulah noticed Kate visibly shudder as she continued, "He said, 'You killed my son.' And then he turned around and walked out. I cried myself to sleep. It was a horrible night. The next morning I was released, and I was going to call Brent to come get me, but Dave Davenport showed up in uniform. He's the detective I told you about who attends our church. He said that he was going to take me home, but first he wanted me to come down to the police station and answer some questions. I asked him why Brent wasn't there, but he didn't answer me.

When I got to the police station, it didn't take long to realize that they were asking me — not questions about an accident, but questions about an alleged homicide. For the next fourteen hours I was grilled about why and how I had purposely driven my son into the lake to drown him. I was exhausted and frantic, but they wouldn't let me go. They kept sending different people in to ask me the same questions in twenty different ways. I kept asking them where Jackson was and had they gotten him out of the lake, but they wouldn't answer me. Finally, it was dark when they let me go. Dave said he would take me home, but I called a cab. When I got there, Brent wasn't there, and he didn't come home at all that night. I cried until I was sick. I didn't sleep at all, even though I was totally exhausted."

Kate stopped. She looked as if she was experiencing the same exhaustion she had been describing. "I don't think I can talk about this anymore today, Beulah," she said with a heavy sigh.

Beulah squeezed her hand. "You don't have to, dear. It is more than enough for one day — more than enough for a life time. Thank you, dear, for sharing that painful experience with me. A burden shared is a burden lightened."

"Just tell me one thing," Kate asked. "Do you believe me?"

"With all my heart," Beulah answered.

Chapter 13

When Kate awoke the next morning, the first thing she noticed was a different kind of light in the room. Grabbing her robe and tucking her feet in her slippers, she hurried over to the window and looked out. Overnight the first snowfall of the season had turned her yard into a winter wonderland. She was thankful that it was Saturday and she didn't have to shovel her driveway and drive to work.

Although she had grown up with winter snows, the first snowfall of the year always held a certain magic for her. She leaned against the windowsill savoring the beauty of the scene before her and wondered if her mother had sat at this very window as a child and watched the same scene with equal wonderment. It was a happy thought and only added to her delight. The snow had covered the landscape with an instant purity, erasing any and all unsightly blemishes. Even the pile of junk in her neighbor's backyard was temporarily transformed into a graceful sculpture garden. I need to be snowed on, too, she thought wryly, suddenly remembering yesterday's emotional afternoon with Beulah.

Was it the magic of the Christmas card scene outside her window, or did she actually feel lighter? She wasn't sure, but this morning felt different for some reason. It was the first time in a long time that she felt excited about a new day. Hurriedly she showered and threw on a pair of jeans, a turtleneck, and a heavy pullover sweater. She dug through her closet for her snow boots, and after pulling on her thickest socks, she laced up her boots.

Without stopping in the kitchen, she raced out the front door and immediately felt the sting of cold on her face. All the bushes were mounded with snow, and the tree branches hung low with their added weight. Next door, little Kevin was already outside, bundled up in a snowsuit with just his face showing. He and Randy were busy building a large snowman. Kate felt the familiar pang in her heart.

A door slammed, interrupting her thoughts. Dee had come out to join Randy and Kevin. Kate quickly turned to go back inside but not before Dee saw her. "Hey Kate!" she called, "Come on over and help us build this snowman!"

"Yeah, come on over!" Kevin chimed in. Randy smiled in agreement.

"Thanks," she answered, "But I need to get some breakfast going."

"No, you don't," Dee said, "I've got extra pancakes right inside. Come on over and finish them up. Then we can play."

"I'd better not," Kate said, but that quickly, Dee had run up beside her and was tucking her arm inside Kate's. "I won't take no for an answer," she said cheerfully as she led Kate toward her house. "Besides, I haven't seen you for a long time."

"Fine," said Kate. She couldn't think of one other thing to add.

As they entered Dee's house, Kate noted that it was small but cozy. The living room was full of toys. Action figures were scattered on the floor. "Don't worry about your boots. I've got to clean later anyway. Just watch your step," Dee said. "Sorry about the mess. It's a losing battle around here." Kate followed Dee into the kitchen, and the aroma of fresh pancakes brought an instant hunger pang. She took a seat at the small, round kitchen table.

"Mmm...they sure smell good," Kate said as Dee pulled a plate out of the warm oven and placed it in front of her. Dee poured two cups of coffee and took a seat across from her.

"Kevin was so excited this morning. He didn't even want to eat breakfast he was so eager to get outside — which is the *only* reason I have extra pancakes!" Dee chuckled. "This is your lucky day!"

It was hard not to catch Dee's enthusiasm for life. She was the bubbliest person Kate had ever met. And why shouldn't she be? She had everything — a happy home, a beautiful little boy, a reason to smile at the future — all the things that Kate had lost. All-too-familiar feelings of self-pity descended upon her, and before she knew what was happening, the fresh excitement of a snowy morning was gone. True to form, her facial expression betrayed her mood change.

"What is it, Kate?" Dee's voice held a note of concern.

Startled, Kate responded with her pat phrase, "Nothing. I'm fine." She forced a smile. "These are great pancakes, Dee."

Dee ignored the ruse. "It's no use pretending because I can see that something is really troubling you."

"It's nothing really," insisted Kate. Memories of reliving part of her ordeal yesterday flooded her. She had no desire to go through that again.

"What do you say we play 'truth for pancakes'?" Dee asked, her eyes twinkling. Kate found herself smiling in spite of her doldrums. "I just did," Kate answered. "I told you that the pancakes are great. That is definitely true."

"Clever," Dee acknowledged. She took a sip of her coffee and continued, "Well, here's something else that's true. I could use a good friend. And you look like someone who might just be one."

Kate blushed at the unexpected compliment. Dee was nothing short of direct, she thought. Kate tried again to keep the conversation light. "How do you know I'm not a serial killer?" she joked.

"Because I knew your aunt," she said. "Remember? She used to love to talk about you. She really loved you."

Kate had forgotten. "What did she tell you about me?"

"She said you were a very caring person and that you used to write to her a lot. She loved getting your letters." Dee paused for a moment as if not sure how to continue. "She, uh, she showed me the picture that you sent her of your family."

It was warm in the kitchen. Kate pulled off her heavy sweater and draped it on the back of her chair. She knew the picture. It was the one she'd had taken right before Jackson's first Christmas. She looked at Dee. "What else did she tell you?" she asked pointedly.

Dee was clearly uncomfortable at the question. She took a minute before she answered. "She told me about the accident. Kate, I'm so sorry about your little boy. I've wanted to say that since the first day I met you, but I just didn't know how to bring it up."

Kate could see the genuine anguish in Dee's eyes. Knowing how uncomfortable this must be for her, she softened. "Thanks, Dee," she said quietly. She knew that she had never written Aunt Belle about what happened after the accident. In fact, she had stopped writing except for the short note in her Christmas card.

"Is it hard for you to live so close to my Kevin?" Dee asked.

"Honestly, yes," she replied. "But there are children everywhere you go, so I know I have to get used to it."

"I hope it's okay to ask this, Kate, but what about your husband?"

"We're divorced," she said matter-of-factly. It was the first time she had ever uttered those words out loud, and she was surprised at how easily they rolled off her tongue. She was surprised, too, at the realization that she did not miss Brent. Even though she was lonely, the peace and quiet of her house far surpassed the cold tyranny and walking on egg shells that she had endured with Brent. She hadn't realized how miserable she had become until he was out of her life. And she hadn't realized that any love she had felt for him had disappeared along with him.

"I hear that divorce is not uncommon after the loss of a child," Dee said.

Especially if the husband is a total cad, Kate thought, but she just nodded. Dee picked up Kate's plate and took it to the sink. "Do you want some more coffee?" she asked.

"No thanks," Kate answered. She wasn't sure why, but she found that she was glad that Dee knew and that she didn't have to go through the ordeal of telling her. She felt lighter, and she was suddenly reminded of Beulah's words, "A burden shared is a burden lightened." That was turning out to be true.

Kate pushed her chair back and got up. She pulled her sweater over her head and smiled at Dee. "I could use a friend, too," she said. "Come on, let's go out and help finish that snowman!"

"Right behind you, Kate," she said, drying her hands on a towel. She looked out the window, then picked up a carrot, a hat, some walnuts, and a long, red scarf that she had set aside earlier. "It looks like they could definitely use our help accessorizing!"

When Kate stepped out on the porch, she saw that the sun had come out. Like diamonds, the snow sparkled and the scene was even more beautiful than when she had first gotten out of bed. Kevin saw her and ran to her. He tugged at her jacket. "Come and help us, Kate!" he cried. Kate took the carrot from Dee and followed Kevin to the snowman. She stuck the carrot in the front of the snowman's head. Dee put the hat on, and together they set the walnuts for eyes.

"He needs a smile!" Kevin said.

Kate and Dee looked at each other and laughed. "Out of the mouths of babes!" Dee said.

Chapter 14

The drive into work on Monday had been an easy one. The fast-moving weather front that had brought all that snow was followed by warmer temperatures and sunshine. All that was left of the snow were large patches here and there in the shady areas.

Kate hummed as she helped Beulah through her morning physical therapy. "My," said Beulah, "You're in good spirits today!"

"Yes, I guess I am," Kate answered, smiling.

"What did you do, win the lottery?" Beulah asked, chuckling.

"No, nothing that grand, actually, but I did have a very nice weekend."

"What did you do?"

"This is going to sound silly, but all I did was build a snowman with my neighbors!"

Beulah grinned. "There can be great joy in simple things," she said.

"You're right. It was just so much fun. I felt like a kid again."

Beulah had a twinkle in her eye as she said, "I think the smartest people are the ones who always keep that little child alive within them. Who says we have to stop having fun just because we get older? When my kids were having their snowball fights and racing down the hills on their sleds — I'm going to confess that when I could spare the time, I was right in the thick of them!"

"Really?" asked Kate. It was hard to picture this handicapped octogenarian racing downhill on a sled.

"I know that's hard to believe looking at me now, but yes, I did. And I had a ball doing it. I'd still be at it with my great grandkids if I could move all my parts and I didn't think I'd break every bone in my body." Kate laughed. Beulah had so much spunk that it was easy to see that her impaired body was the only limitation she had.

"Not to bring up a sore subject, Beulah, but that is why we are doing these exercises — so you can get some movement back into those parts!"

"Well, doggone if I didn't leave myself wide open for that one!" They both laughed. Kate realized that since Saturday she had probably laughed more than she had in the entire year.

"You were right, Beulah," Kate sighed.

"About what, dear?"

"When you said that our burdens get lighter if we share them. Ever since we talked last Friday, I have felt different. Even though it was very hard at the time, afterwards I noticed that things seemed so much brighter."

Beulah was thoughtful for a moment and then asked, "Did you ever see a wolf go after a flock of sheep?"

"No."

"Well, if you had, you would have noticed that the first thing he did was single out a weak or injured one, and then the second thing he did was separate that sheep from the rest of the flock. Once he got it off by itself, the rest was easy."

Kate stopped what she was doing as she pictured the scene that Beulah was describing. She sat down on the edge of the bed. "I was that sheep, wasn't I?" she asked.

"Kate, dear, the important thing is that you're back in the flock," Beulah said with a big smile. "You're a smart girl and you won't let yourself get into that spot so easily again."

"I hope you're right."

"Usually am!" she said with a grin. "And we're done with these fool exercises today! I'm right about that, too!"

Kate glanced at her watch. "Indeed you are — we are done!"

After settling Beulah comfortably back in the living room, Kate brought in the tea she had prepared. It had become their custom to follow the dreaded exercises with a relaxing cup of tea and a visit. Kate poured Beulah's cup and placed it carefully in her hand. "I was proud of you today," she teased. "You didn't complain about your therapy until the very end."

"There doesn't seem to be much use complaining about it. You're relentless!"

"Just doing my job," Kate said, smiling as she sat down. She blew on the top of her steaming cup to cool it.

"I hope I'm not being a pest," Beulah began, "but I would very much like to hear the rest of your story, dear."

"I don't remember where I left off."

"I believe that you had just returned home after being questioned by the police, and your husband wasn't at home."

"Oh yes," Kate said, that faraway look returning to her eyes. Her expression grew somber.

Beulah looked at her intently, "It's all right, dear if you don't want to talk about it right now. I understand that it must be very hard for you to revisit those memories."

"No, it's okay, Beulah. Just knowing that you believe me has made all the difference in the world."

"I'm glad to hear that. It occurred to me that I might be the first person that you have talked to who does believe you."

"Well, almost. There actually was one other person, come to think of it."

"Who was that?"

"Archie Dean, our church maintenance man. I remember it because it seemed so strange. Just before I left town, I went back to the church to get some sheet music I had left in the choir room. I didn't want to run into anybody, so I waited until Brent's car was gone and the parking lot was almost empty. I was bending down in front of the cupboard when he came up behind me so quietly that he actually startled me. I didn't know Archie very well. He was a quiet man, not overly friendly.

"I heard this voice say, 'Pardon me, Mrs. Reed, I just want you to know that I believe you're innocent.' I turned around quickly and saw Archie looking at me. He wasn't smiling, just really serious, but then Archie was like that. Before I could form the words to thank him he turned around and walked out. I got my music and hurried out to find him, but he was gone."

"It must have made you feel good to hear him say that," Beulah remarked.

"Well, yes, of course, but it was so strange because before that I don't think Archie had ever said more than two words to me."

"Just when you think you've got people all figured out, they can sure surprise you. No matter — he's on our side!" Beulah said with a grin.

"True," agreed Kate.

Beulah leaned forward in her chair. "Now back up a bit dear and tell me what happened the morning after you got home from the police station."

Kate took a long sip of her tea and then put it aside. "I kept waiting for Brent to come home, but he didn't show up. Finally, I called the church. His secretary, Angie, answered. She was very cool. She said that he couldn't come to the phone. I told her I *had* to talk to him. And then she hung up!"

"Oh dear," said Beulah.

"Next I called the police station and it took a while before I could get through to Dave. I asked him where Jackson was, and he said that divers had retrieved his body shortly after it had happened." At this point Kate was quiet for a moment. Her eyes were brimming with fresh tears but she continued, "I asked him where they had taken him, and he told me 'Riley's Funeral Home.' Then he said very abruptly, 'Pastor Reed has made all the arrangements; I suggest you check with him,' and then *he* hung up!" Kate was twisting the napkin that she was holding in her lap, fresh anger rising in her.

"I was so frustrated that I sat down on the floor and I just bawled like a baby. I didn't know what else to do. I thought people should be coming over with casseroles or something, but there was no one except a big noisy group of reporters in front of the house with cameras. I didn't dare go outside. I just got up and went into Jackson's room, pulled the shades, closed the door, crawled into the rocker, and cried some more. I don't think I've ever felt so alone."

Beulah dabbed at her eyes with her napkin. "You poor child," she said shaking her head.

"It gets worse," Kate said sadly. "I heard the doorbell ring. I thought it might be someone from the church, so I went to answer it, but it was Dave, and he had a couple of other officers with him.

I opened the door and all these cameras and microphones were aimed at me, and Dave said, 'Mrs. Reed, we are placing you under arrest for the murder of your son, Jackson Reed. You have the right to remain silent…' I didn't hear the rest. They put my arms behind my back, handcuffed me, took me to the waiting cruiser, and put me in the backseat. I couldn't believe what was happening. I screamed at Dave when he got behind the wheel, 'You're making a terrible mistake! Why are you doing this?' but no one would answer me."

Kate leaned back in her chair and let her head fall back on the cushions. She looked up at the ceiling, still finding difficulty in believing it. It had been the second most horrible moment of her life.

Chapter 15

It was the first Sunday after their return from their honeymoon. Brent was going over his sermon notes in the living room, and Angie was in the bedroom struggling with her makeup. She wasn't at all sure what she was going to do. Although the swelling had gone down on the side of her face, there was still a large bruise that no amount of makeup was going to cover. Things had returned to normal between her and Brent, but every time she looked in the mirror she was reminded of what had occurred the day before.

If she went to church, everyone would want to know what had happened to her. If she didn't go to church, then she would be hiding, and she was tired of hiding. If she said that she had run into a door, she doubted that anyone would believe her. The thought of sitting at home on her first Sunday morning when she should be walking in as the new Mrs. Brent Reed really irritated her. Why should she sit home?

She slumped over her dressing table and thought, "I'm ashamed." That thought made her very angry. It didn't seem fair that she had to deal with these kinds of questions a mere week after her wedding or at any time, for that matter. After a night's sleep, the trauma of the event had subsided a bit, and she was beginning to feel resentful of the position that she was finding herself in.

Making matters worse were the memories. The situation was dredging up the terrible fights that had gone on between her mom and dad. She had put those thoughts far away for so long, and now they were back as if they had just happened. Hearing her mother and father fighting had terrified her as a child. Lying in her bed at night, she had put her pillow over her head to stop the sounds of violence, but she had still been able to hear them. In the morning her mother had always worn some evidence of the beating she had received.

As terrible as the beatings were, the way that they were dealt with or rather, *not dealt with*, was in Angie's mind even worse. There was her mom, looking as if she had gone ten rounds with a prize fighter, and nothing had been said about it! Everyone had pretended that there were no ugly bruises on her face. For a week her mom had stayed inside and her father had done the grocery shopping. He was always very meek after one of those episodes, she recalled.

When she got a little older, she had asked her mother, "Why don't you do something about it?" She still remembered her lame response, "He's a good man. He doesn't mean to do it." And that's the way it had stayed until the night that her mother had "fallen" down the stairs. After a week in the hospital and surgery to repair her shoulder and broken arm, the police had finally become involved, and her father had been taken away. Although her mother had refused to press charges, the marriage had ended and so had the cycle of abuse.

With these dark thoughts swirling in her mind, Angie suddenly realized that she could be on the brink of repeating an age-old pattern. For the first time she began to have the tiniest inkling of what her mother had endured. Hadn't she herself been quick to forgive Brent? Hadn't she desperately *needed* to forgive him so she could seek his comfort? Hadn't the thought of being married to an abusive husband been so terrifying that she had put it immediately out of her mind? Was it probable that Brent's abuse was a onetime knee-jerk reaction based on his grief and pain?

These questions made her head spin, but at the hub of that spin was the realization that whatever she chose to do at this moment would have a defining effect on her future. Angie had always prided herself on being a fighter. She knew that if she stuck her head in the sand now, she might very well end up walking the same road that her mother had walked. The very thought of it made her cringe. She stood up, took a long look at her reflection, walked over to her closet and said, "Hmm, what goes well with purple and blue?"

Angie chose the lavender floral print and slipped it carefully over her head. She stepped into a pair of black dress flats and walked into the living room. Brent looked up when she entered. "What are you all dressed up for?" he asked.

"It's almost time for church," she answered.

Brent put his notes down for a second and then picked them back up. "Don't joke about that, Angie," he said frowning.

"I'm not joking," she said as calmly as she could.

He put his notes down again. "Angie, you can't go to church looking like that."

"Why not, Brent?"

"You know perfectly well, why not," he said, irritation creeping into his voice. "What are you trying to do, start something? Look, I've got a sermon to give and I don't have time to play games."

"This isn't a game. I'm going to church with you, Brent," she said firmly.

"No, Angie, you're not," he replied, just as firmly. "We don't need people asking embarrassing questions."

"You mean *you* don't need people asking questions."

"You look awful, Angie. Do you actually want people staring at you?"

"I'm not going to hide, Brent. If I do, I will regret it."

"You will regret it more if you don't," he replied.

"What's that supposed to mean?" she asked.

"People love to gossip. We can't let that happen."

"What do you mean 'we', Brent?"

"I mean 'we', just like I said! We're a team and we have to behave that way."

Angie was getting more irritated by the minute. "If we're a 'team' Brent, then why am *I* the one with the bruises?"

"Oh Angie, stop it. You were pushing my buttons yesterday and you know it. Don't make a federal case out of it."

"Brent, you knocked me to the floor!"

Brent got up and put his notes in his briefcase and pulled his car keys out of his pocket. He walked over to Angie and looked directly into her eyes. "This conversation is over. You are staying home and I will tell you why. Your paycheck and mine are both written by the New Eden Community Church. Without them, we don't eat. Putting my job in jeopardy is nothing short of stupid, and if you give it even a moment's worth of thought, you will come to the same conclusion. I'm going to tell everyone that you are getting over a cold and are tired from our trip. I'll see you when I get back." Brent did not wait for a response. He walked out the door and got into the car.

Angie watched sadly as his car pulled out of the driveway. It really wasn't that simple after all, she thought. As much as she hated to admit it, Brent was right. They couldn't afford to lose their jobs. She stared out toward the street, feeling the isolation and the quiet of the house. And right then she understood what it was she had to do — quietly go about finding a different job. It would take a week for her bruises to disappear, and then she would begin her search.

Chapter 16

On her way home from work, Kate had gotten an idea. She had stopped off at the store and chosen something that she thought would be fun for Beulah. The next morning she walked into work carrying a bag. "I have a surprise for you!" she said to Beulah.

Violet, who was putting on her coat, getting ready to leave, came over to see. Kate pulled a large box out of the bag. "A jigsaw puzzle!" exclaimed Violet. "What a great idea!" There was a picture on the box of a beautiful farm scene with deep green trees, a red barn, and some horses.

"Looks like a lot of work!" remarked Beulah as she studied the box. "One thousand pieces! Are you trying to get me out of your hair?"

Kate laughed. "No, of course not! I bought this for us to do together! My mom and I used to love them."

"Well, I was never one for just sitting, but since I don't have much choice anymore, I guess I might as well keep my one good hand busy," Beulah said. "Thank you, Kate, that was mighty thoughtful of you."

"Can I help with it, too?" asked Violet.

"Of course," Kate said. "I'll look forward to seeing your progress when I arrive in the mornings."

"Thanks!" Violet said. "You two have fun getting it started. I expect to see all the edges done by tomorrow! See you!" With that she waved and was out the door. Kate hung up her coat in the hall closet and pulled out the folded card table that Beulah kept behind the coats. She set it up in front of Beulah's wheelchair and brought in a chair from the kitchen for herself. She opened the box and positioned the box cover on end so they could see the picture as they worked.

Beulah looked at the mound of tiny pieces in the box. "Oh my lands!" she cried. "Where do we start?"

"Haven't you done one of these before?" asked Kate in disbelief.

"Well, it's like I said, I've never been one for just sitting. With four children and a vegetable garden, there was always just too much to do."

"You'll be amazed at how this little mound of pieces will grab your mind," Kate said. "I've been known to work on one of these for hours!" She sifted the pieces through her fingers. "The first thing we do is look for the pieces that have a straight edge," she said as she pulled a couple out. "See? We know that these pieces have to go around the outside edge. Once we get the outside edge done, we can work toward the inside."

"That looks easy enough, I guess," said Beulah as she began looking through the pieces. "Oh look — here are two," she exclaimed with excitement as she laid them on the table.

"You've got the idea," beamed Kate. "See, the fun is in the hunt and then figuring out where all the pieces go."

Beulah didn't answer. She was already too engrossed in finding more edge pieces. Kate smiled, happy that her hunch had been a good one. The two of them sat for the next hour busily pawing through the pieces and laying out the edges. Kate was delighted to see that Beulah was very adept at this. She glanced at her watch, "I hate to mention it, but it's time for PT," she announced.

"I don't feel like doing any physical therapy right now," Beulah said. "We can do it later, or better yet, not at all."

"Come on, Beulah. You know these are doctor's orders. You've got to let me do my job."

"Who are you working for, him or me?" she asked.

"You, of course, but I have an obligation to do what your doctor says. And besides, it really is important to keep those idle limbs moving. You're such a great lady, Beulah, but you sure do give me grief about this one thing."

"When you get to be my age, and just about every part of your body hurts just because it's old and worn out, the last thing you want to do is make it hurt even more," she grumbled.

Kate reached over and patted her hand. "You're right. I can't even imagine what it must feel like to have aches and pains all the time and then have to endure me adding to it. The last thing I want to do is make you hurt."

Beulah softened at Kate's words and the fight went out of her. "Let's get it over with. I know I have to do it," she said with a sigh. "I've always hated whining, and here I am doing it myself!"

Kate pulled the table away and wheeled Beulah to the bedroom where they always did the exercises. She lifted her onto the bed and slowly began the rhythmic routine.

"You're not doing it like you're supposed to," remarked Beulah.

"I don't want to hurt you," Kate said with a look of compassion.

"If it doesn't hurt then it's a waste of time," remarked Beulah.

Kate laughed, "Beulah, sometimes I just don't understand you. First you don't want me to hurt you, and then you want me to hurt you. What's this about?"

"I may be old, but I'm not dumb," Beulah answered. "I know that sometimes pain is the only avenue to healing."

"Well then, why do you fight it so much?" asked Kate.

"Because it hurts! And I'm human," laughed Beulah. "And I'm not much different from you."

"What do you mean?" asked Kate.

"You've been carrying around a boat load of grief and sorrow, and in order for you to heal from that you've got to get it out and deal with it. But do you want to? No — and the reason for that is why? Because it hurts," she said, answering her own questions.

Sometimes Beulah's words of wisdom were like lasers finding their mark before you knew what hit you. Kate let them linger in her mind as she pondered their weight. Finally she said, "You've been right about everything, and you're right about this, too."

"Let's make a pact," Beulah said with a wink, "Let's keep after each other where and when we need to!"

"Agreed," said Kate as she resumed Beulah's normal routine.

"Now that's better," said Beulah. "It's hurting so it's doing some good!"

After lunch Kate and Beulah resumed their work on the puzzle. They were making good progress. "How are you spending Thanksgiving?" Beulah asked.

"I haven't really thought about it," Kate answered, suddenly realizing it was only a week away.

"I have an idea," said Beulah with a grin. "This year my kids have decided to come here and cook the turkey, and I would love it if you would come and join us."

"Oh Beulah, I couldn't. That's your family time and besides, you don't need one more mouth to feed when you'll have so many."

"Well, first of all, I'm not worried about mouths to feed, because I don't have to do any of the cooking," she said grinning. "And second of all, I think of you as family already. I won't enjoy my Thanksgiving if I have to think about you sitting alone at home."

"Don't you think you should check with your family first?" she asked.

"It's my house and I can invite whomever I want," she said. "But my kids are used to extras at the table. It's how they grew up. Besides, Kate, I don't think of you as my nurse. I think of you as my friend. Do you think Violet and I have the kind of talks you and I do? Well, we don't. I knew from the first time I met you that God had sent you to my house."

Kate blushed and her eyes grew moist. "Thanks, Beulah. You've no idea what it means to hear that. You've come to mean a lot to me, too. In fact, in some ways you remind me a lot of my mom."

"Well, it's settled then. You're coming!" Beulah said, her eyes twinkling. "We'll tell Mark when he gets here. I forgot to mention that he's coming by this afternoon."

Kate jumped up. "I'd better see if you have the makings for some cookies, or something," she said as she headed for the kitchen. Before she got there, the doorbell rang.

"That must be him!" Beulah exclaimed with a big smile.

Kate went instead to the door and opened it. Mark stood there with a bakery box in his hands. "Hi," he said, handing Kate the box, "I picked up some of those fancy little fruit tarts that Gram likes." He went into the living room and gave Beulah a warm hug and a kiss on the cheek. "How's my favorite Grandma?" he asked.

"Fine now that you're here!" she said with a grin as Kate took the box into the kitchen to put the tarts on a plate.

"Gram, I need to talk to you — alone," Mark whispered.

"What's this about?" she asked.

Mark glanced toward the kitchen, "About Kate," he answered.

Chapter 17

Kate brought the plate of tarts into the living room on a tray with some forks and three dessert plates. "Would anyone like me to make some tea?" she asked.

Beulah answered, "No need for tea, dear, but I'll tell you what I would like. Would you mind running to the market and getting some whipped topping? These are wonderful but they are even better with a dollop of cream."

"Sure, Beulah, be glad to," Kate said as she headed for the coat closet. She put on her coat and threw her purse over her shoulder. "Back in a minute," she called as she went out the front door.

Beulah leveled her gaze at Mark. "Now what is this all about?"

"I did some checking, Gram. I don't know how to sugar coat this, so I'll just say it straight out. Kate was once arrested for committing a murder!"

"I assume you're talking about her little son, Jackson?"

Mark looked surprised. "Yes, she was arrested in Maryland for his murder just a year ago. The DA didn't have enough evidence so they had to eventually let her go, but she's still considered a suspect. Gram, you could be in danger."

"Thank you for your concern, Mark, but I already know all about it."

"How?" he asked, incredulous.

"She told me herself." Beulah replied. "That poor girl has been through the mill, Mark. What she needs the most right now is for someone to believe her. She lost her mother, her son, her home, her husband, her reputation, and any friends she might have had. I don't know too many people who have had to deal with stress like that."

"What makes you think she's not guilty?" asked Mark.

"I'm a pretty good judge of people, Mark. I would stake my life on her innocence."

"People can fool you, Gram."

"It's been many a year since someone has pulled the wool over my eyes," she answered confidently.

"It doesn't mean it can't happen. There's a lot at stake here, Gram. If she is guilty, then you could have a crazy person here in the house with you. There's no telling what might happen to you!"

"Well, if it concerns you so much, then maybe you need to talk to her yourself. I don't need any reassurance."

"Gram, I think it would be prudent to let her go. We just can't take a chance like that."

"My body might be falling apart Mark, but my mind is clear as a bell. This is my house and my life, and though I appreciate your concern, I find it misplaced."

Mark ran his hands through his thick, dark hair, clearly frustrated. "Gram, please, think about your family. I can't be over in Spokane wondering if I'm going to get a call that someone has poisoned your lunch!"

Beulah laughed. "I think you're getting a bit carried away." Suddenly a frown appeared on her forehead. "You haven't mentioned this to the other family members have you?"

"I just told Mom," he answered. "But I told her not to get involved, that I would take care of it."

"If you want to 'take care of' something, why don't you help this poor young woman? Something's fishy about this whole thing that happened to her. That ex-husband of hers is the one who got her arrested!"

"He's a pastor, Gram! He's a respected member of the community. He knew that she was depressed and mentally not well. I've dealt with lots of cases like this. Some of the 'nicest' people can be cold-blooded killers. Look at Ted Bundy! He worked on a crisis help line for heaven's sake!"

"Say what you will, Mark, but 'something is rotten in the state of Denmark'!"

"Quoting Shakespeare doesn't change the facts, Gram, and I would be totally remiss if I didn't step in and do something."

"Mark I couldn't love you more, but you have to bow to my wishes here. Not only is Kate staying on, but she is joining us for Thanksgiving dinner. You had better get used to the idea."

Mark stood up and stuck his hands in his pockets. He paced back and forth as he said earnestly, "I'm not through with this, Gram. I can't just take your word for it. The stakes are too high."

"Well, well," she said, with a smug smile. "I'm finally getting somewhere!" She paused to reflect, then said, "You're very good at what you do, Mark. I would be deeply grateful if you would put some of your talents to work on the tatters of this poor girl's life."

"I won't be doing it for her, Gram; I'm doing it for you."

"That doesn't matter. What matters is that you're doing it."

Just then the front door opened and Kate walked in. "I've got the topping," she said. "It'll just take a minute to get a spoon."

When she had hung up her coat and disappeared into the kitchen, Beulah leaned toward Mark. "You won't be sorry," she said.

Kate reappeared with a bowl of topping and placed a mound on two of the tarts. "Is it okay if I join you?" she asked before she put any on the third tart.

"Of course, dear," Beulah said, "Sit down and enjoy one of life's great treats."

Kate noticed that Mark seemed troubled. She wondered what she had just walked in on. "Maybe I'll just go in the kitchen and get some things done. I can have it later," she said.

"Nonsense — sit down, right there," Beulah instructed. "Mark and I were just talking about you."

Mark shot a look of alarm at Beulah, but she ignored it. "It turns out that Mark has learned quite a bit about your tragedy in Maryland on his own. He is a detective, as you know, Kate. I think it would be helpful if you could give him your view of the events as you did for me."

Kate was momentarily stunned. She didn't know what to say. She looked at Mark. He clearly wasn't happy about what Beulah had just divulged. She wanted to just disappear through a hole in the floor. There was a long, awkward silence.

Beulah patted her Bible next to her chair. "You shall know the truth and the truth shall make you free," she quoted and then added, "Life is too short for pretense — one needs to just dive in."

Mark shifted uncomfortably in his chair. He turned toward Kate. "Do you want to go somewhere and get some dinner when your shift is over?" he asked. It was very clear by his tone of voice that he was not asking her for a date.

Kate felt like a deer trapped in the headlights. She looked at Beulah who smiled at her and nodded while mouthing the words, "Trust me."

She turned to Mark. "Okay," she said, so quietly that he almost didn't hear it."

Chapter 18

Mark and Kate sat at a small booth in Carmine's, a small Italian restaurant on Main Street. The tables were covered in red and white checked vinyl, and a stubby candle flickering from the top of a Chianti bottle cast a warm glow on the table. A plate of ravioli, no longer warm, sat in front of Kate. They had been sitting there for over an hour, and she had barely eaten two bites. In that span of time, she had brought Mark up to speed on everything that she had previously shared with Beulah.

Telling her story to Mark was decidedly different than talking to Beulah. He asked very specific questions in a businesslike manner, and there were no smiles of compassion — no reaching across to take her hand. She almost felt as if she was back in Dave's office being interrogated. So far, she had been successful in not letting herself cry. Looking around at the other diners chatting amiably at nearby tables was enough of a reminder of what a spectacle she would become if she lost it right here.

After finishing his last forkful of linguini, Mark wiped his mouth with his napkin and took a sip of wine. He looked at her intently as he asked, "Why do you think that Brent accused you of intentionally harming your son?"

"That is the one question that I have struggled so hard to find an answer for. I can't imagine why he did such a horrible thing to me." Fresh anger surged in Kate as her mind traveled back to the awful night. "Even if I hadn't been his wife, but merely a member of his congregation, he should have afforded me the tiniest bit of comfort at a time like that, but there was nothing coming from him but a cold, heartless hatred. In fact, aside from the few words of accusation that he spoke to me in the hospital, we never had a real conversation ever again. It was as if our marriage ended for good in that lake along with the life of our son." Kate took a long sip from her glass of Merlot. She could feel the emotion rising within her and she fought it.

Mark studied her quietly from across the table. In the candlelight his dark eyes and handsome features were hard to ignore, and Kate thought wryly that if her life had not become such a train wreck, she would have been thrilled to be sitting across from such a good-looking man in a cozy restaurant sharing a bottle of wine. But for her the ambiance was wasted. She might as well be sitting across a cold gray table at a police station talking to Dave Davenport.

"How would you describe your marriage before the tragedy?" he asked.

"It wasn't the greatest, that's for sure, but I've never been married before, so I can't really compare it to anything."

"Would you say that you were happy?"

Kate thought about this question for a minute. "Yes," she finally answered, "but not with Brent. I think my happiness had everything to do with Jackson. He was my whole life."

"How were things between you and Brent before Jackson was born?" asked Mark.

"It's almost not fair to answer that," Kate said. "My mom was dying of cancer, and I was in Baltimore most of the time. We hardly saw each other."

"Well, let's back up a little more then," Mark said patiently. "Before your mother got sick, how would you describe your relationship with Brent?"

Kate gave herself a moment to think about his question. "I know this is going to sound strange, but we actually began to develop two relationships: one at home and one for show."

"Can you describe them for me?" Mark asked with interest.

"When we were out in public or at church, he was a devoted, attentive husband. When we were at home, he became more and more this cold, distant person who didn't want anything to do with me."

"Did you do anything to try and resolve that?" Mark asked.

Kate took another sip of her wine and laughed derisively. "What was I supposed to do, go talk to my pastor?"

Mark grinned for the first time. "Ouch," he said putting up his hands in mock surrender.

Kate acknowledged his gesture with a brief smile and continued, "Seriously, it's a little intimidating when you are married to someone in that position whose job it is to give guidance and counsel to everyone else. There was no possibility to talk to anyone about it. Brent would never have allowed that. His image was more important to him than anything. The one time I suggested going to a counselor, he came unglued."

"Did you ever tell anyone about your problems with Brent?" Mark asked.

"There was no one to tell. By the time it started to really become an issue, my mom was very sick and I didn't feel that I could burden her with my issues. The only other people I knew were members of our church, and I didn't dare make noise on that grapevine! Instead I focused on my mom and the baby, and I guess, eventually, I was living in two different worlds myself."

"So, are you saying that no one outside of you and Brent had any knowledge that there were problems between the two of you?"

"There was just my Aunt Belle. I wrote her that we were having some difficulties."

"Where does she live?" Mark asked, with interest.

"She passed away not long ago. She's the one who left me the house I'm living in."

"I'm sorry," Mark said, and then went on, "It sounds to me like you were pretty isolated. I guess anyone could get pretty depressed in that kind of environment."

Kate immediately bristled. She sat up straight and said emphatically, "Not depressed enough to drown my own son, if that's where you're heading!"

"Whoa, take it easy," Mark said gently, "I'm not trying to accuse you of anything. I'm just making some observations." He stared into the candlelight for a moment and then asked, "What do you know about Brent from the time before you met him?"

Kate relaxed a little. "I know that he was adopted. I actually met him in a hospital where I was working in Baltimore. His adoptive father was a stroke patient on my floor, and Brent came in to see him. He never talked about his mother except to tell me once that his parents were divorced."

"Is his father still alive?" asked Mark.

"No, unfortunately he died. That's when it all started. He came into the hospital a few days later with a big bouquet of flowers for the nurses' station and a thank you card. I felt really sad for him, and when he asked me to go out I agreed."

"Did you learn anything else about his life besides his being adopted?"

Kate squirmed a little at these questions. In retrospect they revealed just how careless she had been in her early relationship with Mark. "He said that he didn't really want to talk about his childhood. Because of his parent's divorce, it wasn't a happy time, so I let it alone."

"Did you ever meet any of his friends?"

"No," she said, and then added a little defensively, "He was just finishing up school and said he hadn't had time for a social life."

Mark leaned back against the seat, "Let me wager a wild guess here — you embarked on a whirlwind courtship during which time this man lavished you with gifts and lots of attention, followed by a marriage proposal that took you by surprise because it came so quickly."

Kate hated to admit it, but everything he said was true. "How did you know?" she asked.

"Because I've seen it plenty of times before. I'm sure he had some very plausible reason why it was necessary to get married right away."

"Well, yes. He was interviewing for a job at a church, and he said they preferred that pastors were married and 'settled down.' He said we might as well get married right then because he would have a better chance getting the job, and we could start our lives together. I was so much in love, it didn't make much sense to me to put it off, especially if it might get in the way of him getting a job. But I do remember that my mom was not happy about it. She thought it was too soon. When I told Brent that, he said we knew we were in love, so why wait?"

"What was Brent's relationship like with your mother?"

"Well, after he found out that she wasn't in favor of the wedding, he took offense, and they never did form a good relationship. I don't think he ever forgave her."

"I need something from you," Mark said. "Will you make a list of all the people who had anything to do with the events of the past year and how they related to you or those events and where these people can be found? Don't leave anyone out, no matter how unimportant they seem to be."

"Where do I send it?" asked Kate.

"If you can get it to me by tomorrow, I'll be at Gram's. I'm not going to drive back to Spokane tonight. I'll just bunk at her house."

Maybe it was the wine, or just being out at night, she wasn't sure, but in spite of the unpleasantness of their topic of conversation, Kate wasn't in a hurry to leave. She finished the last of her wine. The waiter had taken away her cold plate of ravioli long ago. She toyed with her spoon and said, "You've been asking a lot of questions. Now it's my turn." She took a deep breath, leveled her gaze at him, and boldly asked, "Do you think I am capable of killing my son?"

It was clear that Mark was taken aback by her question. He was silent for a moment and then answered carefully, "In my line of work, you run into a lot of seemingly nice people who do some pretty egregious things. I've learned to do my homework first and draw my conclusions later. I don't mean to sound harsh, but I think your question deserves an honest answer."

Kate rummaged in her purse and pulled out a twenty and a ten from her wallet. She put them on the table. "This should cover my dinner," she said. "I'll work on your list. Good night." She grabbed her coat and walked away, ignoring Mark as he called after her.

Chapter 19

It took three more days for Angie's bruising to diminish enough that it could be adequately camouflaged with makeup. Those three days she had put to good use by perusing the classifieds and local job postings on the internet. There hadn't been a lot to choose from and very few that even interested her, but she put together a short list of possibilities, made the calls, and set up appointments for interviews. She was relieved to have been able to arrange times during the lunch hour. Brent usually liked to go to lunch together, but she could easily insist that she had some shopping to do. She knew that he would do almost anything to avoid that.

They had only been married a little over a week, and Angie was sad to note that she already had things to hide. It was not the way she wanted things to be, but she didn't spend much time worrying about it. A girl had to do what a girl had to do, she reasoned. No sense stewing. She would worry about the fallout later — and there *would* be fallout. She knew Brent well enough by now to know that.

Once or twice she had considered canceling the interviews. Life was going relatively smoothly, and it was easy working together at the church. With Brent as her boss, she enjoyed a certain freedom that she knew would be gone when she changed jobs. But each time she had reached for the phone she had remembered Brent's words about their paychecks coming from the New Eden Community Church. No, she didn't really have a choice, she realized. There existed within her a deep resolve to never allow her life to end up like her mother's.

Another thing that Angie had done during her three day "holiday" was to set up her sewing machine in the nursery. Brent never went in there anyway, so it was unlikely that he would notice. All she had to do was be careful not to work on her projects when Brent was in the house, and that would give her lots of time as church demands were constantly pulling him away in the evening.

Her first day back she found a mountain of phone messages. On top of that, the water heater went out. It took her awhile to find Archie. He was perched atop a ladder washing windows on the east side of the building. She called up to him, "Archie, we've got a problem with the water heater." He grunted but kept washing the windows. "Well, are you going to fix it?" she asked, irritated by his lack of response.

Archie didn't miss a stroke with his squeegee. "'Reckon so," he said.

"Well, when?" she pushed. "There's no hot water."

"When I get to it," he replied.

What was it about that man that got her so riled? He had no right to talk to her like that; he should be fired, she fumed to herself. She walked off in a huff, comforted only by the knowledge that she was a short-timer.

Lunch time came quickly with all she'd had to do that morning. Her first interview was scheduled for twelve thirty at the offices of Hamilton Insurance Company. It was one of the biggest businesses in Careytown. Angie had dressed carefully that morning, choosing her black suit with a satiny cream-colored blouse. She was a little nervous as she didn't know that much about insurance, but she figured that secretarial requirements were pretty standard across the board.

After meeting Mr. Leonard, she immediately felt at ease. He was a little chubby, had thinning gray hair and glasses and appeared to be a gentle grandfatherly type who was probably about five years from retirement. They chatted for about twenty minutes, and then Mr. Leonard began to describe the job in more detail. "I manage the life insurance division," he said. "It's a large department and I won't lie to you, there's a mountain of paperwork and more forms than you've probably ever seen in your life. I need someone who has a keen eye for detail and accuracy."

"I've never worked in the insurance field before, Mr. Leonard, but I have worked for a human resources administrator, so I'm well acquainted with forms. I'd be glad to provide you with that reference."

"That would be great," he said. He then continued on with several more questions. Angie was pleased that they were well within her comfort zone. Finally, Mr. Leonard asked her, "When would you be available?"

"As soon as I could find a replacement for my current job, a week or two at the most," she answered.

"Well, I don't like to keep people hanging, Mrs. Reed. I like what I've heard so far, and after doing some routine checking on your references, I feel confident that I will have some good news for you shortly." He looked down and skimmed her resume. "You mentioned your current job but the last job you have listed here is two years ago. Where are you working right now?"

Angie suddenly realized that she *had* mentioned her current job without thinking. Now what? Brent would never give her a good reference. He would be so angry that she was interviewing that she knew he would wreck her chances for finding another job. She almost had this job in the palm of her hand, and now, in just a few seconds, she was about to lose it.

"Is there a problem?" Mr. Leonard asked.

Angie was irritated with herself for taking so long to answer, but she was trying desperately to figure out how to handle his question. Finally she said, "Yes, I'm afraid there is. I work for my husband right now and I know he doesn't want me to quit. But I don't want to work there anymore, so I am trying to find another job."

"Why don't you want to work there anymore?" Mr. Leonard asked. He seemed to be genuinely concerned.

"I work at a church, and my husband is the pastor. It just makes it very hard to separate our lives from the business of church life. Unfortunately he doesn't see it that way, but I do." Angie hoped that this answer would be enough.

"You say he's a pastor? I think I might know him. Is his name Brent Reed?"

Angie froze. That he might know Brent was something that had not occurred to her. "Yes," she admitted. "How well do you know him?"

"Not well at all, really," he answered. "He came in about a year ago and took out a life insurance policy on his wife. It was the same day that his son drowned. I remember it because of all that happened right after that. What a tragedy that was."

"Yes," Angie agreed, nervously. "We just got married not ten days ago. I thought it might be best for each of us if we didn't work in the same office. You know how it is, you want to have something fresh to bring each other at the end of the day."

"I take it that you don't want me to call him for a reference?" Mr. Leonard's eyes twinkled as he asked that question. Angie breathed a sigh of relief, "Exactly," she replied.

"Well, you seem to have enough other references here. I don't think I need to complicate your private life anymore than it already is. Why don't you call me tomorrow about this time and I might have news for you." Mr. Leonard stood up and Angie followed his lead.

"Thank you, Mr. Leonard," she said, shaking the hand he offered.

"Call me Hank," he said with a smile. Angie could not help liking this kind man.

Angie thought about little else until lunchtime the following day. She had another interview set up for one o'clock, but first she planned to call Hank Leonard. After getting into her car, she drove around the block and pulled over. She dialed the number of the direct line Hank had given her. After just a few minutes of conversation, she flipped her phone closed and a huge smile spread across her face. She had the job! Without hesitation, she dialed the number of her one o'clock appointment and promptly cancelled it.

A new set of challenges now presented itself. She hadn't expected to find a job so soon, but she was ready nonetheless. Her first action was to call the newspaper and place an ad for her position. Her second was to drive back to the church and post the position in the bulletin that would be handed out on Sunday. It was the third thing that truly gave her trepidation. She was going to have to tell Brent.

As she drove to the deli to get a sandwich, Angie tried to think of different ways to deliver her news. No matter what she came up with, she knew that he was going to be furious. After picking up her sandwich at the drive-up window, she drove to the park and sat in her car while she ate. It was best not to put it off, she reasoned. She also decided that she had to tell him at church where she knew she would be safe. The very thought of what lay ahead took her appetite away. She put the half eaten sandwich back in the bag and drove back to the church.

Brent was in his office when she returned. He smiled when he saw her. "Did you get your shopping done?" he asked.

"I didn't really find what I wanted," she lied.

"What were you looking for?" he asked.

Angie wanted to shout, "A job! And I found one!" but she only smiled and said, "Just girl stuff." She knew that would stop any further inquiries and it did. She walked over to where he was seated at his desk, and she put her arms around his shoulders from behind as she kissed his neck.

"Mmmm," he said.

"Brent, honey," she said softly. "There's something I need to tell you."

"What is it?" he asked as he turned to face her.

Angie took a deep breath and plunged ahead, "I've decided that I would like to work somewhere else," she said. There, it was out.

Brent sat bolt upright. "What are you talking about?" he asked.

"Well, I got to thinking about what you said this weekend, about how both of our paychecks come from the church, and the more I thought about it, I realized that it wasn't a good idea to have our entire income dependent upon one place."

Brent looked at her with astonishment. "Angie, this is crazy. You can't quit. I need you here."

"You need a secretary, Brent. It doesn't have to be me."

Brent's eyes narrowed. "What is this really about?"

"Nothing. It's just like I said," Angie answered, backing away a little. Immediately she wished she hadn't.

"Oh, so now you're afraid of me?" he asked sarcastically.

"Don't make this into more than it is, Brent. I have a right to work someplace else if I want to."

"Look, Angie. Forget about it. Our income is not in jeopardy."

"It was on Sunday," she said and regretted it.

"Oh, so this is some kind of payback? I get it." There was anger in his eyes now.

"No, Brent. It's just what I want to do."

"Well, you can't, so get over it."

"Yes, I can. I've already put an ad in the paper for your new secretary."

"What?" Brent got up and began pacing. "You had no right to do that without talking to me first," he said angrily.

"The reason I did that was because I knew that you would do just what you're doing right now — flipping out!"

Brent came over to Angie and looked her directly in the eye, "Do you have any idea how this is going to look?"

"That seems to be the only thing you care about," Angie retorted.

"That's not true!" He exclaimed. He walked over to the window, stood for a moment. When he turned back around, Angie was surprised to see his whole demeanor had changed. It was almost eerie, as if a switch had been tripped. "I need you here with me, Angie," he said softly. "I love you. Your place is beside me."

"Brent, just because we work at different places doesn't mean we don't love each other. Millions of couples do that. In fact, very few work together."

Brent walked toward Angie and took her into his arms. "You belong here with me," he whispered.

"I'm quitting, Brent," she said evenly, "My mind is made up. I'm not leaving you; I'm just leaving my job, for heaven's sake."

Abruptly he took his hands off of her. She could see that his anger had returned.

"No!" he shouted.

"Yes," she answered, without emotion. "I already have another job."

"You have betrayed me," he hissed. Angie couldn't believe what she was hearing.

"And *you* are overreacting," she said.

Brent stood rigidly staring at her. His face was flushed. "Who hired you?" he asked.

"Sorry," she answered. "I'm not about to divulge that yet," she paused and then added, "for obvious reasons."

"You're going to regret this, Angie," he warned.

"How?" she asked, daring him to answer.

Brent did not respond. Instead he roughly pushed her aside and strode through his door which had not been completely closed. Archie Dean was standing right outside the door and Brent almost ran into him. "What are you doing here?" Brent asked brusquely.

"Water heater's gone bad," he said. "Need a new one."

"Well, don't just stand there, replace it!" Brent said angrily as he continued out the door.

Archie remained where he was. Angie had to step around him in order to get to her desk. "I'll order a new one," she said. Archie didn't answer. He just stood there looking at her. She wanted to pick up her stapler and throw it at him, but instead she said coldly, "That will be all, Archie." He nodded, turned and walked out but not without looking back at her over his shoulder. He shook his head as he walked away, and Angie barely heard what he muttered to himself, "You reap what you sow."

"Crazy old man," she mumbled, but her thoughts didn't linger on Archie. She was more concerned about Brent. Although she was relieved that the dreaded conversation was behind them, she knew she would be a fool to think she had heard the last of it. Worse than that was the nagging fear that her brand new marriage had just sailed into treacherous and uncharted waters.

Chapter 20

Heavy, dark clouds hung low overhead as Kate drove to work in the morning. Matches my mood perfectly, she thought. A biting wind was howling out of the north dropping the chill factor into the low twenties. Her car heater hadn't really gotten going until she was almost to Beulah's and she was freezing.

As she pushed open the front door, she heard the sounds of conversation in the kitchen. There she found Mark and Beulah at the table having coffee over the remnants of breakfast. "Good morning, Kate!" Beulah said, full of good cheer. Having her grandson with her always seemed to bring a lift to her already high spirits.

"Morning," Kate said, looking directly at Beulah. She avoided eye contact with Mark, but she could feel his gaze upon her. She busied herself picking up the plates and carrying them to the sink.

"Sit down and have a cup of coffee," Beulah said. "The dishes can wait a bit."

Kate was not interested in sharing a table with Mark again. And why, she wondered, did Beulah have this innate talent for yanking her out of her comfort zone all the time? She decided not to cooperate. "I think I'd better get the sheets started in the washer," she said. "You two enjoy your visit." Leaving no time for a reply, she exited the kitchen and headed for Beulah's room.

Beulah looked at Mark. "Okay, what have you done?" she asked with a sigh.

Mark grinned like a school boy with his hand in the cookie jar. "Nothing, Gram; don't look at me like that."

"Out with it," she said firmly.

Mark shrugged his shoulders as he answered, "She asked me a question last night, and I guess she didn't like my answer."

"What was the question?" Beulah asked pointedly.

"She wanted to know if I thought she was guilty."

"Let me guess — you said 'yes'?"

"No, I didn't. All I said was that I liked to do my homework and draw my own conclusions later. I was just being honest. I had no idea it was going to upset her so much."

"Well, I'm all for telling the truth, but Mark, this poor girl doesn't need one more person doubting her credibility. Can't you see how painful that is for her after all she's been through?"

"Sorry, Gram, but I've been trained to focus only on facts. Trust me, I didn't know it was going to set her off like that."

Beulah rolled her eyes, "Men!" she said in exasperation, shaking her head.

Mark was quiet for a moment and then he spoke, "You're important enough to me so that I really want to check her story out, Gram. Since you refuse to let her go, I've got no choice. I've got some time off coming, and I'm going to go out there and see what I can learn."

"Well, I can save you a lot of time and money by telling you that what you're going to find out is that ex-husband of hers is a first-class moron!"

Mark laughed. "No one can fault you for not being loyal, Gram," he said.

Beulah smiled but then got serious again. "You go do what you've got to do. All I ask is that you really *do* keep an open mind. Sometimes cops make up their minds and then go out and find facts to support *their* theories. I don't want you doing that to this nice young woman." There was a note of warning in her voice as she continued, "I'm very serious about that, Mark."

"I'm not *that* kind of a cop," Mark replied defensively.

"I know that," she said kindly, but added, "See that you don't turn into one." She reached over and patted his hand. Her voice softened as she said, "Thank you for looking out for me. It means a lot. But promise me that you'll look out for Kate, too. She's in sore need of that."

"How about I do this, Gram — I promise you that I'll do my best, and then we'll let the chips fall where they may."

Beulah frowned. "Stubborn as the day is long," she muttered.

Kate walked in and started loading the dishwasher. Mark stood and walked over to her. "I didn't mean to upset you last night," he offered. Kate didn't turn around.

"That's fine," she said without emotion. Mark turned around and looked at Beulah, shrugging his shoulders as if to say, "I tried." She winked at him in return.

Mark turned back to Kate and asked, "Did you have time to make that list?"

She turned around then and dried her hands on a towel. "I'll get it," she said and disappeared into the other room. In a minute she was back and handed him a long white envelope.

"Thanks," he said, then walked over to Beulah. He bent down and gave her his customary hug. "I've got to get going." He walked to the doorway and turned to Kate, "Bye," he said. She nodded. A small smile played at the corner of her mouth.

When he had gone, Beulah said, "He's really a fine man. Don't be angry with him."

Kate sighed and leaned her back against the sink. "You know, Beulah, I don't think I'm angry at Mark. I think I'm just angry period."

"Well, it seems to me that you've a right to be. And I think it's a real good thing that you're figuring that out. As long as you know what to do with it, anger can be a positive thing."

"I've never heard anybody say *that*," Kate remarked.

Beulah replied, "The way I see it, when you finally get good and mad, then usually you do something about it. It's when you don't feel anything that you're in a bad way, because you're just an inert lump going nowhere."

Kate laughed. "Don't make it sound so attractive!"

Beulah laughed too. "Just calling a spade a spade," she said.

Using a wet cloth, Kate wiped the table in front of Beulah and removed the empty coffee cups. "I have an idea," Beulah said. "Why don't we move into the living room and put that puzzle table in front of the window? We'll get better light that way. It's such a dreary day, and it's hard to see over by the fireplace."

Kate stood still and didn't answer. She had purposely avoided that window and its view of the lake, and Beulah knew it. "Why are you doing this?" she finally asked tersely.

Beulah smiled at her and asked gently, "Aren't you angry that you can't look at something as beautiful as that lake? Don't you ever want to be able to enjoy that beauty ever again?"

Pain flashed in Kate's eyes. "Of course I do, but how can I?" she demanded. "All it does is remind me of losing Jackson!"

"You were in a car when the accident happened, but I still see you driving a car," she said.

"That's different," Kate said. "I have to drive."

"I see," remarked Beulah. "So, it is a choice."

There was silence as Kate processed those words. Beulah had set her trap so deftly that Kate had fallen head first into it. Finally, she looked at Beulah and asked, "Are you saying that I don't have to feel this way?"

"I think you just said it yourself, my dear, except you phrased it as a question."

It was clear from Kate's furrowed brow that she was trying hard to understand this new concept. "But — but I don't see how," Kate stammered. "Every time I look at a lake, *any* lake, I just get terrified. It's involuntary!"

"I think it's possible, Kate, that you have allowed your grief and your pain to attach itself to that innocent body of water. It's like a scapegoat. By avoiding the lake, you feel that you are somehow safe from pain. It's a little trick that our minds sometimes play." Kate walked over and sat down next to Beulah. She was quiet and listened as Beulah went on, "The pain isn't in the lake, dear." She paused for a moment and placed her good hand over her heart, "It's in here."

Reflexively Kate took her own hand and held it to her heart. She sat very still and her eyes glistened. In her mind's eye she was seeing herself as a young girl standing at the edge of the swimming pool, her mother's outstretched arms reaching toward her from the water, "Jump, Katie!" she had encouraged. "I'll catch you!" But she had been afraid to jump, to leave the certainty of the pool deck for the unknown of the water that she knew was over her head. It was no different now. Beulah, she realized, was giving her a similar challenge. As long as she continued to identify the lake with all of her angst, she didn't have to deal with it, but acknowledging that she carried it within her own heart seemed too horrible to contemplate. "Jump Katie!" her mother's voice sounded in her ears once more. "I'll catch you!"

The sound of her mother's voice was so real. Kate felt her presence as if she were actually there. She hesitated a few minutes more until she heard it again, "Jump!" she said. She laid her head on the table and great sobs began to shake her body. All the anger and grief that she had tried to hide from washed over her in giant waves. She cried and cried. All the while Beulah had her hand gently upon her arm. Her eyes were closed.

Long minutes passed. Finally, her sobs became quieter and gradually subsided. She felt drained but strangely peaceful. The familiar knot inside of her was conspicuous only by its absence. She sat up, her face and arms soaked from tears. She pulled a handful of napkins from the holder on the table and did her best to wipe her face. Beulah was smiling at her, a look of deep compassion in her eyes.

"You've been so kind to me" Kate said.

Beulah ignored her statement and said, "It's an important day — one that I've been waiting for."

"Thank you," Kate said, "for caring so much."

Chapter 21

Mark sat in the back row in the New Eden Community Church. He had spent the previous day driving around Careytown, familiarizing himself with the area. Now he listened as Pastor Reed began his sermon. Opening his Bible, the pastor read aloud, "'Wives, submit to your husbands as to the Lord.' From the book of Ephesians, Chapter 5 verse 22." He paused for a moment and searched the faces of the congregation. "Dear friends," he said, "It's just one small line from a very big book, and yet it can make the difference between having a home filled with peace or living in a war zone. Which one do you think God wants for you?" He continued talking about the merits of a wife's role in the home and how important it was for her to place herself in submission to her husband — that she would be blessed mightily if she obeyed.

Observation was a critical tool in Mark's work. Seeing what other people didn't notice was key. He listened and watched Brent connect with his congregation. He observed whether people were yawning, distracted, or listening attentively. He found the pastor's choice of subject matter interesting in light of his recent conversation with Kate. Watching his mannerisms, he noted that Brent was a good speaker, not without charisma. He was young, dynamic, and it appeared that he was popular with the congregation.

Coffee and donuts were served that morning in the fellowship hall after the service. Mark decided to hang around. A few people came up to him and introduced themselves. In response to their inquiries he mentioned that he was in town on business. After a few pleasantries, they moved on. He noticed an attractive blonde woman at Brent's side. He guessed her to be his wife as both wore wedding rings and Brent stood close enough to her to suggest that kind of intimacy.

His attention was diverted by a middle-aged man in work clothes at the back of the room. In contrast to the smiling faces around him, he seemed unfriendly. Mark watched him enter a closet, and reappear with a mop. He walked over to a sizable puddle of juice on the floor that some women were trying to soak up with paper napkins. When he had cleaned it up, he returned the mop to the closet but he didn't leave right away. He lingered for a few moments, staring at the backs of Brent and the woman at his side. As if she could feel his penetrating gaze, the blonde woman turned around and looked back at him. She frowned and leaned toward Brent, whispering something to him. He then turned to look, but the man had already gone.

Mark put down his coffee and slipped out the door. He walked down a hallway, looking into each room he passed. They appeared to be mostly Sunday school classrooms. When he reached the end of the hall there was a closed door on the left. Mark opened it quietly and found a large storage room with shelves full of decorations and boxes. He looked behind the door and was startled to see the same man who had just wielded the mop a few minutes ago. He had a half eaten donut in his hand. He stared up at Mark and said nothing.

Mark was quick to extend his hand, "Hi, I'm Mark. You must be the maintenance man," he said cheerfully. The man wiped his hand on his pants and shook Mark's hand. "Archie Dean," he said matter-of-factly and continued to eat his donut. He did not stand up.

"I was wondering if I could ask you a few questions," Mark said.

"What about?"

"How long have you worked here?" Mark asked.

"Who are you, and why do you want to know?" Archie looked intently at Mark.

"I'm investigating the drowning of the pastor's young son that occurred a little over a year ago."

"Who you working for?" asked Archie.

"I'm not really working for anyone. I'm just trying to determine if there was any guilt on the part of the boy's mother."

"Why?" Archie asked, his eyes narrowing.

Mark had a gut feeling and he went with it. "She's working for my grandmother, and I need to know if my grandmother's in good hands or not."

"You a cop?" Archie asked.

"Yes, but not from around here. I'm Detective Matson. I work out in eastern Washington."

Archie thought for a moment, all the while searching Mark's eyes. Finally he said, "Can't talk here."

Immediately Mark's antenna went up a notch. "Name the time and place," he said.

"There's a diner way out on Route 10. Ruby's — about ten miles south. I lock up here at noon."

"I'll be there," Mark said. He backed out and closed the door behind him.

Mark saw a short hallway that connected to another one and he followed it. The other hallway led to a couple of offices and a reception area for a side entrance. A name plate on one of the doors read "Pastor Reed." The door was closed. Just then he heard footsteps coming from the other direction, and Brent and the blonde entered the reception area. They were not smiling, and both of them were startled to see Mark.

Instantly, Brent's demeanor changed, and a wide smile opened on his face. "Can I help you?" he asked. "I'm Pastor Reed. This is my wife, Angie. Are you a visitor?"

"Mark Matson," he said, shaking his hand. He nodded at Angie. "I'm just in town for a short while."

"Welcome. What can we do for you?" he asked.

Mark hesitated. He had a hunch that he needed to hear what Archie had to say before he began questioning either of them. "I'd like to come in and talk with you tomorrow if that's all right?"

"Is it urgent?" he asked. "Mondays I'm not usually in the office."

"How about Tuesday?" Mark asked.

Brent turned to Angie. "Take a look at my calendar and see what I've got on Tuesday," he said.

Angie went to her desk and started her computer. She clicked open the appointment calendar and scanned it. "You have four o'clock free," she said.

"That will be great," Mark said. "I'll see you on Tuesday." He quickly let himself out the side door before there were any more questions to answer. He checked his watch. He had a good half hour before Archie would even be done at the church, so he decided to explore a little more. He made a right turn out of the parking lot.

Right away he realized that this had to be the stretch of road that Kate had traveled on that fateful night. She had mentioned turning right out of the parking lot and heading away from the direction of the town. This area was all rural. He passed a couple of driveways with houses set far back from the road on the right side. Tall trees lined the road on both sides. Up ahead he saw the bridge.

He slowed as he neared the bridge. The trees were cleared within about 500 feet of the approach. Mark pulled his car over on the shoulder and stopped. He got out and walked slowly toward the bridge. Across the road he saw a clearing that matched the area where he was standing. On both sides, the bank running down to the water was quite steep. It was so steep that he couldn't get close to the water's edge without risk of losing his footing and sliding down. By the angle of descent, it was his guess that the water was deep even at the shoreline. As he looked down at the water from up above, he couldn't help but think of the last moments of that little boy's life, and he grimaced.

The wooden bridge looked as if it had been there for a long time and needed to be replaced. Had it been a newer one, it would surely have had extended guard rails preventing a car from entering the lake. Mark walked back to his car and reached in for his camera. He photographed the area from several different angles until he was satisfied he had enough. From the corner of his eye he saw a car approaching the bridge. He looked over just as the car slowed down to a crawl. Through the window he recognized

Angie's blonde hair. He saw that Brent was driving. Quickly the car accelerated and continued on over the bridge.

Mark looked at his watch and realized that he had spent more time there than he had planned. He got back in his car and pulled across the road into the other clearing. He backed into the road again and headed back in the direction of the church. He did not want to risk missing his appointment with Archie.

Chapter 22

Archie was seated at a back booth in the diner and he looked nervous. Mark had planned to be waiting for him but it hadn't worked out that way. Now he was just glad that Archie was here waiting for him. As he slipped into the booth opposite Archie, he was annoyed that he had to sit with his back to the room, *not* a choice he ever made willingly. He liked to keep his eyes open and know what was happening around him.

A waitress approached and put two menus down. Mark didn't even look at his. Before she could say anything he said, "I'll have a BLT and a Coke."

She looked over at Archie expectantly. He started to open his menu but instead pushed it aside. "The same," he said. She picked up the menus and left.

There was an awkward silence for a minute, and finally Mark asked, "What can you tell me about the first Mrs. Reed?"

Archie said, "Let me see your badge."

Mark chuckled to himself. This guy wasn't going to make things easy. He dug out his credentials and showed them. Archie studied them for a few seconds and then just grunted. He looked up. "She's a nice lady," he said.

"Did you know her very well?"

"Just the times she'd come around the church. In my job you can tell the nice people right off because the others just look right through you like you're not even there."

"Well, my grandmother sure likes her," Mark offered, hoping to put him at ease, "And she prides herself on being a good judge of character. I prefer to do a little leg work before I make up my mind." He smiled but Archie didn't return the smile.

"Do you have any thoughts about the tragedy regarding the little Reed boy?"

Archie shook his head slowly back and forth. "Shouldn't a' happened," he said solemnly.

"How do you think it happened?" Mark asked.

"Boy drowned," he answered.

"Yes, I know. What I meant was do you think it was an accident?"

"Yes and no," he answered cryptically.

"Can you explain what you mean by that?"

"That's all I'm going to say about that right now." Archie folded his arms across his chest. Mark understood by that move that he was holding on to something that he didn't want to share. Archie didn't look like a guy that could be easily pushed.

The waitress reappeared with a tray. She placed their Cokes and sandwiches before them. "Can I get you anything else?" she asked.

Mark looked over at Archie, but didn't expect a response and there wasn't one. He smiled at the waitress and said, "No thanks." She returned the smile, picked up her empty tray, and left.

For a few minutes both men silently ate their sandwiches. Mark was thinking of how he could get Archie to open up, but he was doubtful that he could get him to budge on something he'd already made up his mind about. He decided to change the subject entirely. "What can you tell me about the new Mrs. Reed?" he asked.

"She works at the church. She's his secretary," he answered.

"Has she worked there long?"

"Over two years now."

"Were you surprised when she married the pastor?"

Archie didn't answer right away. Mark had already observed a pattern in Archie's responses, and he could tell that this question held some kind of significance, but he didn't know what. Interviewing was like fishing, he thought. You threw out a lot of worms never knowing which one was going to get the bite. He waited patiently for his answer.

Finally, the one word answer came, "Nope."

"Why didn't it surprise you?"

Again, there was a wait. Archie looked at Mark carefully as if he was trying to size him up. "Who you working for?" he asked.

"I already told you, I'm on my own time right now. This is personal."

"How do I know that for sure?"

Mark pulled his cell phone out of his pocket. "Would you like me to call my eighty-five-year-old grandmother out west and let her tell you?"

Archie looked down and shook his head, "Nah." He was quiet for a time and then he said, "I've had this job for over twenty years. It's not the Ritz, but it's comfortable, and I know it real well. I don't want to lose it."

"Why do you think you would be risking your job to answer my question?"

"Because the pastor's my boss and he'll fire me if he finds out what I know."

Mark sat up, immediately alert. "I can assure you that I won't be divulging to Mr. Reed any information that you provide. You have my word on that. What is it that you know?"

Archie looked really uncomfortable. He looked around. Finally he said, his voice almost too low to hear, "He and that new wife of his was carrying on a long time before that poor boy died."

Mark sat back in his seat at this unexpected bit of information. "Are you sure?"

"Saw 'em with my own eyes! Disgusting!" he spat. "I wasn't spying or nothing, but I sort of happened upon 'em by accident. It was just after quit'n time and I was late getting out of there. They didn't see me, but it was clear what they was up to. That was no way to be treating that nice wife of his." He shook his head back and forth, "No way at all!"

Mark could see that Archie was pretty agitated. "I can imagine how upsetting that would be to discover. You've been carrying this around for a long time; I'm sure it hasn't been easy. Is there anything else that you can tell me?"

Archie thought for a minute and then said, "I'll trust you with this much and see what happens." He pulled out his wallet and took out some bills. As he laid them on the table he said, "I gotta be somewhere."

Mark took a card out of his wallet, circled a number, and handed the card to him. "You can reach me at this number — anytime." Archie nodded, took the card and hurried out. Mark sat for a moment, absorbing the information that had just been dropped on him. Suddenly, this whole thing had just gotten a lot more interesting, he thought.

Chapter 23

It was early Sunday afternoon, and Angie was cleaning up the lunch dishes. Brent had just left to visit a hospitalized church member, and she was glad that he was gone. Nothing had been right since her announcement that she was changing jobs. She had known that he was going to be angry when she told him, but she had not imagined that he was going to stay that way. Since that day, he had treated her as if she wasn't even there.

This was not how she had envisioned the start of her marriage — the one they had planned and waited for so long. Maybe she should have talked to Brent first about the job change, but then she reasoned that he would simply have forbidden it, and they would have been right back at square one.

Angie placed the last dish in the dishwasher and dried her hands. She walked out onto the back porch, sat down, put her feet up on the porch rail, and began to review the troubling thoughts that had been plaguing her for the last couple of days. The most troubling was the complete change in Brent's demeanor. He had certainly had his moody days before they married, but he had never completely shut her out the way he had just recently. And then there was the physical abuse. She was still having a hard time grappling with that episode. The hardest thing to deal with had been the difference in the way he behaved when they were alone as opposed to when they were around other people. He was like two different people, and he seemed to move effortlessly between the two personas.

She would have loved to have been able to talk about it, but every time she tried he just froze her out. She was reluctant to push too hard, and she hated to admit it was because she was afraid. And then there was that episode on the drive home from church earlier. As they had approached the bridge, they had spotted a car parked alongside the road. Brent had slowed to a crawl and stared at the young man who was walking nearby. When they had realized who it was, instead of giving a friendly wave or something, Brent had just floored it. When she asked him why, he had just stared straight ahead and said nothing. What followed was a silent lunch during which they ate their meal together but very much apart.

How could she be so miserable so soon after her wedding? Who was this man she had married, and how would they ever manage to get back to where they should be? These were questions that played in her mind. She folded her arms over her chest, feelings of frustration rising in waves within her. She could not escape the thought that this was how her mother had lived, and now it was her turn. Was this how it was in all marriages? It didn't seem possible.

Angie sat there for a few minutes more and then decided that she would feel better if she got busy. She remembered the fabric she had bought a while ago and thought this would be a good time to start the new curtains that she had planned for the kitchen. Brent was going to be away most of the afternoon, and she could work in the nursery without him knowing about it. She got up and went into the house.

When Angie opened the door to the nursery, she was startled to find that the sewing machine and her box of sewing supplies were no longer there. At first she wondered if her mind was playing tricks on her, but as she scanned the room there was no sign that she had ever put anything in there. She crossed to the closet and opened the door — nothing. She looked behind the rocker — still nothing. Angie closed the door and started her search.

She went through every room in the small house fairly quickly, checking closets, under the bed, anywhere those things could be stored. A panicky feeling crept up within her. The only place left to look was the garage. Angie hurriedly walked through the kitchen, out the door, and across the grass to reach the unattached single car garage. She opened the door and looked. All she saw was the usual stuff. As she walked around, she checked every box to make sure that her things weren't inside. She moved anything that could possibly have something behind it. Still nothing.

Exhausted and defeated, she walked back toward the house and spotted the two garbage cans sitting next to the back porch. She opened the lid to one of them and saw nothing unusual. Halfheartedly she checked the other one and froze. The remains of her smashed-up sewing machine lay in pieces inside, along with torn and soiled pieces of her new fabric and what remained of her sewing supplies.

For a few moments Angie didn't move. She just stared in disbelief at the wreckage in the can. The sheer violence of it unnerved her, and she was afraid — afraid suddenly of what it meant to her. She could no longer trust this man who was her husband. And she asked herself what kind of man would do this.

Angie told herself that it was just a piece of machinery, but she couldn't help feeling that the violence was really intended for her, and she shuddered. She put the lid back on the can and went inside to grab her purse. When she came back out, she got into her car and backed out of the driveway. She didn't know where she was going to go. She just knew that she needed to be someplace else where she could think.

Driving aimlessly, she tried to get her panic under control. Like Alice in *Alice in Wonderland*, she found herself catapulted into a strange and different world, but this one was not full of happy surprises. Up ahead she saw a diner and decided she needed a cup of coffee. She pulled into the parking lot and maneuvered her car into a parking slot. Before she could open her door, she was surprised to see Archie Dean walking out. Quickly, she hunched down a ways in her seat and stayed right where she was, hoping that he wouldn't see her, and when she saw him get in his car and drive away, she was satisfied that he had not. The last thing she had expected was to run into Archie way out here on Route 10.

With a heavy heart, she walked toward the entrance. This was one she had never been to, and she had pulled in because she felt comfortable that she wouldn't run into anyone she knew this far from town. Well, she had been wrong about that! She was just thankful that she hadn't arrived a few minutes earlier.

She walked inside, glad to get out of the cold. She felt chilled and wondered how much that had to do with the November air as opposed to what she was feeling in her heart. A hostess led her to a small booth and she slid in. She wasn't at all hungry, but she picked up her menu anyway. When she did, she was surprised to see that her hands were shaking. Quickly she put it down. As she did, she noticed a man approaching her booth, and when she looked up, she was surprised to see it was the same man that she and Brent had met earlier that day in the church office. The diner had been a bad idea.

Hurriedly, Angie picked up her menu again and looked down, hoping that she would be as lucky with him as she had been with Archie a few minutes before. Out of the corner of her eye she saw him stop as he reached her booth. She did not look up.

"Mrs. Reed?" he asked.

Grudgingly Angie looked up. "Oh, hello," she offered with a weak smile that didn't reach her eyes. Her hands continued to shake and she put the menu down and quickly slid her hands down onto her lap, hoping that he hadn't noticed.

"Are you by yourself?" he asked. Angie nodded.

"Do you mind if I join you for a few minutes? I would like to ask you a few questions."

Angie peered up at him, wondering who this man was and what he was about. She didn't answer right away, and he apparently took that as a "yes" and sat down across from her. Oh great, thought Angie, just what I need.

"Who are you?" she asked bluntly. She hadn't meant to be so abrupt, but her feelings were raw and revealed more than she wanted them to.

"I'm Detective Mark Matson," he said. "I'm not from around here."

"What are you doing here?" she asked.

"I'm trying to get some answers about a case I'm researching," he answered.

"What case?" she asked.

"Wait a minute," Mark chuckled. "I was going to ask you a few questions." He paused for a moment and searched her eyes. "You seem to be upset," he observed. "Is something wrong?"

"No, I'm fine," she lied.

Mark waited a moment. He could see that she was uncomfortable, but he felt that an opportunity had just been dropped in his lap, and he couldn't walk away from it. Acting on a hunch, he asked, "How would you describe your husband?" He was actually more interested in her reaction to his question than her actual answer. He watched her intently.

Angie stiffened, started to say something, and changed her mind. Finally she said, "He's very popular with the congregation." There was no enthusiasm in her voice.

Mark smiled. "I take it that he's not very popular with you right now."

"It's not been our best day," Angie said.

"Want to talk about it?" asked Mark.

Angie's trembling had stopped, and she felt much better being in this crowded place full of people with the noise and clatter of dishes and friendly conversation. She sat up straighter and said, "Look, I don't know you from Adam. Why would I discuss my personal life with you?"

"I understand," Mark said. "It's just that you seemed pretty upset, and I thought I might be able to help in some way. Sometimes all anybody needs is a good listener."

"A detective?" she asked sarcastically. "The only person worse would be a reporter."

"Yes, but I have the advantage of not being from around here. And I have the added advantage of not knowing anyone in this town. You probably couldn't find anyone right now more objective than me." He was being half playful and yet his voice held a note of seriousness. He pushed on, "In my line of work I've learned to detect fear pretty easily. Something or someone has frightened you badly. Maybe I *can* help."

The desire to tell all was strong in Angie. She wanted desperately to talk to someone about what had happened today, but she did not know this man. He looked kind and helpful, but she knew now that looks could be very deceiving. "I appreciate your offer to help," she said, "but no thank you."

Mark pulled a card out of his wallet and handed it to Angie. "This is my card," he said. "If you change your mind, don't hesitate to call my cell number. Anything you tell me will remain confidential." She took the card and looked at it. "Thank you," she said softly.

The waitress arrived and asked them what they wanted. Angie ordered a cup of coffee. "Nothing for me," Mark said. "I've got to be going." The waitress left. Mark got out of the booth and stood up. "I meant what I said. Don't hesitate to call me." He smiled and said, "I hope your day improves."

Angie watched him walk away. She couldn't help wondering what he was doing in Careytown, who had hired him, and why. When her coffee arrived, she sipped it eagerly to try to warm up. The hot mug felt good in her hands.

The question in her mind that she couldn't escape was what was she going to do next? Her first instinct was to tear into Brent and let him know just how angry she was, but she understood she was no longer that normal new bride dealing with a mundane frustration. There was a well of anger in him that was much deeper than anything she had seen since her childhood days with her father. That sixth sense she had developed as a child now told her it was imperative for her not to trigger that anger.

A second option was to pretend that she had not discovered the destroyed sewing machine and supplies. It had been several days since she had looked in that room, and it would be believable that she simply had not done any sewing yet. That would give her time to think and would postpone what promised to be a very ugly scene.

There were two things she was absolutely certain about. One — she had never been more miserable, and two — she was not going to wait until she had found a replacement. She was going to start her new job right away. Brent could find his own secretary. In one week her whole world had changed so much that she didn't even recognize it. As she gazed out the window of the diner, she whispered to herself, "This is for you, Mom. I'm not going to fall into that same hole you fell into." She wanted desperately to have a good cry but it was too much of a luxury, not to mention embarrassing. She had to pay attention, and she had to stay strong.

Chapter 24

With her freshly baked pies in a basket in the backseat, Kate drove to Beulah's house. In light of what she supposed everyone now knew about her and her recent past, she was nervous about meeting Beulah's family. Things hadn't gone all that well with Mark, and she could just imagine what it would be like to have a whole group to deal with. Having Thanksgiving dinner at home alone was preferable to what could turn into an "inquisition" or equally uncomfortable, polite but cool rejection. Unfortunately, Beulah had refused to take no for an answer when she had repeatedly offered excuses. If it hadn't been a double celebration, including Beulah's birthday, she might have gotten away with it.

Mentally she reviewed the names of Beulah's children. In the order of their birth, there was Laura, Sarah, Adam, and Melanie. She could only hope that they turned out to be as nice as their mother. There would be a group of grandchildren to meet as well — all in all, a bit overwhelming all at once. Kate pulled into the driveway and noticed a group of cars already parked. It looked like she was the last one to arrive.

Carrying her pie basket on one arm and her gift bag over the other, Kate rang the doorbell. Even though she let herself in every work day, somehow it didn't seem appropriate today. A woman who looked to be in her mid-sixties opened the door. "Hi," she said with an inviting smile. "You must be Kate! I'm Laura. Happy Thanksgiving!" She took the pie basket from Kate. "Ooh, these look delicious. Thank you." Kate returned the greeting and followed her into the living room that was full of people. A football game was playing on the television, and there was a level of noise and activity in the house that gave Kate a small glimpse into what this house had been like years ago.

On the periphery sat Beulah watching everything around her, and Kate didn't think she had ever seen such a contented look on her face. She saw Kate come in and quickly exclaimed, "Kate! Happy Thanksgiving! I'm glad you're here." She motioned for people to quiet down and she continued, "Everyone, I'd like you to meet my friend, Kate." Glances turned her way, and the men and boys stood up. Everyone was quite welcoming, and Kate relaxed a bit.

A woman close in age to Laura came in from the kitchen. She had a wooden spoon in her hand. "I'm Sarah," she said.

A man offered his hand, "Hi, I'm Adam." He looked to be quite a bit younger.

Finally, the one who had to be Melanie came into the room from the kitchen. "I'm Melanie — the baby," she said with a grin. "Welcome! We're glad you could come. Mom has told us how much she has enjoyed getting to know you."

Kate thanked her and then it was time to meet the grandchildren, some of whom seemed to be much closer to her age. Laura introduced Karen and Dara, "These are two of my three," she said. "Mark couldn't be here today and we're all mad at him!" she teased. Adam introduced his wife, Leann, and their two, Chuck and Lisa. Melanie introduced her husband, Bill, and their boys, Kyle and Kurt. There were girlfriends and boyfriends aplenty, and Kate knew she wasn't going to remember most of their names. She decided to just do her best.

"I'm happy to meet all of you," she said. "And I thank you for including me today. She walked over and squeezed Beulah's hand then turned to Laura. "I'll bet you could use another hand in the kitchen."

"Follow me. All volunteers are gratefully accepted," Laura said.

Laura was attractive and still young-looking for a woman Kate knew had to be in her mid-sixties. There was an energy about her that Kate found appealing. She hoped she would have that when she was her age.

The kitchen turned out to look nothing like the peaceful place it usually was. Every inch of counter space was crammed with bowls and pans and chopping boards. The women came in along with Kate and returned to their tasks. The men stayed in the living room near the television, which didn't surprise Kate at all. It was easy to see that everyone felt very at home in this house. And better yet, they seemed to feel very at home with each other. This is the kind of family that you read about, Kate thought wistfully. She suddenly wished that she had sisters and brothers, too.

Any qualms that Kate had held about being rejected quickly evaporated. If they had anything against her, they were disguising it very well. She worked alongside the women as they put the meal together, and by the time it was ready to be served, she felt that she belonged. It was the strangest feeling as she had just met these people only a couple of hours before. Amazing, she thought.

The number of people prevented everyone from sitting at the table. Beulah and her children and their spouses had a place there, and the rest took a tray and found a seat in the living room which adjoined the dining room. Kate positioned herself toward the back of the buffet line and reached for a tray, but Laura stopped her, "No, Kate, we have a place set for you at the table."

Kate blushed. "No, Laura. That should be reserved for family."

"Today you're a guest and guests are seated at the table. No arguments," she said firmly.

Kate was reminded of how much she sounded like Beulah and how useless it would be to argue. "Thanks, Laura," she said. When she took her plate to the table, she found that she was seated next to Laura. Everyone gathered around behind those who were seated, their trays in hand while Beulah offered a prayer of thanksgiving. Kate found herself touched by Beulah's words, surprised that she had allowed herself to feel that way. She was surprised a lot lately. Ever since that day at Beulah's kitchen table that the floodgates had opened within her, she felt different about almost everything. One of the best things was that she could look at the lake without fear. Tears of gratitude began to fill Kate's eyes, but she blinked them back. She did not want to embarrass herself in front of everyone.

Dinner was actually fun. There was laughter, good natured teasing, and banter and stories from younger days. Beulah was right in there holding her own. Those seated in the living room came over to the table on their way for seconds and lingered, coming in and out of the conversations easily. Kate was startled when she realized what was absent — tension. It had become so much a part of her life before she had come to Lake Pendant, that she had nearly forgotten what it was like for it to not be there. She could breathe, and it felt wonderful not to have to measure her words or anticipate reactions.

After the meal, Kate helped carry the plates into the kitchen. Cleanup was swift with such a large group of helping hands. The younger ones pitched in, and in no time the kitchen was back in shape. Laura and her sisters put the pies on the dining room table and set a stack of plates and some forks nearby. This was obviously a routine way of serving desert because no one had to be told it was there. Some helped themselves, and others wanted to wait until they had room for it. Everyone found a spot in the living room, either on the floor or on the furniture. It was clear that this was a football family as the game was getting a lot of attention.

Laura leaned toward Kate. "Come on in the kitchen," she said with a wink. Kate followed her. They sat down at the table. "I wanted to tell you that I feel terrible about what has happened to you. Mom has explained a little of it to me, and I hope that's okay with you. None of the others know anything."

"It's okay," Kate said. She had expected it. She was relieved to hear that everyone didn't know. She wondered what this was leading to and started to feel a little nervous again.

"I know that Mark didn't show you much compassion," she said. "I apologize for that, but that's Mark. He's so focused on facts sometimes that he forgets about feelings." Laura was obviously trying to put Kate at ease and she appreciated it.

Kate could see Beulah's kindness in Laura's eyes. "I want you to know that your mom has been wonderful to me," she said. "I don't know where I'd be if I hadn't happened into this job. She's gone out of her way to help me deal with a lot of the baggage I've been carrying."

"Well, that's Mom," Laura said. "She's got a heart as big as that lake out there." She looked toward the window.

They sat in silence for a moment, and then Laura turned her gaze away from the window and back to Kate. "I talked to Mark this morning," she said. "He's taken quite an interest in things in Careytown. That's why he's not here. He said he needed more time to dig a little deeper."

Kate looked up, startled. What had he meant by that? She was afraid to ask, so she said nothing. She could just imagine everyone painting her as a murderess.

Laura interrupted Kate's thoughts. "I think Mark has begun to see things a little more from your point of view."

That was indeed a surprise to Kate. "What did he say?" she asked, curiosity trumping any caution she had.

"Not much, just that he's got some suspicions about your former husband that he thinks are worth chasing down. Mark's got a nose like a bloodhound when he's working. If he thinks there's something there, more often than not, there usually is." She gave Kate a heartfelt smile and continued. "I just want you to know that not all marriages are bad. You're young, Kate. You will have a chance to try again one day."

"Nothing could be further from my mind," Kate said emphatically.

Laura sat up straight, striking a telltale "Beulah" pose. "It looks like that man already stole a lot from you, Kate. Don't let him take your future too."

Melanie stuck her head into the kitchen and announced, "It's half-time. Let's sing Happy Birthday to Mom now and give her our presents."

"Great, Mel. We'll be right in," Laura answered. She and Kate stood up.

"Thanks, Laura," she said. "You're a lot like your mom. That's about the highest compliment I can give you."

Laura leaned over and gave Kate a quick hug. They walked into the living room. Melanie had already stuck a candle in a piece of pumpkin pie. As she knelt down and held it before Beulah, they joined the others in a chorus of "Happy Birthday." "Happy Eighty-sixth, Gram!" Chuck shouted.

"Make a wish, Mom!" Melanie said.

Beulah looked around the room, her eyes twinkling. "What else is there to wish for?" she asked, "but to have all of you gathered around me?" There was a round of applause as Beulah blew out her candle.

Chapter 25

With the curtain pulled back just a little, Angie watched Brent pull out of the driveway and head to work. She needed to get herself in gear quickly if she was going to make it to her new job on time. She had told Brent that she was not feeling well and was going to stay home. Now she had to dress in double time.

Things had been surreal since Sunday afternoon. Having made the decision to say nothing about the sewing machine, she had returned to the house and pretended that she had been out doing some shopping. The following day, Brent had busied himself on his day off with a couple of household chores that he had been putting off. Angie had baked bread and made a pie — anything to keep busy.

All the while she had worked in the kitchen, her mind had sifted through the events of recent days, and she had grown increasingly more uncomfortable. At the bottom of all the turmoil lay a great sadness and a feeling of loss. How could Brent do what he had done? It seemed so out of character for the Brent she had fallen in love with. And yet, she knew all too well that her own father had led a hidden life behind the closed doors of their home. Why should she be so surprised?

I guess I never believed that it would happen to me, she had thought as she had kneaded the dough, punching it down much more ferociously than necessary. While the dough was rising, she had taken a short walk, and called Hank Leonard at Hamilton, and told him that she could start work the next day. He had been pleased.

Angie hadn't dared tell Brent what she was doing. She knew he would have followed her and there was no telling how he might try to sabotage her new position. She stepped into her shoes and gave herself a last check in the mirror. Satisfied, she went to the back door, grabbed her coat and headed out. She felt a little panicky, not because she was starting a new job, but because she had entered a whole new existence, and she felt like a fugitive. She also couldn't get out of her mind the violence represented by her destroyed sewing machine. It had taken a lot of time to save up enough to purchase that machine. Not only was she angry, but a feeling of danger still lingered and she couldn't seem to shake it.

When Angie passed the church, she was relieved to see Brent's car in the parking lot. She checked her watch. She had ten minutes to make it to work on time. It wouldn't do to be late on the first day. With a minute to spare, she pulled up to the building and managed to arrive at Hank Leonard's office right on the dot. She breathed a sigh of relief.

The morning passed quickly with her Human Resources briefing and filling out required forms. By early afternoon, she was learning some of the tasks associated with her new job. The most amazing thing to Angie was the stark contrast in her new environment. It was, quite simply, normal. People were friendly and Hank proved to be patient and kind. For the first time in days, she relaxed a bit and began to enjoy herself.

At promptly five o'clock, she cleaned off her desk and leaned her head into Hank's office. "Is there anything else for today?" she asked.

He looked up and smiled. "No, you go on home," he answered. "You've put in enough for the first day. Tomorrow we'll knock off early and get a head start on the holiday. Good job, Angie, and welcome to the office."

"Thanks, Hank. Good night. I'll see you tomorrow." She retrieved her purse from her bottom drawer and left. As she walked out of the building, she could feel the familiar tension return. She knew it was customary for Brent to work past five, and she was banking on that to have time to beat him home, but she wasn't stupid enough to think it would automatically work out that way.

How had her life become this mess of fear and anxiety so quickly? She still couldn't figure it out. She had thought by marrying a pastor that she would be guaranteed not to repeat the life her mother had endured, and now she was thinking she might have been wrong about that. Already she felt forced to lie about the most insignificant things — why she was going out, where she was going.

As if things weren't crazy enough, she had to contend with Thanksgiving. In just two days she had to deal with a major holiday in the midst of a marriage in crisis. They had been invited to the Woodruff's, members of their congregation, and she wouldn't have to cook, but the inevitable "happy couple" charade was getting harder to endure.

Passing the church, Angie was relieved to see Brent's car still in the parking lot. The office door opened and a man emerged. Angie recognized Detective Matson immediately. She had forgotten that he had a four o'clock appointment with Brent. What if he had mentioned seeing her at the diner? For a moment she panicked, but then she reasoned that he was in the business of obtaining information, not giving it out.

As soon as she got home, Angie ran to her closet and changed into a pair of jeans and a sweatshirt. She then went to the kitchen to start dinner. Pulling her biggest pot out of the cabinet, she filled it with water and put it on to boil. Rummaging in the pantry, she found a jar of spaghetti sauce and a package of spaghetti. She remembered that there was half a loaf of garlic bread in the freezer and she took that out. Adding a couple of green salads would complete the meal. She was hoping to have it ready when Brent arrived.

Twenty minutes later, Brent walked into a kitchen filled with the aroma of garlic bread and spaghetti sauce. "Hi," Angie said. "I hope you're hungry, because I have a lot."

Brent took his coat off and didn't answer her. He hung it on the hook by the back door. "You seem to be much better," he stated.

"I'm a little better," she lied.

"I tried calling you four times today. You didn't answer," he said flatly.

Angie tensed up. "I went out for some more Ibuprofen," she said.

"I called at ten a.m., at noon and twice in the afternoon," he said, staring at her coldly. "And besides, we have a whole bottle of Ibuprofen."

"I know. I dropped it and they went all over the bathroom floor and I wasn't going to put them in my mouth after that," she said, grateful that she could think so fast. Brent stared hard at her for a moment and then said nothing more. He left the room. Angie leaned against the sink and exhaled.

In a moment he was back. "How come there are no pills and no bottle in the wastebasket?"

Anger flickered in Angie but she forced herself to keep calm. "Because," she said, "I actually dropped the bottle in the toilet."

"Why did you say you dropped it on the floor?" he grilled.

"Because I thought you would be angry that I flushed it down the toilet," she explained. She thought to herself how easy lying could be once you started. In an attempt to change the subject, she asked, "How did your four o'clock go with that guy we saw on Sunday?"

"Fine," he answered. But Angie could see by the clenching of his jaw that he was lying as well. She knew better than to push it. She put the last plate on the kitchen table and the two sat down. After a rudimentary prayer of grace, they began to eat in silence. Though she said nothing, inside Angie's thoughts were shouting, how can you be such a hypocrite? What's wrong with you? She wanted more than anything to challenge him, but she didn't dare. She wanted to shout, "How dare you treat me as if I'm not even here!" but the truth was she was afraid.

When Brent had finished his meal he looked up at her. "I have your replacement," he said matter-of-factly.

"Who is it?" Angie asked, surprised. She couldn't imagine that he had found someone so fast, but she was incredibly relieved and tried not to show it.

"The Woodruff's oldest daughter, Amy," he said. "She came in today and asked to fill out an application. I hired her. She starts tomorrow."

Angie wanted to do cartwheels. She couldn't have asked for a better turn of events. Amy was a beautiful brunette about twenty-two, and Angie knew Brent didn't have to think long about hiring her. She found, surprisingly, that she wasn't even jealous, just grateful.

"You'll need to come in and train her," Brent said. Angie froze. She had not anticipated this, and she chastised herself for overlooking such an obvious thing. She tried wildly to think of anything she could say that would get her out of it, but her mind went blank. Finally she said, "I still don't feel very well, and I have to bake some pies tomorrow to take to the Woodruffs."

"You seem perfectly healthy to me," Brent said coldly.

"It's not that hard a job," Angie said. "Amy can figure things out as she goes. If she has any questions, you'll be there to help her. And she can call me with questions."

"What are you saying? You're not coming back?" Brent asked, raising his voice a notch.

Angie felt trapped, like an animal backed into a corner. She was all out of excuses and lies. She felt the panic rising within her, and she fought it with anger. This whole scenario was insane, and she couldn't believe that she, a newlywed, was caught in this impromptu web of deceit. She returned Brent's angry glare with one of her own and felt liberated to be speaking the truth to him for the first time in days. "No, I am not coming back," she dared to say.

Brent reached across the table and gripped her arm. "You will do what I tell you to do," he said icily as he increased the pressure of his grip. Angie tried to pull away, but his grip was too firm. His fingers were digging into her flesh and it was painful.

"Stop it, Brent!" she exclaimed. "That hurts!" But he did not let her go.

"You are going to train Amy, and you are starting tomorrow," he shouted.

"Who are you?" she screamed at him. "Why are you being like this? Let me go!"

He held on. "You have to calm down, Angie," he said evenly. "And you need to know your place."

Tears of rage began to run down her cheeks. She clawed at his hand trying to get him to release his grip, but he just squeezed harder. "You're hurting me!" she cried. She tried to get up, but his hold on her arm was so firm that she couldn't move without hurting more. Her shoulders shook as she cried. She buried her face in her free hand. She wanted to throw her water glass in his face, but she was terrified of what he would do in return.

"Do we have an understanding?" he asked.

"Yes," she cried, willing to say anything to be free of his grasp. Finally, he let her go. She grabbed her coat and purse off the hook and ran out the back door. Running to her car, she got in and backed out. She had nowhere to go, but she couldn't subdue her desire to flee. For the second time in three days she found herself in the same situation. She headed for Route 10 and the diner. She needed to think.

Chapter 26

The day after Thanksgiving had dawned clear but cold. Kate had the day free since Beulah's family was still in town. As she sipped a cup of hot tea in her kitchen and finished a muffin, she decided that staying inside was going to be the plan today. It was way too cold to be walking around town or venturing out. She would leave that for the skiers.

After cleaning up in the kitchen, Kate decided to start going through some of the closets and getting rid of things — a project that she had put off for a long time. Although her Aunt Belle had been a tidy person, she was also a "saver" and the closets were full.

Kate was a little surprised to find that she was eager to attack this job. Before, she had strenuously avoided it, feeling unable to delve into Aunt Belle's things. But today she knew the time was right, and she felt more like her old self than she had in a long time. She had a new strength and vitality, things that had eluded her since she had fled Maryland two months ago. Smiling, she thought of Beulah and how much her time spent with the wise woman had helped to bring her back to herself. She felt safe. Lake Pendant was like a cocoon, a place where she could be free to be herself once again. She hadn't realized how far she had traveled from being that person who had so joyfully and impulsively married the handsome young pastor.

With a sigh, she forced thoughts of Brent out of her mind and opened the hall closet, as good as any place to start. There were several boxes on the shelf and she carefully pulled them down and stacked them next to the couch. When she opened the first one, she was delighted to find it was full of old photos. They were black and white pictures from the forties and the fifties. She recognized her mother and her aunt standing together holding Easter baskets and dressed in fancy dresses with patent leather shoes and lacy socks. Others included her grandparents and their two girls on a trip to the Grand Canyon; some were taken at a lake and there were assorted ones from Christmases past.

For the first time in a long while, she felt "connected" again to family. Even though they were gone, they belonged to her and she to them, and it grounded her, placing her within their little group much as she had seen Beulah yesterday firmly fixed in the midst of her clan. It was a little sad but at the same time still a good feeling to know that she had a place, a beginning — that she was a part of a unit and that she would see them again one day.

This last thought surprised her as she had diligently pushed all thoughts of anything spiritual out of her mind after her dealings with Brent. It was funny how just a few old photos could so quickly bring back to life feelings and beliefs she thought she had successfully buried. She found it strangely comforting to recognize that they were beliefs she still owned, ones she had shared with all the loved ones in the photos on her lap, and she recognized for the first time that they represented the strongest threads that connected her to all of them. Brent had taken so much from her — why had she been foolish enough to let him steal that from her, too? She shook her head in disgust.

There were several more boxes of photos and some slides as well. As she held the slides against the light, she saw that they were more early images of her mom's family. Her grandmother wore a dress in all the slides and a shiny, tan 1948 Chevrolet appeared in quite a few of them. She hoped she would find a slide projector somewhere in the house so she could see them better.

Carefully she carried the boxes back to the closet and put them on the shelf. Half the morning was gone, and she hadn't gotten rid of one thing. She turned next to the antique rolltop desk in the living room. There were several deep vertical slots under the rolltop that were each filled to capacity with envelopes and letters. She pulled the waste basket around to her side and got ready to fill it. Copies of outdated invoices were pitched, and she had a sense of accomplishment as one-by-one the slots were emptied.

Kate next turned to the drawers. The top one she ignored with its assortment of the usual office supplies. In the second drawer, a deeper one, were bundles of letters held together by rubber bands. She noticed the first bundle was all in her mother's handwriting. Eagerly, she removed the rubber band and opened the first letter.

Her mother described a recent heavy snowfall and how she had been battling a head cold. It was her next words that caught Kate's interest:

I am very concerned about Kate's plans to marry a man she barely knows. Brent is a good-looking fellow and appears quite friendly, but I can't shake a feeling I get when I am around him — as if he is "acting" the part. I've tried to tell Kate, but she is so in love that she won't listen. I'm afraid that this will be something she is going to regret. How I wish her father was alive. I know he would know how to handle this.

Kate let the letter drop to her lap. Why hadn't she listened? Why had she been so willing to ignore her mother's warnings, a woman who loved her without reservation while she allowed herself to be led by someone she didn't know hardly anything about? Thinking back, she had to admit there had been little inklings of doubt within her, but she had chosen to ignore them or find ways to rationalize them. When Brent had not wanted to spend time with her mother, she had reasoned he was just being overly sensitive to her concerns for her daughter. When he had gotten irritated with her for trying to include some of her nursing friends in their evenings out, she had bought his line that he just wanted time alone with her, and like a fool, she had been flattered.

She put the envelope back and pulled out another one, this one dated much later. This time there was no talk about the weather. Her mother had gotten right to it:

Dear Belle,

My heart is so heavy with worry about Kate. She seems to be changing before my eyes. The happy, vibrant girl is slipping away, and in her place is someone I hardly recognize — a girl with little emotion except for an ever-present sadness.

When I ask her about it, she just says they are adjusting to married life and I should give them time. I don't ever remember walking around like that after I married Bill...

Kate sat still and her eyes grew moist. She had been so wrapped up in her own misery that it had never occurred to her that her mother had suffered, too. How glad she was that her mother had not lived to see what had eventually happened, had not had to suffer the terrible loss of her only grandchild, and had not had to watch as her only daughter was thrown into jail.

She read through several more letters. They were a chronicle of the last years of her mother's life from within her own heart. It was gut-wrenching at times for Kate to see how much of her suffering she had kept from Kate.

In the bottom of the pile was a letter she had clearly written during her final days. Her handwriting showed unmistakable indications of weakness as she had penned:

Dear Belle,

The doctors are doing all they can, but I can see in their faces that they have little hope. I am desperately hanging on for the birth of my grandchild, and I pray that I will.

It is strange to have all these contrasting emotions fighting for a place within me.

The joy of the impending birth, coupled with the sadness that I won't live to see this little one grow up, is something that is at war constantly within my heart. Worse than that is the knowledge that I am leaving Kate at a time when I know she needs me the most.

I had a call from Brent this morning. He said Kate is spending too much time up here with me and I should tell her to not come up as often. He said she is needed at the church. It is hard to fathom the coldness in that man's heart. I doubt if he has one. I'm so glad I can vent to you, Belle and that my thoughts are safe with you. I can't mention this to Kate, not when she is already so unhappy at home. This little one has put a spark back into her eyes and I don't want to spoil that for her or ruin what little time we have left together...

Kate slammed the letter down on the desk. Unbridled anger flooded her like a tsunami. How dare he! The self-centered jerk! If only she had known about this she would have had something to say to him. How could he have said such a thing to her dying mother — a woman who didn't have a mean bone in her body? She wished with all her might that she had left him then and brought Jackson to Lake Pendant. He would be alive today.

Thoughts of Jackson brought fresh tears to her eyes, and the sadness overpowered the anger. Her arms physically ached to hold the sweet little boy one more time. She was so lost in her memories, that it took her a minute to hear the sound of someone banging loudly on her front door.

Quickly Kate wiped her eyes with her sleeve and went to the door. She saw through the little window that it was Kevin, and there was panic in his eyes. She opened the door, and he rushed in talking as fast as she had ever heard him, "Kate come quick! Mommy's hurt!" He tugged at her sleeve.

Together they ran next door. As they entered, Kevin ran to the kitchen and Kate followed. She found Dee lying on the kitchen floor next to an overturned stool, her head bleeding. She was unconscious. Kate grabbed a roll of paper towels off the counter, tore off several sheets, and folded them quickly. She firmly pressed these to Dee's head wound. Next she checked her pupils and found them dilated, indicating a possible concussion. Dee's eyelids fluttered. Sounding half asleep she mumbled, "Kate?"

"You're okay, Dee. Looks like you've had a nasty fall off that stool."

"What stool?" Dee asked, looking confused.

Kevin appeared visibly relieved to see his mother talking. "Mommy was reaching for her big bowl up there!" He pointed to a cupboard over the refrigerator. "The stool fell over and she hit her head there." Again he pointed, this time to the metal edge of the counter. "Mommy, are you okay?"

Dee reached out and took Kevin's hand and gave it a squeeze. Slowly she sat up. "I'm a little dizzy," she said. Kate kept the compress against her head. Dee looked down and saw the little puddle of blood on the floor. "Uh-oh," she said. "No wonder my head hurts so much."

"I'm going take you over to Pendant General. You need to be checked out and get stitched up." She took Dee's hand and guided it to her paper compress. "Here, keep pressing on this." Kate found a clean towel and a little bag clip and wrapped the towel around Dee's head to hold the compress in place. She fastened it tight with the clip. "It's not pretty but it will do until we get there," she said as she helped Dee to her feet.

Together the three of them walked to Kate's car. The hospital was only a few blocks away, and they arrived in just minutes. Dee was put on a gurney and wheeled through the doors of the ER treatment area. Kate knew she couldn't leave Kevin alone in the waiting area, so she remained with him.

After what felt like hours but was probably only one, a nurse came out and told Kate that they were going to admit Dee for observation overnight. She did indeed have a concussion, and doctors wanted to watch her for any sign of increased swelling in her brain. It took another hour for Dee to be placed in a room upstairs and finally, she and Kevin could go see her.

"How do you feel?" asked Kate.

"Like I've gone ten rounds with George Foreman," Dee answered, with a sleepy grin. Her head was wrapped in layers of white gauze. Kevin's eyes were big as he took in the sight. Dee reached for the little boy, "Come over here, Kevin. It's not as bad as it looks, honey." He quietly got as close to his mother as he could, threw his arm over her, and buried his face in her blanket. "I'm going to be fine. You were a brave boy to go get help like you did. Daddy will be so proud of you!" She patted his head. "That reminds me. I need to call Randy. He's working a job down in Lewiston. Can I use your cell phone?"

Kate fished her phone out of her purse and handed it to Dee. She made the call and after repeatedly assuring Randy that she was going to be okay, she finally hung up. She handed the phone back to Kate and quietly looked at her for a long minute.

"What is it?" Kate asked, aware that something was on Dee's mind that she was having trouble putting into words.

Dee lifted Kevin's chin. "I think it's time that you used the bathroom. Better go do that."

"I don't need to go, Mommy," he said.

"Yes, you do," she answered with a firm tone to her voice.

Kevin sighed, "Okay," as he dutifully disappeared into the little bathroom.

Dee pulled herself higher up on her pillow. "I don't know how I can ask you this, Kate, knowing what I know about your situation. I just don't know what else to do. Do you think you could watch Kevin for me until Randy gets home tomorrow?"

"We haven't talked in awhile, Dee. A lot has happened — good things. I'm stronger now. Not only can I do this for you, but I was going to insist if you didn't ask. I would love to watch Kevin for you. He's a great little guy, and it will be fun for us both. Besides, I don't really want to spend the rest of the day sorting through Aunt Belle's stuff."

A smile spread across Dee's face. "Thank you, Kate. I owe you one. And I'm glad to hear that you're ready to start living again." She winked at her. They heard the door open and Kevin came back in. "Did you wash?" asked Dee. Kevin nodded and held up is hands.

Kate stood. "Hey Kevin, what do you think about getting a hot dog and seeing a movie?" His eyes lit up and he looked at his mother.

Dee smiled and nodded. "Kevin's been dying to see that new animated feature playing in town."

Reaching out, Kate took his small hand in hers. It was still wet but she didn't care. It felt so very good to have a little boy's hand resting in hers. Together they walked toward the door. "I'll call you later, Dee. Try to get some rest."

Dee had already closed her eyes.

Chapter 27

It was Sunday afternoon. Kate was finished with her weekend "to-do" list and decided to check on Dee. After putting on her heavy coat, she walked over and knocked on the door. Kevin opened it and was excited to see Kate. "Mommy!" he yelled. "Kate's here!"

Dee walked out from the kitchen and smiled. Her head was still bandaged. "I still look like a character from a horror movie, I know," she said, laughing. "What are you up to?"

"I just wanted to see how you are doing," Kate answered.

"I'm great except for this really ugly hat!" she said, pointing to her bandage. "Doctor says I can get the stitches out in a few days."

"That's great news. I hope that you won't be going for any more stuff in that high cupboard again, at least not without a sturdy ladder!"

"I think I learned my lesson. I shudder to think what might have happened if Kevin hadn't been here. And I'm really thankful that I have a nurse living right next door!"

"I was glad to help. And I was really glad to be able to spend time with Kevin. He's a lot of fun." Kevin smiled with pleasure at her praise. "We had a great time at the movie, too, didn't we, Kevin?" He nodded and she continued, "I hope that you'll come over and play again soon."

He smiled a big smile. "Can I, Mommy?"

"Sure, anytime. But right now, why don't you go see what Daddy is up to?" She gestured to Kate, "Come on in and sit with me while I finish frosting this cake," Dee said.

"What's the occasion?" Kate asked.

"There really doesn't need to be one in this house. If I don't make something sweet and gooey every couple of days, I hear protests from Randy and Kevin."

Kate remembered the days when she had made cookies for Jackson. That had been so much fun. Licking the bowl was a favorite thing for him, and he couldn't wait until the last cookie had been dropped on the cookie sheet so he could swirl his little finger around the inside of the bowl. "I used to enjoy that, too," Kate said wistfully.

"Oh, I'm sorry," said Dee, her face instantly sad.

"Don't be, Dee. I'm not looking for sympathy. I'm just remembering out loud. It's a good feeling to be able to talk about that time again. For so long I didn't dare go there. Having Kevin with me this weekend was like a breath of fresh air, and it helped me. Thank you for letting me take care of him."

"Thank you, Kate. You really saved the day for both of us. With Randy out of town, I don't know what I would have done without you." Dee stopped frosting for a moment and said, "You know, I have noticed a big change in you. Whatever that old lady is doing for you, it sure is working."

"When I think back to where I was when I first met Beulah, I have to admit that I have come a long way. She has a way of homing in on things, and she's not shy about it, thank goodness. I'm grateful. I've let go of a lot of the fear and feel more like myself than I have in a long time. There's only one area that still troubles me."

"What's that?" asked Dee as she swirled the last dab of frosting on the top of the cake.

"I'm ashamed to say that I haven't driven across the bridge since I first came into town."

"That's understandable, Kate. It reminds you of a terrible accident. I'd feel the same way."

"It's not just that. It's that I can't remember what really happened before I went into the water. I've tried and tried but there's nothing. I'm leaving the church parking lot, and then I'm in the water fighting to get Jackson out of the car. Why can't I remember what happened in between?"

"Well, if you hadn't showed me the overturned stool and Kevin hadn't told what happened to me the other day, I wouldn't have remembered it either. When I woke up I didn't know what had happened. It's not unusual after you hit your head to be a little fuzzy about things."

"I think it's more than that — like I've pushed it so far down that I wanted to make sure I couldn't remember."

"That's putting a lot of blame on yourself that you don't need, Kate." Dee observed.

"Maybe so, but I've finally gotten to the place where I feel strong enough to deal with it. And according to Beulah, truth is the way out of this maze I've been wandering around in. I do want out, Dee."

Dee sat down and wiped her hands on a towel. She reached her hand across the table and put it over Kate's. "You poor thing, you've been through so much. Why don't you just let it go? It won't change anything. Why put yourself through all this again?"

"I don't know, Dee. I just feel like something is driving this. I feel like I can't really get free until I remember it all and finally know how I could have driven that car in the lake. I haven't told you this, but the whole town, including the police department, thought I did it on purpose!"

Dee's eyes opened wide. "Impossible! How could they think such a thing?"

"Because my husband told them that I had been very depressed and that I had intended to kill Jackson. They believed him."

Dee shook her head. "I thought your experience was horrible enough before, but I can't imagine having your own husband turn on you at time like that. Why would he do that?"

"I wish I knew, Dee. We hadn't been getting along very well for quite a while, but I never imagined that he would do anything like that."

Dee took off her apron and ran some water in the bowl, leaving it in the sink. "Come on, Kate. You and I are going for a drive."

"Where?" asked Kate.

"Across the bridge," she said. She hollered down the hallway, "Randy, Kate and I have to go somewhere. We'll be back in about an hour. Can you keep on eye on Kevin?"

"Sure, you two have fun," he hollered back.

Kevin came running in and asked, "Mommy, can I have some cake?"

"Have Daddy cut it for you — and only *one* piece," Dee said sternly. They put on their coats and walked out to Dee's car.

Kate was walking slowly. "I don't know about this, Dee."

"This is what friends are for, Kate. You need a little help right now and I owe you one. Come on, get in."

Kate dutifully obeyed. She could feel the anxiety rising within her, just as it had the first day she had driven into town. She knew that she needed to conquer this fear, but there was no doubt that it was very real. The Long Bridge was just a few minutes from their neighborhood. In no time they were approaching it. Kate felt her breath quickening, and her hands were clammy. She wanted to close her eyes, but she forced herself to look. The water spread out in both directions and the panorama would have been beautiful had she not been so frightened. Her heart was beating fast as Dee followed the traffic onto the bridge. In an instant her mind traveled back to that night. She could not keep the images out of her head — swirling black water closing in on her, the desperate search for Jackson, the swim to the surface as she was running out of air. She put her hands over her eyes and hung her head.

"You okay?" asked Dee.

"It's always the same," Kate answered just above a whisper. "The water is the first thing I see." They drove across the bridge and Dee turned the car around in the restaurant parking lot, the same one that Kate remembered pulling into before she had driven into town that first day. Dee entered the highway and headed back over the bridge. Kate found that it wasn't as bad as the first time. When they got to the end, Dee pulled into a big gas station and once again turned the car around. She waited for the traffic to clear and pulled back onto the road, heading across the bridge again. This time Kate kept her eyes open the whole time. She forced herself to look out over the water, suddenly remembering what Beulah had told her, that the water wasn't her enemy.

When they had crossed the bridge, Dee pulled off into the same restaurant parking lot and parked. She opened the door. "Come on, change places with me," she said as she got out. She walked around to Kate's door and opened it. "You can do this."

Kate got out and went to Dee's side and slid in. She buckled her seat belt and put the car in gear. As she pulled out onto the highway and approached the bridge her eyes got wide. "Dee!" she exclaimed.

"What is it?" Dee asked.

"I just 'saw' something — a flash of red!"

Dee looked around. "Where? I didn't see anything red," she said.

"No, I didn't actually *see* it; I saw it in my head."

"What was it?"

"I don't know. It was just a flash of red right in front of me, and I remember now that night I swerved when I saw it and tried to stop." Kate had slowed to a crawl and the car behind her honked. She realized that she had braked as she was remembering. She picked up her speed again. "I remember hitting it as I swerved!" she exclaimed. "That must have been when I hit my head!"

"You said you tried to stop. Why couldn't you?" Dee asked.

"I don't know. The car just wasn't stopping. I swerved but I didn't have enough time."

"But you said that there were no other cars around."

"When I got up to the road there wasn't anyone there. I don't understand what I saw or where it could have gone. Could I be imagining it?"

"I don't think so, Kate. I think something was in that road in front of you. Maybe it was a hit and run."

"Maybe," she said, chewing on her lower lip. Suddenly she realized that she was at the other end of the bridge. The anxiety had all but disappeared due to her concentration. She turned the car around yet again and drove back on to the bridge as if it were a city street. She turned and smiled at Dee. "Big day," she said.

"Definitely a big day," Dee agreed.

"Thank you, Dee."

"You're welcome, Kate. I think the rest will come to you soon. It's a little like priming the pump. Once you get a trickle going, it's just a matter of time."

"I think you're right, Dee. I'm not so afraid to know anymore."

"Just let it come. It will." Dee said. "Now I think we'd better get home before too many people see me looking like this!" Kate laughed. Dee continued, "Besides, we need to celebrate with a piece of cake — if there's any left!"

Kate felt she had literally and figuratively crossed a bridge. There was a new strength within her and it felt good. Whatever came to her in the days ahead, she had a newfound confidence that she would be up for it.

Chapter 28

On the day before Thanksgiving, Angie had called Hank Leonard and told him that she was sorry, but she couldn't come into work as she was not feeling well. Hank had been understanding and had told her that it was a short day anyway. She should just take care of herself so she would be able to enjoy the holiday the following day. It had been hard enough to call in sick after the first day on the job, but she had felt doubly bad lying to her new boss and having him be so kind in return.

After sitting at the diner the day before and sorting through her options, Angie had come to the conclusion that she had few. Going against Brent right now was not smart. She needed to wait until she could think more clearly about what to do. What was clear to her was that she had no idea of the actual depth of his anger or where he might go with it, and she didn't want to trigger any more of its ugliness.

Maybe she was paying for her affair with him before the marriage. It had been her first time to get involved with a married man, something she had sworn she would never do. She wasn't even sure how she had let that happen. There had been such a gradual response to Brent's charm until the feelings growing inside of her had reached a fever pitch.

Angie remembered that day very well. She had accompanied him to an appointment. They had stopped for a bite to eat on the way back, and when they were at lunch he had looked at her in a way that had made her insides go crazy. Later in the car, he had pulled off the highway and driven down a country lane and parked. She remembered feeling nervous, like a teenager and a combination of fierce desire and guilt were doing battle within her. He had told her that his life with Kate was very unhappy, that the marriage was all but over, and soon it would be resolved, but she was not to tell anyone. He had said that he felt safe sharing this with her — that he trusted her. Then he had reached over and tenderly taken her hand in his. She had not pulled it back. She realized now, that had been the very moment of a pivotal decision, and she had let it pass — the very moment when she had taken the turn down the road she was now traveling with such regret.

She could have resisted, *should* have resisted she knew deep down, but the idea that a man like Brent wanted her — that there might be a future with him, that she might be able to live a life so different from the one she had grown up in overpowered her sense of reason and right. In the span of that fateful moment, he had kissed the back of her hand softly and then leaned over and kissed her lips. All her resolve had collapsed, and she had given in to the hunger for him that had been building for a long time. She had kissed him back with all the passion that had been building within her. From that point on, everything had changed, and their secret lives had begun.

In her booth in the diner, as she sipped her coffee, she had wondered for the first time if Kate had been enduring the same treatment that she was receiving. It had been the first time that she had thought of Kate with anything besides contempt. All of Brent's subsequent talk of Kate had been so negative that Angie had come to believe the woman was a total witch. Now she wasn't so sure. She had laughed derisively at the sudden realization that a man who would seduce her while married to another woman could certainly do the same to her. How could she have been so stupid? Quite easily, she had remembered. She had gone down willingly and without a fight.

With all of these thoughts tumbling around inside of her mind, Angie had decided that the time for being stupid was over. She needed to have all her wits about her now in order to keep from falling into yet more traps. But the one thing she had no clue how to handle was her love for Brent. She had to admit to herself that in spite of how he had been treating her, she still loved him. It had sounded crazy to her that this could be possible, but it was true. And in that instant, she had seen clearly that this was what her mother had gone through — why she wouldn't leave her husband in spite of Angie's pleas to get away. For the first time she felt she was truly walking in her mother's shoes, and she understood.

She had paid her check and returned home. The house had been quiet, and there had been no more conversation with Brent. The next morning she had dutifully gone to the church and had begun training Amy. She was a lovely girl, beautiful in fact, and as she watched Brent display his charm — the same charm that he had poured out on *her* early on — she wondered just how long it would be before he would be telling Amy about how terrible his marriage was with Angie.

Fortunately, Amy was a quick study, and by the end of the day she had absorbed enough information to handle the basics of the job. Angie did not intend to give it one more day.

The following day as they had shared the Thanksgiving meal with Amy's family, Angie had watched Brent's behavior with a newly discerning eye. He had been charming, witty, and the center of attention, something she now realized was very important to him. Amy clearly thought the world of him, as did her parents. Even Angie had been taken in at times. As Brent had treated Angie with respect and fond attention, she had let herself believe for a moment that all was well with them once again. Her spirit had soared, and she had felt happy again, as if her world was returned to normal. It wasn't until they were in the car on the way home that she had been sharply brought back to reality by Brent's withdrawal and his coldness. It had all been an act, and it had felt like having a cold bucket of water thrown over what had been up to that point, one of the best Thanksgiving days she had ever experienced.

Love or no love, Angie had decided right then that she could not live this double life. She knew all too well how it ended. All she had to do was think of her mother and the years she had wasted until the only things she had left were bitterness and regret. No, she and Brent would have to have a very serious talk, and things were going to have to change if she was going to stay with him.

That was for sure. In the meantime, she would do all she could to stay under his radar. Getting her new job had been the first smart thing that she had done in a long, long time.

Chapter 29

After having a way-too-big piece of Dee's cake, Kate returned home, tired but exhilarated in her achievement of another victory over her fears. As she stretched out on the couch and closed her eyes, her mind kept going back to those seconds before the accident. As hard as she tried, she could not remember anything more, but she knew that it was all there — somewhere, if only she could get to it.

Her reverie was interrupted by a knock on the door. She hoped it wasn't Kevin. As much as she enjoyed the little guy, she was just too tired for the energy of a four year-old. For a few seconds she considered not answering but the person was persistent, knocking again, only louder this time. When she got to the door and peeked through the window, she was surprised to see Mark standing on her porch. She ran her hand through her hair and opened the door.

"Hi," he said. "I was just on my way back from the airport and was hoping that you would be home. Is it okay if I come in?"

"Oh, sure. Sorry," she said, opening the door wider and moving to the side. He was the last person she expected to see on her doorstep after the way their dinner had gone. She wished she didn't look like such a frump and then just as quickly she wondered why she cared. "Have a seat," she said, "Can I get you anything?"

"No thanks. I just wanted to talk to you for a few minutes if you have time."

"Sure," she said, taking a seat across from him on the rocker. "What's up?"

Mark looked down and tapped his fingers on his knees. "I, uh," he started, then lifted his head, "I feel badly that I made you out to be like you were some kind of criminal."

Kate had her arms folded. "Don't worry," she said with a hint of sarcasm, "I'm used to it."

"Yeah, I can imagine," he said with remorse. "I've had a chance to talk to several people in Careytown, and I know it must have been really rough on you to be treated that way. You sure didn't need any more from me."

"Why the change of heart?" she asked, one eyebrow raised.

"I've learned some things that the general public didn't know about your situation. It's made all the difference."

"Oh, like the fact that Brent Reed is a total jerk?"

Mark laughed. "Yes, for starters." He could see that Kate still had her armor up. "Look, Kate," he continued. "I really am sorry, and I hope that you'll forgive me. Whatever happened that night, I feel strongly that you had nothing to do with it."

Kate wasn't sure how to respond. She tucked a strand of hair absentmindedly behind her ear and was silent for a moment. Finally, she looked at Mark and said quietly, "Thank you." There was an awkward silence between them for a moment as each one searched for the next thing to say.

Mark was the first to break the silence. "I'll admit, I went to Maryland to check your story out. I tend to be pretty protective when it comes to my grandmother. But when I started doing some digging, I realized that there might be a lot more to this whole thing than meets the eye. Now my investigative juices are flowing, and I want to keep at this thing for a whole different reason."

Again she raised an eyebrow as she asked, "And that would be...?"

"Well, partly because when I'm chasing a story down I get to a point where it's like the tail wagging the dog. I just can't leave it alone until I get at the truth."

Kate pressed him, "And?"

"And I want to help you if I can."

Now it was Kate's turn to squirm. She hadn't been prepared for this turn in the conversation. She found it totally disarming. "I don't know what to say."

"You don't have to say anything. I just wanted you to know that we're on the same page now. I know it took me a little while to get to this point, but better late than never." He grinned, and she found it impossible not to return his smile. He was silent for a moment and then continued, his expression turning serious, "I've been hurt, too, Kate. I know what that feels like."

"Beulah told me," she said.

He glanced up quickly. "I should have known! What did she do, give you my whole life story?"

"No, not really. She just told me about your marriage and how unhappy it turned out. I'm sorry. I know how stupid you can feel when you believe in the wrong person."

"That's exactly how I felt," he said, with fresh enthusiasm. "No one has ever understood that before."

"Well, I sure do," she answered, suddenly remembering her mother's letters she had read a few days before. "My mother tried to warn me, but I didn't listen. I still can't believe that I would jump so quickly into a marriage with someone I barely knew."

"Don't be so hard on yourself," Mark said. "I was warned too, and all I could see was the cover, never mind the book." He looked down at his watch. "Say, it's almost five, why don't we go somewhere for dinner?"

"We've already tried that, remember?" she teased.

"Even more reason why we need to do it again until we get it right," he answered with a smile.

Kate still wasn't all that hungry after that huge piece of cake she had eaten, but she found that she didn't want this conversation to end. "Let me just change into something a little nicer," she said as she got up. "I'll just be a minute."

Mark took her to a place she had not been before. It was cozy with lots of wood beams reminiscent of a lodge and had a large fireplace blazing. Being a Sunday night after a holiday weekend, there weren't many people there. They were seated at a small table near the fire. "This is lovely," Kate said. "I've always wanted to come here."

"It's a favorite with the ski crowd," Mark replied.

"Do you ski?" she asked.

"When I have time. I haven't been able to do much in the past couple of years. What about you?"

"Same with me. My parents were skiers, and when I was little we went almost every weekend."

"We should go sometime," he said.

"That would be fun," she replied. Kate had this strange feeling that her life was taking an abrupt turn, and she wasn't sure where it would take her. She was eager to find out, but then she reminded herself of the mess that she had made of things not so long ago. She decided to pull the conversation toward safer ground. "What did you learn in Careytown?" she asked.

You could see Mark visibly change gears as he thought of how to answer her question. "Well, I found that you have one strong ally," he said.

"Who's that?"

"Archie Dean."

"Oh, yeah. That's something I could never figure out because I didn't know him well at all."

"Apparently, Archie doesn't say much, but he doesn't miss much either."

"What do you mean?"

"He figured out that Brent isn't all he makes himself out to be."

"I don't see how. Brent always made a huge effort to look good at church."

"That would be when he knew others were watching."

"Did Archie see something he wasn't meant to?"

"You could say that."

"What did he see?"

"I'm not sure you're ready to hear this," Mark said thoughtfully.

"Too late. You've come this far, you're going to have to spill it, ready or not," she said firmly.

"Ordinarily I wouldn't pass this kind of information on, but as a friend, I think you have a right to know. You just have to agree not to divulge where this information originated."

Kate leaned forward with a keen interest. "Of course."

"Some time before the accident, Archie observed Brent and Angie having some kind of romantic liaison." He watched Kate intently to see the impact of this information. When she didn't respond, he continued, "I don't want to hurt you anymore than you already have been, believe me," he said, reaching across the table to put his hand over hers. She left her hand under his, receiving the comfort that it implied.

"It makes perfect sense," she finally said. "He wasn't at all interested in me anymore. In fact he barely talked to me. It was as if he had pulled a shade down on a window — only the window was me."

"I'm sorry, Kate. I know the feeling all too well." She smiled in gratitude. It did feel good to know that he understood. Mark took a sip of his wine and then said, "I need you to do something for me."

"Sure. What is it?"

"I need you to tell me everything you can remember from the time you left the church that night until you woke up in the water."

"It's so funny you should ask me that today," she said. "My neighbor Dee and I spent the afternoon driving back and forth across the Long Bridge until I got comfortable with it. It was when I changed places with Dee and got behind the wheel that I remembered something new. I remember seeing a flash of red. I don't know what it was, but there was something in front of me, and I swerved."

"Back up a little bit. Tell me from the time you left the church."

"Well, I always parked on the street in front of the church. It was kind of understood that it was *my* space and people left it for me. I was the first to leave because Jackson needed to get home to bed. I loaded up the Pac 'N Play and got Jackson in his car seat. He was pretty fussy because he was so tired." Kate paused a moment remembering her last cherished moments with her little boy. Mark closed his hand around hers. She continued, "There was no traffic.

There never was that time of night on that road. I pulled out and headed east toward the bridge. I opened the window even though it was chilly, because Jackson always liked to feel the wind and I thought it would distract him. It was dark. I could see the bridge coming up, and I wasn't paying much attention as I'd driven the road so many times. It was straight and boring. I know now that I saw something red, and I think I swerved and hit something. That's all I can remember until I felt the water."

"Do you think it was a car?" Mark asked.

"I can't tell. All I remember is the color red. I've tried and I just can't seem to get the whole picture."

Mark was silent, his brow furrowed. Kate stared at him for a moment, and then asked, "What are you thinking?"

"I don't want to say just yet," he said.

Kate leaned back in her chair and thought for a moment. Then she suddenly sat bolt upright and exclaimed, "Wait a minute — Angie has a red car!" Mark didn't say a word.

Chapter 30

It was the second week of December, and the temperatures had been holding in the twenties for the past five days. Kate was getting used to wearing three or four layers of clothes when she ventured out. It was a Saturday, and she and Dee had made a date to do a little Christmas shopping in town while Randy stayed home with Kevin.

As quaint as the town was with its little old shops scattered within blocks of each other, Kate was suddenly wishing for a modern indoor mall where it would be warm. "Brrrr…" she said as she clutched her collar together against the biting wind.

"Yeah, I'm cold too," Dee said. "Why don't we break for lunch and warm up?"

"Good idea," Kate answered as they both spotted Patsy's Pies, a little sandwich shop.

The windows were frosted, and it was warm inside. They slid into one of the pine booths but kept their coats on. "I think I'm frozen through and through," Kate said. They both ordered coffees when the waitress appeared. She was carrying a pot and filled the two cups already on the table.

"We can't make coffee fast enough today," she remarked with a smile, leaving them each with a menu. In a couple of minutes she was back with her pad and pencil. "Are you ready to order?" she asked.

"I'll have the chili," Kate said.

"Vegetable soup and half of a turkey sandwich on wheat for me," added Dee. The waitress picked up the menus and left.

"So," Dee said. "Don't you have something you want to tell me?"

"Like what?" asked Kate.

"Like who is that terrific looking guy that I've seen coming to your house lately?"

"Oh, you mean Mark."

"Well, whatever his name is, he's gorgeous! Who is he?"

"He's Beulah's grandson."

"Well, that doesn't explain what he's doing at *your* house," Dee said with a wink. "Tell me more, come on."

"He's a detective and he's working on that case involving my accident back in Maryland."

"Pardon me for being a little slow, but what could he possibly have to do with that?"

"He's just interested, I guess."

"Yeah, I'll bet he's interested," Dee said with a big grin. Kate blushed. "Well? Are you?" Dee asked eagerly.

"I don't know how to answer that. It's almost as if I can't trust my own feelings anymore. The last time I did that I got into a heap of trouble."

"You were a lot younger then, and you're a lot wiser now, Kate. I think you should give yourself a little more credit. Tell me about him."

As the waitress arrived with their lunches, Kate moved her coffee to make room and waited until the waitress left. "He and I have one thing in common," she said. "We've both made fools of ourselves for love."

"There are a lot of people in that club!" Dee laughed. "Tell me — what do you feel like inside when he's around? Do you have butterflies?"

Kate thought for a moment and then answered, "I feel safe."

Dee finished a bite of her sandwich and said, "Of all the things I thought you might say, I never would have guessed that one."

"It just sort of popped out," Kate said, blowing on her hot bowl of chili to cool it. "I'm surprised myself."

"Considering what you went through with Brent, I guess it's not all that surprising that it would be something important to you. Were you afraid of Brent?"

Kate didn't answer but Dee saw something in her eyes that told her she was holding back. "Hey, it's me, Kate; you can tell me. Did he ever hurt you?" Kate remained silent as she looked down at her chili, avoiding Dee's gaze. "Kate, please answer me, hon. Did he hit you?"

A small tear slid down Kate's cheek, and she quickly brought her napkin to her face and wiped it away.

"Oh, Kate, I'm so sorry for badgering you. Now look what I've done." Dee was clearly remorseful. "You don't have to tell me anything, really. Try to forget that I ever asked."

Kate looked up and smiled. "It's okay, Dee. I'm finally wising up to the fact that hiding stuff doesn't work in the long run. Unpleasant things have a way of rearing their ugly heads when you least expect them." She stirred her chili. "The answer is yes. I've been so ashamed that I've never told a soul."

"Why should *you* be ashamed?" Dee asked indignantly. "You were the victim."

"You don't know what it's like with some people, Dee. People like Brent can make you feel as if you *do* deserve it. They mess with your head to the point that you don't know what to think anymore."

Dee's eyes were full of compassion as she answered, "I hope that you know now that no one deserves that, Kate, *ever*." Dee's countenance changed as she thought about what she had just said. "I'd like to give that guy a piece of my mind. Creeps like him should be sent to jail."

"I'm the one that ended up there," Kate said. She laughed at the irony.

"What? How?" Dee asked, clearly shocked.

"Brent accused me of deliberately driving my car into the lake, and the police believed him." She paused and added, "I told you he was good at it."

"Didn't you tell them that he was an abuser?"

"The officer handling the case thought I was lying. That was clear right away. Apparently, Brent had done a real hatchet job on my character by the time I got a chance to try to say anything. It didn't help that the officer was a member of our church."

Dee slumped back against the booth. "My gosh, Kate. Every time I think I've heard the worst, you trot out something more ghastly. I can't believe that you had to endure all of that, especially when you had just lost your son. What kind of animal was he?"

"I'd say the worst kind, Dee. Only I didn't realize it until it was too late. You can't imagine what it was like to have the whole town, let alone the whole church, think that you are a killer."

"How did you ever get out?"

"When they finally realized that they didn't have any evidence, they had to let me go."

"How long were you in there?"

"Just a few days, long enough for Brent to pack up my things and put them in storage."

"What happened then?" Dee asked.

"I went to Baltimore and rented a small apartment. They gave me a job at the hospice where my mom lived until she died. They knew me there. I just basically shut down and did what I had to do to pay the rent. That's where I was when I learned about Aunt Belle's passing. As soon as I found out that she had willed me her house, I decided to come out here and try to start a new life. I wanted to get as far away from Brent as I could."

"I guess it's a good thing I didn't know all that back then," Dee said. "I wouldn't have known what to say to you. It's bad enough right now."

"You've managed to say all the right things, Dee. You can't know how grateful I am for your friendship."

Dee smiled at her in gratitude. "Right back at you," she said softly.

The waitress arrived and asked them if they wanted pie. "That's the only reason I came in here," Kate admitted. She ordered the chocolate cream. Dee ordered the lemon meringue. "Lord knows, we are in dire need of a little sugar right now," she said with a chuckle.

As the waitress left with their plates, Dee leaned across the table and said, "Enough about El Creepo, tell me more about New Guy."

Kate laughed. Dee had a knack for lightening the mood. "Well, he's kind and he's smart," she began. "I think he might be interested in me, but as I said, I don't trust my own feelings anymore. It could be that his interest is mostly in the case."

"Doubt it," Dee answered swiftly. "That's my gut talking. Do you like him — I mean as in, are you interested?"

"I have to admit that I feel very good when I am with him. I can totally be myself, and that feels so good. It's just hard to let my guard down when it comes to my emotions. I've had it up so long."

"Don't keep it up too long, Kate. Even the nicest guys get tired after a while."

"You're right, Dee. I need to be more trusting. It's just so hard after what's happened."

"Maybe so, but you won't ever be able to unless you make up your mind to do it."

The pies arrived and they didn't waste any time digging their forks in. "As good as this pie is, Kate, the love of a good man is way better!" Dee laughed, adding, "And not fattening!"

Kate agreed. "And unlike this pie, Dee, you're good for me," she said.

Chapter 31

Late afternoon the following day, Kate was busy stoking the fire in Beulah's large brick fireplace. Beulah had become a devotee of jigsaw puzzles and was working on the finishing touches of her tenth puzzle since Kate had brought her the first one.

"I'm going to get this one done today, I can just feel it!" she exclaimed with enthusiasm.

"I think I've created a monster," Kate replied with a laugh. "You've turned puzzles into a full-time job."

"Can't help it," she said. "It keeps my mind sharp and I get so involved I don't think of my aches and pains. I've got you to thank for that," she added with a wink.

"Well, I'm glad I followed my hunch that day to pick one up for you." The fire was catching once again as Kate poked it and rearranged the wood. She stepped back and brushed her hands off against her jeans. Just then the doorbell rang. "Expecting anyone?" she asked.

Beulah was so engrossed in her search of a puzzle piece that she didn't look up. "That must be Mark," she said. "He said he was coming by."

Kate quickly brushed her hair back and smoothed her shirt as she went to the door. "Hey there," she said as Mark stomped the snow off his boots onto the mat. "I didn't know you were coming today."

"I knocked off early. Actually, I wanted to talk to you."

Kate was pleased to hear that but curious, too. "What's up?" she asked as she took his coat and hung it in the closet.

"In a minute," he said, as he passed her, "First, I need to give Gram her hug." He walked over to Beulah and stood there for a second while she tried fitting a piece in a spot on the puzzle.

"Just a second, Mark, I've almost got a home for this one!" she said, not taking her eyes off the puzzle. Mark looked back at Kate and shrugged.

"Those little pieces have taken her over," Kate replied. "I've given up!"

Beulah settled the piece neatly into its spot and reached her arm up to Mark. "Now then, give me my hug!" she said smiling. Mark leaned over and embraced her. "You know I'm always glad to see you!" she remarked. "I can't help it if Kate got me hooked on these things!"

Mark sat on the couch and Kate felt comfortable enough now to sit down next to him. She waited for him to start the conversation. "I have a favor to ask you," he said.

"What is it?" Kate asked.

"Now I know that this is asking a lot, and you're probably not going to want to do this, but I think it's pretty important, so please at least consider it."

Kate wondered what he could be leading up to. She looked over at Beulah who was back at work on her puzzle. "Go on," Kate said.

"There's a guy in Careytown that I am convinced knows something important about the night of your accident. I can't seem to get him to open up to me, and I have a strong feeling that he just might talk to you."

"Who is it?"

"Archie Dean."

"Why do you think he would talk to me?"

"Because he approached you before you left town and stated his belief in your innocence. A guy like Archie doesn't step out like that unless he has some pretty strong feelings about something." Mark looked intently at Kate as he asked, "Will you go to Careytown with me this week and see if you can get him to open up on what he knows?"

Kate felt as if he had just asked her to go over Niagara Falls in a barrel. "Mark, I — I — It's just not possible. I have a job. I can't just pick up and leave on a moment's notice."

Beulah continued concentrating on her puzzle but muttered, "I'm giving you the week off. Laura is coming for a visit."

"Oh, so this is a set up?" she remarked. "You guys have already decided for me ahead of time?" There was irritation in her voice.

"No," Mark answered. "It's not like that. All I did was work the details out for you in case you were willing to do this. It would help me a lot, and in the long run, I think it will help you."

"How could it possibly help me to be catapulted back to a place where I lost everything? Nothing is going to change what has happened. Nothing is going to bring back one thing that I have lost!"

"How about your good name?" Mark asked.

"Who cares what any of those people think of me? I'm never going back to Carreytown, ever! And I never want to see those people again." She folded her arms firmly across her chest.

Beulah laid down the pieces she had in her hand and turned to Kate. "I think anyone can understand how you feel Kate. It is a huge thing to ask of you. I know I've already asked a lot of you. But if you're honest, and I know you are, you have to agree that I haven't asked anything of you that hasn't ended up being good for you."

"I'm feeling a little outnumbered right now," Kate replied, an edge to her voice, "And I fail to see how it could be good for me to be plunged back into a town where everyone thinks I'm a criminal."

"Kate," Mark said gently. "I can promise you that you don't have to see anyone but Archie. We'll arrange to meet him out of town, and no one will even know you are there. You can be sure that *if* Archie agrees to talk to you, he won't be telling anyone about it."

There was silence as Mark and Beulah waited for her response. Everything in her fought against returning to Careytown. She had experienced victory against some of her fears and felt that she had gained ground in finding her way back from the darkness of her grief. The thought of falling back into that darkness again was too much to comprehend.

Beulah broke the silence. "Kate, you've come a long way. You are not the same girl you were when we first met. If I didn't think you could handle this, I can assure you that I would have never let Mark ask it of you. But I think that for you, going back is like me finding the last few pieces of this puzzle. You left Careytown in disgrace and despair. If you go back in strength, things will be forever changed in the way that you remember the place and the people. And if you play a part in vindicating yourself, then you will have achieved something very meaningful in your future."

Kate knew Beulah well enough to know that she had never steered her wrong. If she was right about this, then maybe she needed to be open to it. She looked at Mark and asked, "What do you think really happened that night?"

"I don't know enough yet to answer that, but I can say that I don't think it was an accident. And by that, I don't mean that I think you are responsible. There is information out there that needs to be pulled together, and I think when it is, you will be very glad we took the time and effort to go after it."

"What if you're wrong, Mark? What if the whole thing blows up in our faces? I have a lot more to lose than you do."

"Kate," he began and paused for a moment, "you've already lost the things that matter most."

There was no getting around the truth of that. But there were other things at stake. "What if they try to arrest me again?"

"It's not going to happen. In fact I learned that Sgt. Davenport jumped the gun on your arrest. He took some heat from that in the department and isn't about to repeat that mistake." Mark reached over and took Kate's hand. "I'm going to watch out for you, Kate. I promise you'll be safe."

The feel of his hand on hers always sent a current through her. It warmed her and gave her chills at the same time. *How was that possible?* She had to admit that she *did* feel safe with Mark. Just his presence gave her a courage that she didn't ordinarily have. It suddenly occurred to her that here he was taking time off his job, going out of his way to help her, and she wasn't even willing to help him. She felt ashamed.

"When would we leave?" she asked quietly.

"There's a six o'clock flight out of Spokane in the morning. I'm staying at Gram's tonight, and I can pick you up early in the morning. Can you be ready?"

The thought of flying across the country with Mark and spending time with him was very appealing to Kate. When she thought of it in those terms, she wasn't nearly as afraid. And if she only had to see Archie, then she could certainly manage that. "I can be ready," she said feeling a surge of excitement at the prospect of being alone with Mark. "But I'd better get on home. I've got a lot to do if I'm going to make an early flight like that."

Mark smiled. "Thanks, Kate. You won't be sorry."

Beulah was grinning too. "That's my girl!" she said. "Why don't you go on home and get yourself ready. Mark's staying here, and Laura will drive down as soon as I give her the call."

Kate stood up and went to the closet for her coat. She turned back over her shoulder and said, "You two make a pretty formidable team."

Mark and Beulah looked at each other and laughed. "Go on, scoot!" Beulah said.

Chapter 32

After getting up at three in the morning, driving an hour and forty-five minutes to the airport and flying across the country with layovers, Kate was tired when they finally reached BWI airport in Baltimore. She had been able to doze a little on the airplane and had been surprised when she awakened to find her head resting on Mark's shoulder. It had felt so good that she had kept her eyes closed for a few more minutes, feigning sleep until the flight attendant had come by to tell them to prepare for landing. Shaken out of her euphoria, she had chided herself for acting like a teenager.

The drive to Careytown took another hour and forty minutes — plenty of time to be reminded of why she was there and what she had to do. While Mark had one thing on her agenda, she had another, which she considered even more important. When they reached the outskirts of town, she asked him to pull into a supermarket parking lot.

"I'll just be a minute," she said as she got out of the car. Mark didn't ask any questions and seemed content to slip his seat back and catch a nap. After about five minutes, Kate reappeared carrying a large bunch of cut flowers in bright colors.

"What's the occasion?" he asked.

"We have just one more stop before the hotel," she answered. "The cemetery is just two miles up this road and a block to the right." Mark blushed and put the car in gear and didn't answer. Kate could see that he was embarrassed by his question, but she didn't know what to say to make it better, so she remained quiet, too.

Pinewood Cemetery was just as she remembered it, small but pretty, with well-maintained lawns and large trees now leafless in its winter setting. Patches of white still lay under the trees from the last snowfall. It was near dusk, and they didn't have much daylight left. Kate indicated a good place to park and Mark pulled to a stop. With her bouquet in hand, Kate got out and walked over to a small headstone with a little lamb carved on it and a cross. *Jackson Samuel Reed* was spelled out under the lamb. Gently she laid the bouquet in front of the headstone and then stood before the little marker. She had never thought she would get to visit his little grave again when she had headed west; standing here now brought back afresh her sense of loss. She should have waited, she thought. She wouldn't have been so tired tomorrow. But waiting had been out of the question.

Tears washed over her cheeks and fell freely to the ground as she stared at his little marker, remembering the sweet-faced, happy little boy who had brought her so much joy. She hadn't expected this to hit her so hard and then wondered why she should be surprised. Jackson had been her whole life — her reason for getting up in the morning and her only happiness. Her shoulders shook from the wave of grief that passed over her.

Suddenly she felt a pair of hands resting lightly on her shoulders. She hadn't heard him approach, but she knew it was Mark. There was such great comfort in his touch, and she felt her tears subside as calmness flowed through her. Kate was so used to being alone in her grief that she didn't know what to do. She dug in her coat pockets for a tissue but found nothing. Before she could figure out what to do next, Mark had produced a folded handkerchief and offered it to her. When she turned toward him, she was surprised to see that his eyes were moist. For a long moment, as they stared silently into each other's eyes, it felt as if the pain passed back and forth between them. By some unknown catalyst, it was somehow lightened in the process.

As if they had done it a thousand times before, Mark pulled her toward him and held her close, stroking her hair with tenderness. She remained in his embrace, unwilling to leave the first truly safe place she had been since Jackson had died. Tears continued to course down her cheeks, but they felt different, and she wasn't sure what they meant. She felt an odd mixture of sadness, joy, comfort, peace, and pain all rolled into one. Finally, her tears were spent and she looked up at him. "Thank you," she whispered. "I really needed that."

He smiled at her, his arms still around her. She sensed that he didn't want to let go either. "I needed it too," he said. Together they turned and walked slowly, arm-in-arm, back to the car. As Mark helped her inside, she glanced at his handkerchief, now a mess of mascara and makeup. "Uh-oh," she said. "I don't think you're going to want this back."

"Keep it," he said with a wink as he slid into his seat. "I have more."

They were quiet as they drove to the hotel, each aware that something had altered between them. They had entered, for a few brief moments, an incredible place where nothing had mattered but the two of them. It had felt like another dimension, and as such, the intensity of the emotions seemed like a slice taken out of a different time and place. Kate did not know what to say as these thoughts played in her mind. Mark was the first to retreat to the safety of the mundane. "I've booked two adjoining rooms at the Hillside Inn. I hope that's okay. I want to be near enough to make sure no one tries to bother you."

"Who's going to protect me from you?" she asked playfully.

Mark reached over and grabbed her hand. "No one will ever need to do that," he said, his tone serious. "I mean that Kate." She squeezed his hand in response. She didn't think he could possibly know how much that meant to her.

Kate awoke to a tapping on the connecting door. She pulled on a robe and went over and opened it to find Mark already dressed. "I've got breakfast in my room," he announced. "Scrambled eggs and bacon, toast and orange juice. Get it while it's hot!"

"I'm such a mess," she said, hiding halfway behind the door. "Can I get a shower first?"

"Food will be cold," he said. "You look great to me. Come on, let's eat. You can dress later." She followed him into his room where a table was set with two covered plates.

"It does smell good," she admitted. She was hungrier than she thought and it didn't take her long to finish everything on her plate.

"What's happening today?" she asked.

Mark wiped his mouth with his napkin and leaned back in his chair. "I thought it might be good to drive around a little. I'm hoping that it will jog your memory a bit about what happened that night."

"I've tried so hard to remember, Mark. If I haven't been able to in all this time, I don't think I ever will."

"Don't forget what happened when you drove with Dee on the Long Bridge. You *did* remember something else. I think it's just a matter of time before the whole picture falls into place. We can't give up yet."

"Maybe you're right, but I can't help feeling that I don't remember because subconsciously I don't *want* to remember. What if I'm protecting myself from something really horrible?"

"You're strong and you're smart, Kate. You're not going to fall apart if you recover a bad memory. In fact, I think it will release you from the fear of it altogether."

"I hope you're right about that," she said with a tinge of doubt. Kate stood up. "Thanks for a great breakfast, Mark. Give me twenty minutes and I'll be ready."

"Great," he said. "I've got some calls to make in the meantime."

With her eyes shut, Kate stood under the shower head and let the water cascade over her head. As she reviewed how her day had begun she was again amazed at the dichotomy of feelings that tossed about in her mind. How could it be that she had just shared a breakfast, in her bathrobe, in Mark's hotel room? And how was it that she felt as if she had done it a million times before? Try as she might, she couldn't figure out how she felt so completely at ease with this man, especially when she had already decided that men were not safe. Amidst all of her best intentions, she found herself completely letting her guard down around him. It was as if something took over when they were together, something bigger than both of them, and she became a willing partner without even offering a fight.

It felt a little like sitting down next to a box of chocolates. You knew you shouldn't indulge, but with them right in front of you, it was impossible not to sample them. And once you sampled one, it tasted so good that it was just too hard not to have another and another. Chocolate was definitely a weakness of Kate's, but now she realized that it wasn't her only one. She resolved to try and be a little more disciplined when it came to both.

Within half an hour, she and Mark were in the car and winding through town. It felt so strange to be back here with all the familiar landmarks. A feeling of heaviness descended upon Kate right away. It was as if time had stood still awaiting her return. She had to fight to remind herself that she was just a visitor, and this part of her life was now behind her, but that proved difficult.

As they passed the New Eden Community Church, Kate stared at the building. There was Brent's kingdom, she thought wryly. His little world where he ruled. If the people only knew what she knew about him, he wouldn't be "king" for very long. But no one would ever believe her, not after his expert job of character assassination. She was so lost in thought that she didn't realize they were almost at the bridge. Mark pulled the car over as he had done the day he first visited the site.

"I thought we'd park here for a moment, if that's okay," he said.

"Sure, it's fine," she said. She knew that Jackson wasn't there and that's all that really mattered to her. Thanks to Beulah, she understood that it was a body of water, not a sinister entity — an accident scene, nothing more.

"Want to get out?" he asked.

"Okay," she said. She opened her door and stepped out even before Mark got out of his side. She stood and looked at the steep bank rolling down into the water. *If I set a ball down right here,* she thought, *it would roll right down into the water. Nothing would stop it.* She didn't move any closer, afraid of the incline. As she peered at it, she asked herself how she could have let her car go down that embankment. She couldn't even imagine.

"Had enough?" Mark asked as he came up beside her.

"I'm trying to understand how this could have happened, but I'm at a total loss."

"Don't force it," Mark said as he led her back toward the car. "It will come on its own, probably when you least expect it. That's how these things usually work."

They drove on into her old neighborhood and parked across the street a short way down from her house. A pang of sadness hit her as she remembered Jackson playing in that same front yard. "One day my life was just normal and routine," she said wistfully, "and the next, everything about it had changed forever."

"Was it really 'normal and routine'?" asked Mark.

"Maybe not to some people, but to me it was all I knew."

"If you hadn't had Jackson, how would you have described your life here?"

Kate thought for a moment. "Far from normal. Touché, Detective Matson."

"I have to wonder," Mark mused. "Is it much different for the current Mrs. Reed?"

Just as he said that, the front door to the house opened and Angie appeared. Instinctively, Kate slid down in her seat, but not far enough that she couldn't see over the dash. At the same time, Mark picked up a map and held it up to cover his face. Kate noticed it had a small hole in it which Mark had strategically placed at eye level. "I see you're always ready," she remarked with a grin.

Angie was bundled up in a heavy coat and wore a scarf over her head, tied at her chin. She walked out to the mailbox, placed an envelope in it, shut the door, and raised the red flag. As she turned and stood back up, Kate and Mark both noticed a large bruise on the side of her face that the scarf didn't completely cover. Had they blinked for an instant they would have missed it. Angie walked quickly back to the front door and disappeared inside.

Kate was silent. Mark peered over at her, waiting for her to say something. When she didn't, he asked, "Was that a part of your 'normal and routine' family life, too?"

She looked over at Mark. She didn't have to reply. He could read the answer on her face.

"She may not be your favorite person, but that woman probably needs help," he said. Kate still didn't answer, but she knew from experience, what was going on inside of that house. Finally she said, "I can't believe I'm saying this, but I actually feel sorry for her."

Mark pulled away from the curb. As they passed the house, Kate looked down the driveway and spotted Angie's red car parked near the back door. Kate frowned. There was something bothering her about that car, and yet she couldn't say what. She decided to keep it to herself.

Chapter 33

Angie sat at her dining room table, her fingers drumming on the wooden table top. She stared outside at the cold, gray sky and fumed. She might as well be in prison, she thought. Her big outing for the day had been the short walk to the mailbox.

As much as she swore that she would not let it happen again, here she sat, sporting the results of yet another episode of Brent's explosive, unpredictable anger. She had actually prided herself on how she had "handled" him these past few weeks, as if she could contain whatever monster lay within him. She now understood that it had been a foolish foray into denial and a putting off of the inevitable. She could no more control him than she could control the weather. And there was something else, too. His outbursts appeared to be escalating toward more violence. Since this last argument, she realized that she was living in fear. It had been so subtle that she hadn't realized it building, but with nothing to do but look out the window and think, she had been forced to see it for what it was.

The crazy thing was this last fight had started over something as innocuous as a jar of pickles! Angie had put her favorite, bread and butter pickles, on the table with the hamburgers for supper the night before. Brent liked dill pickles. He had gotten angry that she had not bought the kind he liked. Tired from a long work day, Angie had snapped back sharply, "If you're that crazy about dill, why don't *you* buy some?" With that they were off and running. More angry words were exchanged. Angie's tension from the past weeks finally erupted in a loss of self-control, and she had made a huge error. In the heat of battle, she had said she thought he was crazy, and she wished that she had never married him. The back of his hand had hit her face almost before her sentence was finished, and she had been knocked completely out of her chair. As he had walked past her lying there on the floor, he had kicked her so hard in the back that she had laid there for a full ten minutes before she was able to get up.

With these horrible events playing over in her mind, she had to ask herself, "What am I still doing here?" She knew the answers now only too well. She hadn't been able to save enough money yet to rent an apartment, and furthermore, she didn't want to stay in Careytown anyway. Her idea to keep a low profile and wait things out until she had enough money to leave wasn't going to work. Angie had never felt more trapped.

A cordless phone sat on the table in front of her, and for the past two hours she had been debating about whether to make a phone call and who to call. She still had the card from Detective Matson. He had told her to call him anytime. But what good would it do to call an officer who lived across the country? She thought about calling the police, but hesitated because she knew that Brent and Sgt. Davenport were friends, and she didn't trust what would happen if Dave called Brent. If Brent could do this to her over a jar of pickles, there was no question that something worse would happen if she reported him to the police.

Angie wished with all her heart that she had made friends in this town. When she looked back, she could see that her whole life had revolved around Brent. Because they had been involved in a clandestine affair, she had avoided cultivating close relationships with anyone else. Brent had made it clear that his job and hers would be in jeopardy if anyone had found out. It had just been easier to keep to herself. Now she was forced to realize that she didn't have anyone she could run to. If only she could go to her mom. She of all people would understand, but Angie knew that her mom couldn't help her now. A stroke had left her without the ability to speak, and she was living a bleak existence in a crowded nursing home in upstate New York.

It wasn't hard to look back now and see where she had gone wrong. With the eyes of experience, Angie saw clearly now that a pastor who would willingly enter into an adulterous relationship couldn't have been a true man of God to start with. At the time, all she had seen was a man who was offering her love and making her feel like she was the most special person in the world. She had been blinded to anything else. Her little world at the New Eden Community Church had been so small, and with no one to challenge her distorted thinking, the journey to this point in time had been all but inevitable. And now she sat alone at her table, friendless, a prisoner in her own home and her life in complete shambles.

Her hands twisted in anguish as she considered her options, none of which seemed possible. One thing she felt sure of, however, in the light of this new day, was that *not* taking any action would be the second biggest mistake of her life. Who knew at what point Brent would step over the line and injure her permanently? Or even kill her? That had seemed highly unlikely before, but she now knew that she couldn't discount it as a possibility, not if she was being truly honest with herself. The fact that she had not left when the violence began had given Brent a certain security that his actions could continue without reprisal. And Angie could see that, as a result, he had become more brazen in his subsequent attacks.

As the clock continued to tick in the silence of her house, Angie realized that in a few hours Brent would be home once again. Then what? Would there be a repeat? Would they slide back into the silent coexistence of the previous few weeks? It was impossible to guess. She was so afraid, but worse than that, she realized she had become the same inert woman that her mother had been — someone whom Angie had looked upon with a total lack of respect for her unwillingness to remove the both of them from the hands of a tyrant. This last realization was the thing that finally spurred her into action. To see clearly what she had been reduced to was a blow even more painful than the physical ones she had received the night before. Before she could give it anymore thought, she picked up the phone and dialed the number on the card in front of her.

Angie spent the next hour throwing as much as she could fit of her clothes into her suitcase. She made numerous trips to the car, throwing in her most precious belongings, deciding what she could live without and what she couldn't along the way. It reminded her of the time that she and her mother had been forced to leave town as a hurricane had approached. It was amazing how few things they had owned that were truly irreplaceable. Angie focused on her work wardrobe, photos, and personal files. Brent had already taken care of the sewing machine, she thought angrily.

Her first stop was the bank where she and Brent held a joint account. Angie withdrew as much cash as she felt she could without attracting attention. She then went to the new bank where she had recently opened a private account in her own name and deposited the funds. When that was done, she drove out Route 10 to the diner where she had last talked with Detective Matson. It was the place he had asked her to meet him when she had called him earlier.

She saw him way in the back, sitting at a booth by himself. Angie pulled her scarf forward in an attempt to hide the hideous bruise that covered half her face. Quickly she slid into the seat opposite him. Her hands were shaking.

"I'm glad you called," Mark began. "I just got into town yesterday." Angie didn't answer. She felt so embarrassed that she couldn't even look at him. "Angie," he continued, "There's something you need to understand. In my business, I've talked to many women in your situation. Please don't feel at all embarrassed. I only want to help you. What can I do for you?"

Finally, Angie looked up. "I don't know," she answered. "I've spent the whole morning trying to figure out what to do, and all I could come up with was the idea to call you. When you told me to pack my things and meet you here, I came. I don't have any plan beyond this very minute, I'm ashamed to say. My life has become a total mess. Just a few months ago I was a happy bride on top of the world. And now look at me." She pointed at her face.

"I take it it's not the first time," Mark responded.

"No, it's not. And I'm ashamed to say that, too. I should have left the first time it happened, but I had just gotten back from my honeymoon!"

"That day I saw you here at the diner — had you just had a run in with your husband?"

"Yes," she hung her head again, remembering that awful day. "I discovered that he had wrecked my sewing machine — all because I had dared to put it into the room of his little boy who had died. It's not like we have tons of room in that house."

"Could I ask you something about the night Brent lost his little boy?"

"I don't know anything about it. I was at my apartment. I heard about it later that night."

"Did you see Brent at all that evening?"

Angie didn't answer right away. She seemed to be trying to decide what to say. Finally Mark said, "I can't help you unless you help me. If it helps, I already know that you were seeing him at that time."

Angie's head came up suddenly; for a second there was a look of shock in her eyes. Quickly, she recovered. "I don't know what you're talking about," she said.

"Let's cut through all that," Mark said quietly. "Neither one of us has the time for it. Did you see Brent that evening?"

"Who told you we were seeing each other?" Angie insisted, unwilling to let it go.

"I'm a detective, Angie. It's my job to find these things out. Let it go at that. Now, will you tell me — did you see Brent that night?"

"He came over to my apartment," she answered solemnly.

"What time?"

"Seven o'clock, same as always."

"Do you mean that he came over every Wednesday night, or every night?" asked Mark.

"Every Wednesday night; that was when Kate had choir practice. She never missed. It was our night together." Angie was wistful, remembering when her time with Brent had been exciting, happy, and fun.

"Was he there the whole evening?" Mark asked, interrupting her memories.

"Yes...wait, no. He went out to put some gas in my car."

"What time did he do that?"

"Gosh, I don't remember."

"Well, was it early in the evening, or later?"

"I think he'd been at my place for about an hour."

"Did you ask him to go put gas in your car?"

"No. He just offered to do it. I thought it was pretty nice of him."

"How did he seem when he returned?"

"He was upset. Some guy had hit my car when he went in to pay at the gas station. But he was gone by the time he came back out. Brent felt really bad that it had happened while he was driving my car."

"Did he call the police and report the hit and run?"

"No. It wasn't that bad. He said it would be more trouble than it was worth."

"Did he offer to have it repaired?"

"Yes, of course."

"*Did* he have it repaired?"

"Well, actually no. That was the night his boy drowned and all hell broke loose around here after that. Later on we never seemed to get around to it."

'Besides your car being struck, was there anything about Brent's demeanor that night that seemed unusual?"

Angie thought back. It had been so long ago, it was hard for her to remember. Kate's plunge into the lake had forced most other memories out of her mind. After a moment she said, "Now that I think about it, he did seem a little restless. That's why I think he went to buy gas. He just wasn't in the mood for anything else that night, if you know what I mean." Angie looked a little embarrassed at her admission, and then was struck by something. "Why all these questions about that night?"

Mark leveled his gaze at Angie and asked another question, "Do you think Brent is capable of murder?"

"No!" she protested but quickly realized that was one of the reasons that she was sitting here in this diner right now. In a dejected voice, almost inaudible, she continued. "Yes, I do." A chill ran down her spine.

"There's someone I think you should talk to," Mark said. Angie immediately froze. Could this be a double cross? Was Mark a friend of Brent's? Wild fear flashed through her and she thought about bolting for the door. Mark could see the panic in her eyes and quickly said, "Don't worry, I can assure you that I'm not about to compromise your safety."

"Who is it?" she asked, relaxing somewhat, but still on alert.

"Kate," he answered. "There is no one in this town who understands your current predicament better than her."

Chapter 34

Kate waited nervously in the Laundromat next to the diner. She flipped through a magazine as if she was waiting for a load of wash to be done, hoping that no one she knew would come in. It wasn't likely, but anything was possible, and she wished Mark would hurry up and call her. She had been through the same magazine five times now.

When the call finally came, she jumped at the sound of it. After the quick call she gathered up her purse, got up, and walked the short distance to the diner. They were in the back, exactly where he had told her she would find them. The whole thing was a bit awkward, but she had agreed and would do her best. She sat down next to Mark as he made room for her.

"Hello, Angie. It's been a long time," she said, as evenly as she could. It was hard not to think about this woman's part in the breakdown of her marriage.

"Hi, Kate," she responded, not meeting her eyes.

"Well, I gather by now you know a lot more about Brent than you did when you married him," Kate said.

"Yes," Angie answered, her hand resting against her bruise in an attempt to hide it.

"Do you still believe all the lies that he probably told you about me?"

"I — I don't know what to believe anymore," she answered honestly. "Nothing is like it's supposed to be, that's the only thing I'm sure of."

Kate felt a pang of sympathy for Angie. The woman was caught in the same web she had been caught in, no matter how she'd gotten herself into it. "I could probably sit here and describe your life with Brent word for word: the long, cold silences, the 'public' face of affection and cheer, the withdrawal of love and affection, and the times when his rage boiled over and found its mark. How am I doing?"

Angie nodded silently. Kate decided to be brutally honest with her. "Look, Angie. It's no secret that I feel betrayed by your affair. But if I'm being truly candid with you, I have to say that things weren't any good before you ever entered the picture. Was I depressed? Sure, to some extent. I felt about the same way you feel right now. The difference between you and me is that I had Jackson. He was the love of my life. Every wonderful feeling I experienced came as a result of having him for a son. That is why I was able to stay in that miserable excuse for a marriage. Brent would never have let me take him away. I knew that."

"Then why did you put him in the car and drive into the lake?"

Kate wanted to strike the woman for her question, but someone had already beaten her to it. Looking at Angie's bruise she immediately felt guilty about her reaction. "It was an accident," she said as calmly as she could.

"But there were no skid marks at all. You didn't even try to stop!" Angie said accusingly.

There was an element of anger seeping into Kate's voice as she answered, "Why would I willingly endanger the only person who brought such incredible joy into my life?"

"You read about it all the time," Angie said. "Women go nuts. It happens."

"It didn't happen to me," Kate said icily. She looked at Mark as if to say, why are we having this conversation?

Mark took his cue and entered the conversation. "Angie, the whole point is that you need to be asking yourself right now what Brent is going to be saying about you when he realizes that you have left him." It was as if a light bulb turned on in Angie's brain. Immediately she realized the similarities between hers and Kate's experiences.

"Wow, I never thought about it that way," she answered. She remembered how Brent had painted Kate to be such an unstable woman, capable of anything. She had felt so sorry for him, having to live in that situation. Now she realized for the first time that she would undoubtedly be a victim of the exact same treatment. She also saw that the person sitting across from her now in no way fit the description that Brent had provided of her. In fact, if anything, Kate was doing an admirable job of controlling herself in the midst of Angie's accusations. "I'm sorry," Angie said. "I had no right to say those things to you, Kate."

"It's okay, Angie. This is a real low point in your life. I understand that." Kate's eyes softened and the anger that she had been holding a minute before left her. She continued, "That was the whole reason that Mark wanted me to meet with you. He felt that if you could talk to someone who had been on the receiving end of the same treatment by the same man, it might help you to stay firm in your decision to leave. At any rate, it would be harder for you to rationalize a reason for going back for more of the same. Brent is not going to change, Angie, and you're not the reason that he is the way he is. Once you see that, you will understand why you have to protect yourself."

"Kate is right, Angie," Mark chimed in. "This is a very important moment in your life. What you do or don't do right now will have a huge impact on your future happiness. The fact that you agreed to leave is a good start. It's the first step in getting your life back."

"What's next?" Angie asked. She felt like she'd been in an accident of her own and she couldn't think straight.

Mark answered. "I've contacted a women's shelter, and they are preparing for you right now. It is completely secure. No one can get to you there. You can remain there until you are able to make more permanent arrangements. They can also provide you with the kind of counseling that you need right now to deal with this."

Relief flowed through Angie. "How can I ever thank you?" she asked and meant it.

"You can file a police report and get a restraining order," Mark advised.

"I don't know about that," Angie said fearfully. "Brent would go absolutely ballistic, and to make things worse, Sgt. Davenport is a friend of his."

"Let me take care of that," Mark said. "And if I'm right, Brent is going to go ballistic anyway, so you might as well be protected when he does."

It all made so much sense to Angie. The trauma of the past twenty-four hours was starting to turn into a plan, and she felt better already. She was going to need to be strong. And she was going to have to come clean with her boss, Hank. He needed to know what kind of threat she was under. She just hoped that it wouldn't interfere with the good relationship that they had established, but something told her he would be very understanding.

As they stood to put on their coats, Angie put her hand on Kate's arm. "I'm so sorry for everything that happened to you," she said. "And I'm sorry for my part in it. It must have been terrible for you." She was genuinely remorseful, and Kate was touched. Angie went on, "It's hard for me to believe that you would be willing to help me after what I've done to you."

"I've learned some important things recently about reaching out to others. A very wise old lady has helped me see how life-changing that can be." She winked at Mark. He smiled knowingly in return.

Chapter 35

This was by no means Mark's first visit to the Careytown Police Department. He had introduced himself on his first trip out. It had become clear to him right away that the general consensus within the department was that Kate had gotten away with murder. They based this on three things: the absence of any skid marks on the car's path down to the lake, Pastor Brent Reed's information about Kate's mental frame of mind, and Sgt. Davenport's personal belief that Brent's integrity was without question regarding his statements to the police.

As Mark parked the car he turned to Angie. "I think it's best that you go in and make this report on your own."

"Why?" Angie asked in alarm. "They won't believe me. I know how Dave Davenport feels about Brent. He'll tell Brent right away, and then Brent will come after me. It's not that big a town. How long do you think I can stay hidden?"

"Angie, they have to file a report if you make the accusation. They don't have any choice. It's routine procedure. Besides, you have visible evidence to support your accusations, and probably medical too. I've seen the way that you hold your arm against your ribs and wince in pain. I wouldn't be surprised if they find out you have some broken ribs. I just don't think it wise to link my investigation of Brent with your complaint. They are two separate things. The last thing you need is for the department to think that you and I are trying to build a case against Brent together."

It was not something that Angie wanted to hear, but she understood. "I'm scared," she admitted.

"That's understandable," Mark answered. "Any woman would be. But you've got to believe that you are doing the right thing. The only way that men like Brent continue to get away with these things is by women suffering in silence and in fear. It's up to you to break the pattern, Angie. You're the second woman that we know of who has suffered at his hand. If you don't stop him, there might be more."

She knew he was right, but now, sitting in front of the station, she realized that this was going to take a kind of courage that she had underestimated when they had talked about it back at the diner. Her instincts were to run and hide, and Mark was asking her instead to put her dirty laundry out into the public square. There was a cold knot of fear in the middle of her. "What are you going to do?" she asked.

"I'm going back to the hotel. This will probably take quite awhile. When you are finished, call me on my cell and I will come back and pick you up. If you run into problems, call me as well."

There was such an odd mixture of emotions competing within her. Fear, embarrassment, anger, and dread played like unruly children in her mind. She opened the car door and painfully climbed out. "I'll call you," she said.

When Mark arrived back at the hotel, Kate was waiting. She was happy to see him. As he walked in she found herself once again admiring his rugged good looks, and a shiver of excitement involuntarily traveled through her. This was something that was happening all the time.

"How did it go?" she asked, revealing nothing of her inner thoughts.

"I dropped Angie off," he said. "She'll call me when she's done."

"I thought you were going to walk her through this," she said, surprised.

"I thought better of it. I don't like the way they've got their minds made up about Brent. They already know I'm checking into your case, and I didn't want to cast any shadows on Angie's situation."

"That's probably wise. I've heard that Dave Davenport has a lot of influence. In his eyes, Brent can do no wrong. I can't imagine how he's going to handle Angie's accusations."

"Well, we know one thing for sure. He's not going to be able to say they didn't happen. It should be interesting."

"What now?" Kate asked.

"You need to get in touch with Archie Dean," Mark said. "Ask him to meet with me, and ask him if he will tell me everything that he knows about your accident."

"Where do you want to meet him?" she asked.

"At the diner; it's where he wanted to meet the first time." Mark pulled out his cell phone and selected the number of the church that he had programmed into his phone. After asking for Archie he waited while they went to find him. Finally, he was on the phone. Angie heard Mark say, "Hello, Mr. Dean. It's Mark Matson. I'm back in town and there is someone who wishes to speak with you." He handed his phone to Kate.

"Hello, Archie, this is Kate," she said. She could tell by the long pause that he was surprised to hear her voice after all this time. When he finally responded, she asked him if he would help her out by meeting with Detective Matson once more. Archie hesitated. "There are people standing next to you aren't there?" Kate asked. When he said yes, she asked, "Can you meet at the diner on Route 10 today? Please, Archie, I need for you to tell him everything you know. You name the time, he'll be there. And Archie," she paused for a second, "This would be a great help to me. I really need you. Will you do it?"

His answer came quickly, "Five thirty," he said and then the call abruptly ended.

Kate gave the phone back to Mark. "Five thirty," she said with a grin. "He was long winded today!"

"I knew he couldn't turn you down," he said, then added, "How could anyone?" Kate smiled at the compliment, at the same time wondering what, if anything, it implied. Mark looked at his watch. "Angie is going to be tied up for a while with photos, statements, and medical evaluations. That should give me enough time to meet with Archie. If I leave now I can be there a little ahead of him."

"Do you want me to come?" Kate asked.

"No. I have no idea what he has to tell me, and I don't want him holding anything back because you're there. If he wants to see you, we'll set up another meeting." Mark still had his coat on. "I'll see you later."

After Mark left, Kate decided to get rid of the chill with a hot, leisurely soak in the tub. She had been eyeing the nice Jacuzzi in her room since she had checked in. As the tub filled Kate pulled off her layers of turtleneck, sweater and jeans and put on the white terry cloth robe that was hanging in the closet with the name of the hotel embroidered on the front. She turned the radio on and found a channel with soothing music. It was good to have a little down time in the midst of all that had happened.

When the water was at the right level, Kate lowered herself into the steaming liquid and immediately felt her muscles begin to relax. She rolled a towel and placed it behind her neck, and laid back, eyes closed. The first thing to enter her mind was Mark, and she realized that he had actually never left her thoughts. There was no denying that she felt a very strong attraction to him. And she thought that he was attracted to her, but she wondered — could she be imagining it? Since their intimate moment at the cemetery, he had been all business. Maybe she was allowing herself to make more of this than was actually there. After all, she reasoned, they had connecting rooms, and in the twenty-four hours they had been here, he had never attempted to take advantage of that situation.

Kate thought she had better be careful with her emotions. How could she be sure of anything right now? Thrown back into the place where her whole world had come crashing down not all that long ago, it would be easy to become confused about almost anything. She reasoned that she was going to have to find a way to stop thinking about him all the time. That was going to be very hard to do when they were together so much.

With all the discipline she could muster, Kate shut Mark out of her thoughts. When all thoughts of him were gone, she was surprised to find her mind flooded with thoughts of Jackson. Overanalyzing, she wondered if she was using Mark to keep from thinking of the terrible things that had happened to her in this place. This was not working, she realized quickly. Even when she deliberately put him out of her mind, he returned through a back door!

For the first time since she had left the cemetery, she allowed her thoughts to linger on her little boy. Driving by the house that morning, she had been reminded of so many things: the little picnic that the two of them had shared in the back yard under the old oak tree, Jackson's gleeful shrieks as he splashed in the inflatable wading pool during his last summer, and his inspired efforts at building the lopsided and very short snowman the following winter. Her tears fell into the water and became one with it. For a moment, she imagined that she was actually bathing in a collection of the sum of all her tears shed for Jackson. If only she could see him and hold him for one more minute, one more second!

The all-too-familiar ache traveled down her empty arms, and suddenly the water wasn't made up of tears any longer, it was now lake water and she was frantic in it. She got out quickly and pulled the drain knob.

After drying off, she put her robe back on and curled up on her bed. Through the sheers at the window she noticed that darkness had fallen and the street lights were casting an eerie glow through the curtain. She suddenly remembered what Mark had told her about Jackson's room — how Angie had said that Brent had kept everything exactly as it was when Jackson died. She would give anything to go back in time and stand in that room — to touch his toys and sit on the side of his little bed as she had every night before he went to sleep. Maybe for just a moment she could pretend that he was just away, that he was coming back soon. The longer she thought of it, the stronger her desire grew. She would find a way to do that, she decided, no matter what. Exhausted from her spent emotions, she fell into a troubled sleep.

Chapter 36

Archie Dean arrived at the diner at exactly five thirty. Mark was seated at the same booth in the back that he and Archie had shared at their first meeting, only this time, Mark had the seat facing the room. He met Archie's gaze as the man walked toward him.

"Thanks for coming," Mark said as Archie seated himself. "I took the liberty of ordering you a cup of coffee."

Archie nodded and took a sip, no cream, no sugar. "Where is Kate?" he asked.

"She's at the hotel. I don't know what you have to tell me, but I wasn't sure it was something you wanted to share in front of her."

"Why is she in town?" Archie asked.

"I asked her to come," Mark answered. "I think there is more to what happened to her than anyone knows. To be honest, I thought you might be willing to tell me what you know if the request came from her. She's a fine woman and she deserves to know the truth. You might be the only person who can help us answer the questions that we have."

"She was there," Archie said flatly.

"She doesn't have any memory of what happened right before she went into the water," Mark explained. "I don't know if she ever will be able to recover those memories, so I'm doing the best I can to piece things together through other means."

"I told you before, I don't want to lose my job," Archie stated.

"If my hunch is correct, I don't think that is going to be an issue for you," said Mark.

"I can't pay my bills on your 'hunches'," Archie replied.

"You're right. But there are times when we're called to do the right thing no matter what the consequences are. I believe this is one of those times." There was a heavy silence between the two men. Archie continued to drink his coffee. The waitress appeared, topped off their cups, and left. Mark broke the silence by asking, "How are things at the church?"

"Pastor's wife quit. He's got a new girl workin' there. He likes 'em pretty."

"Why do you think his wife quit?"

"Trouble in paradise, I reckon."

"What do you think about the possibility that what happened to Kate might in some way happen to Angie, too?"

"*She* deserves it!" Archie spat.

Mark leaned back in his seat. This was not going to be any cake walk, he realized. He leaned forward once again and put his finger tips together, his arms resting on the table top. "As much as you think Angie deserves that, I think Kate deserves to know the truth about what happened to her and her son. And I think deep down, you agree with me."

"She's a nice lady," Archie conceded but left it at that.

"But not nice enough to make any sacrifices for," Mark added. Again, the silence descended upon them. Archie stared down into the depths of his coffee mug. Mark decided it was time for a different tactic. "Are you aware, Mr. Dean, that it is a crime to obstruct justice and withhold evidence?"

Archie looked up quickly. "What are you talking about?"

"What I'm talking about is the fact that if you have information about a crime and don't provide it, you're obstructing justice. It doesn't matter if you are protecting a person or a job. It's still the same thing."

Archie's fingers tapped nervously against the side of his coffee mug. He seemed to be trying to decide how to respond. When he didn't say anything, Mark continued, "When it all shakes down — and it will, it always does — do you want the authorities to be looking at you as the man who protected a possible criminal or as a man who helped bring him to justice?"

"I've had that job for twenty years," Archie said. "I don't know nothin' else."

Mark stared hard into the man's eyes and said, "That little boy had his life for only two years, Mr. Dean. Sometimes it's not all about us." This time, Mark let the silence hang between them.

After a very long pause, Archie sighed and then he began to speak. "I had to go back to the church that night 'cause I had forgotten to reset something. When I drove by the front of the church, I was surprised to see Angie's car parked partway down the block. I parked in the back like always and let myself in with my key. There wasn't anyone in the office, just the choir people singin' in the church. I don't know what it was, curiosity I guess, but I went downstairs and to the front of the building and stood in the dark and looked out the basement window. That's when I saw him."

"Saw who?"

"I didn't know at first. He was dressed all in black and was down under Kate's car, like he was some kind of grease monkey. I figured he was just fixin' somethin'. I stayed there at the window and watched 'til he crawled out from under. That's when I seen his face. It was Pastor Reed. He was lookin' around like he didn't want no one to see 'im. He shoved some kinda tool in his pocket and hotfooted it down to Angie's car. Then he drove off."

"What time was this?"

"It was about half past eight."

"What time did choir practice end?"

"I finished what I was working on about ten after nine, and when I came up from the basement it was all dark. I stopped hearin' footsteps up there about nine."

"Which way did Mr. Reed go when he drove away?"

"Toward the bridge."

"Why didn't you come forward when you heard about the accident?"

Archie scratched his head, almost like a nervous habit rather than trying to alleviate an itch. "When I seen what they was sayin' about Kate I knew there'd be nothin' but trouble for me if I talked. Looked to me like Pastor Reed had the police department in his hip pocket. Still does."

"Do you have anything more to add?" Mark asked.

"One more thing." Archie took a large swig of coffee, draining his cup. "I went out front of church the next day, where Kate's car was parked the night before. There was stuff in the street. I wiped some up with a rag and took it downstairs. It was brake fluid."

"Are you sure that's what it was?"

Archie looked insulted. "I been working on machines since I was a kid — all kinds. I know brake fluid when I see it."

"Do you still have that rag?"

"I'm sure it's down there somewhere."

"It's very important, Mr. Dean. It's evidence."

Archie looked at Mark soberly. "It's the first time I told this to anyone. Sayin' it all out loud, I don't know, it sorta makes me see that I shoulda said somethin' a long time ago." He pulled out a graying handkerchief and blew his nose. "Please tell Kate I'm real sorry I let her down — real sorry." He hung his head.

"You can make it up to her," Mark said.

"How's that?"

"Give a signed statement to the local police. It's what they'll need to reopen this investigation."

"I'll do it."

Mark threw down a couple of bills on the table top. "Come on, Mr. Dean, follow me down to the police station. We need to take care of some unfinished business."

Archie smiled as he got up, a faint one, but a smile nonetheless. It was the first time Mark had ever seen the man smile. He looked as if a heavy burden had lifted from his shoulders. "Kate will be proud of you," Mark said. Archie nodded and followed him out.

Chapter 37

It had been a very long afternoon for Angie. After filling out copious forms and answering numerous questions, she had been taken to the hospital for an evaluation of her injuries. She learned that she did, in fact, have two broken ribs. Now, with her chest taped tightly, she was being escorted back to the police station. It was past dinnertime, but she wasn't in the least hungry. The whole ordeal had removed her appetite. Having her bodily injuries photographed from all angles had made her feel like nothing more than a piece of evidence, and she didn't know how to process the truth of that.

As she walked back into the entrance to the police station, she was asked to wait as there was one more officer who wished to speak with her before she left. Tired and achy, she sat down and waited. She felt sad and uprooted, her anger replaced by a feeling of hopelessness. There was nothing at all that she could think of to look forward to, and she didn't remember ever having that feeling before.

As she picked at some lint on her coat, Sgt. Dave Davenport walked up to her. "Angie?" he said. She looked up and her face fell. Why had she been silly enough to believe that she could have avoided this meeting in such a small police department? Instinctively she put her hand up to hide her bruising but quickly realized that it was a useless gesture and let her hand fall to her lap. Dave sat down next to her. Quietly he said, "I've been reading your statement. I just don't understand how this could have happened."

"That makes two of us," she said in a small voice already weary of too many questions.

"But we're talking about our pastor," he said. "A good man; it doesn't make sense. Are you sure that you're not protecting someone else?"

Angie turned and gave him a withering look. With a voice dripping in sarcasm she said, "Yeah, it was really Santa Claus, and I didn't want all the kids to be disappointed."

"Look, Angie, I don't mean to offend you. It's just that it's my job to ask unpopular questions sometimes."

"Dave, it's been a rotten month, a horrible week, and a very depressing day. If you don't have anything important to say, I want to go home. Oh, wait. I can't do that, can I?" The edge of sarcasm still lingered in her words.

The door opened and a gust of cold air washed over them. They were both surprised to see Mark and Archie walking in. At the sight of Sgt. Davenport and Angie, Archie hesitated until Mark put his hand upon his shoulder and guided him forward. The sergeant stood up. "Detective Matson, what brings you to town?" He glanced with curiosity at Archie.

"Sgt. Davenport, this is Archie Dean, maintenance man for the New Eden Community Church. We need a word with you. It's important." Archie's face was a mixture of apprehension and confusion as he looked first at Sgt. Davenport and then at Angie, her face bathed in a nasty bruise, looking the worst he'd ever seen her. He looked back at Mark with a frown but said nothing. Angie stared at her hands lying in her lap.

"Come this way," Sgt. Davenport said, gesturing toward the door to an office. He turned to Angie, "I'm sorry. We'll have to talk another time."

As Archie followed Sgt. Davenport into the office, Mark looked back at Angie, pointed to his watch, and shrugged.

She mouthed the words, "It's okay. I'll wait."

With the door closed behind them, the men seated themselves in the sparse office furnished with a table and four chairs. "What's this about?" Sgt. Davenport asked.

Mark began, "As a fellow detective, I know we can have real strong feelings about a case, and sometimes from out of the blue, some new evidence surfaces that forces us to change our whole premise. This is one of those times, Sgt. Davenport. What Archie is about to say is something that you're not going to want to hear, but when you do, it is going to change how you view the case of the drowning of Jackson Reed."

Sgt. Davenport looked up at the ceiling. It wasn't exactly an eye roll but as close as his professional demeanor allowed him. He sighed. "We've been over this ground before, Detective Matson. Remember, this is our town. We've got a pretty good idea of what happened here."

"Hear him out, Sergeant, please," Mark said. He nodded at Archie and the man began to tell his story of that fateful night. As he did so, Mark watched the sergeant's face carefully, but he was a seasoned officer and gave no hint of what was going on in his mind. When Archie had finished, he took out his handkerchief and mopped his brow. He was clearly uncomfortable.

Sgt. Davenport sat for a moment and then asked, "Mr. Dean, do you have some kind of grievance against Pastor Reed?"

"No sir, he's just my boss." He leaned forward and added, "And I ain't lyin' if that's what your tryin' to say!"

With his arms folded across his chest and leaning back in his chair, Sgt. Davenport ignored the remark and asked casually, "Are you sure there's been no incident that might make you want to seek revenge against the man?"

Archie's face was getting red, "No!" he said emphatically. "I do my job and stay out of everybody's way. That's what I've done there for twenty years." Mark remained silent, knowing better than to interrupt a fellow officer during questioning.

Sgt. Davenport pushed on. "Let me put this question another way, Mr. Dean. Has Pastor Reed ever done something that made you really angry?"

"Yes, sir."

Sgt. Davenport leaned forward, an eagerness in his voice as he asked, "And what was that?"

"He cheated on his first wife with that hussy sittin' in the other room," he pointed toward the door, "the one he married next! And him supposed to be a man of God!"

"And who told you that piece of gossip, Mr. Dean?"

"No one. I seen it with my own two eyes."

This time there was a discernible register of surprise on the face of Sgt. Davenport. "When and where did you see this alleged indiscretion?"

"In the church, after hours, about a year before Kate's car went into the lake."

"How do you know you weren't mistaking what you saw for something else?"

Archie had an exasperated look on his face. "I maybe don't have no fancy diploma, but I sure as hell know when two people are gettin' it on!"

"Mr. Dean, I find it strange that you didn't come forward with all this information right after that car went into the lake. What do you have to say about that?"

Archie sank back into his chair, all his outrage seemingly deflated by this one question that penetrated his conscience. He stared at the table top for a moment and then spoke, "I was just plain scared."

"Of what?"

"I knew that you and Pastor Reed was good friends and I didn't think you'd believe me. I didn't want to lose my job. And when Kate got out of jail, well, I figured there was no point. Wasn't goin' to bring that little boy back."

"What made you decide to speak up now?"

Archie crooked his thumb in the direction of Mark. "Detective Matson. He made me see that it wasn't right what I done."

"Are you prepared to sign a written statement regarding the information you provided tonight?"

"Yes sir."

"Well, we'll get it drawn up. Please have a seat out front while I speak to Detective Matson."

Archie nodded, got up from his chair, and with his hand on the doorknob he paused and looked into the eyes of Detective Davenport. "Can I ask one question?" he said.

"Of course," Sgt. Davenport replied.

"You believe me?"

Sgt. Davenport looked away from Archie as if he was trying to retrieve some formulated response designed for questions such as this. Finally, he glanced at Mark who was watching him intently and turned back to look at Archie. Slowly and silently he nodded his head up and down.

When the door had closed behind Archie, Mark was the first to speak. "I know this has not been easy for you to hear."

"You got that right, detective."

"Call me Mark, please."

Sgt. Davenport nodded. "Uh, Mark," he said, scratching his chin, "with all that's transpired today, I've got no alternative but to make the recommendation to the chief that this investigation be reopened."

Mark exhaled, visibly relieved. "I'm glad to hear you say that. I've been doing some searching on my own, and all signs point to Brent Reed being far different in reality than the image he projects to the public." He added, "You may want to question Kate. She'll tell you that she suffered physical abuse while married to him. In light of what you've seen today of the current Mrs. Reed, it fits as truth. With Brent's affair, and his position as pastor, he's got motive."

"That affair is just one man's word against a clergyman."

"If you question Angie Reed, I think you'll find that she corroborates Archie's story."

The sergeant appeared to be still reeling from the turn of events. "But he would never try to harm his only son," he protested.

"Agreed, but it's my opinion that he expected his son to be at the babysitter's that night. The sitter cancelled at the very last minute, after Brent had left the house. Kate made the sudden decision to take the boy with her to choir practice, something she'd never done before."

"But what about all the people who supported Brent's claim that Kate was deeply troubled and severely depressed?" His brows were drawn together as if he was trying hard to put together a puzzle.

"I believe Brent is probably a classic narcissist, and as such, he's a master manipulator. He knows what to say and when to say it to achieve the responses that he wants. Kate was definitely deeply troubled by the state of her marriage and her life as a battered wife. But the one thing that kept her going was her love for her son. That boy was the center of her life."

"How do you know so much about her?" Sgt. Davenport asked.

"She's been in the employ of my grandmother, as a nurse. I've had a chance to get to know her over a period of time. In reality, she doesn't line up with any of the things Brent said about her; quite the contrary." Mark sat up straight in his chair, running his fingers through his hair. He continued, changing the subject abruptly, "How soon do you think we can get a warrant to check out that car at the bottom of the lake?"

Dave Davenport smiled wryly, "One of the benefits of living in a small town is that everyone knows everyone else." He pulled a cell phone out of his pocket and pushed a couple of buttons. He spoke into the phone, "Charlie, Dave here. Can you get a crew together to pull a car out of the lake tomorrow? Yeah, it's pretty deep and it's been there a long time. Yep, that's the one. Thanks, buddy. See you then." He flipped the phone shut with a smug smile. "Try that in the big city," he said.

Mark wanted to ask why they hadn't brought the car up right after the accident, but he felt he knew the answer to that was a pure and simple rush to judgment, and it didn't make Dave look good. There didn't seem to be any point in putting him back on the defensive just when Mark needed his full cooperation. He stood and stuck out his hand. "Thanks, sergeant. It's been a big day. I appreciate what you've done here."

"Call me Dave," he replied, shaking Mark's hand. "I'll call you in the morning when I've got things set up."

"What about Brent?" asked Mark.

"I'll call him in first thing in the morning. His wife has filed a complaint against him. Boy, I'm sure not looking forward to that." He shook his head once and went on. "After we get the warrant and forensics gets a chance to go over that car, we can decide how we want to proceed. Now I've got to finish up with Mr. Dean. Could you send him back in?"

"Sure," Mark said as he fished a business card out of his pocket, handing it to the sergeant. "See you in the morning." When he stepped into the outer area, Archie and Angie were sitting as far apart as possible. Angie's head was resting against the wall and her eyes were closed. He walked over to Archie. "You need to go back in there. You've got paperwork."

Archie stood up quickly. "What happens now?" he asked.

"You'll sign a statement and then you can go home. Tomorrow you'll go to work just as you do every day."

"But what about…?" he stopped short of saying Brent's name as he glanced at Angie.

Mark put a hand on his shoulder. "I don't think we need to be as concerned as we were earlier. I want you to know how much I appreciate your help. It makes all the difference." Archie nodded and went back into the small office.

With a slight tap on her shoulder, Mark woke Angie. "Let's go," he said. "Sorry about keeping you so long." He helped her to her feet and they walked to the car. "Do you want to get something to eat?" he asked.

"I just want to crawl into bed," she answered, "and forget that this day ever happened." They rode the rest of the way in silence. When they reached the safe house, Mark thanked her for her courage and waited until she had gotten safely inside before he drove off. When he arrived at the hotel, he imagined that Kate might be upset that he had worked through the dinner hour and hadn't called her. Instead, when he peeked into her room he found her sound asleep. He quietly turned her lights out and returned to his room. He was actually relieved that he didn't need to talk any more about this case tonight. Morning would come soon enough.

CHAPTER 38

The clock read six thirty when Kate awoke. The room was still dark. She didn't remember falling asleep or pulling a cover over herself. She was still in her bathrobe, and a strong hunger pain shot through her, reminding her that she had slept through dinner the night before. As she lay there, she stared at the gray dawn outside her window. Soon the parking lot lights would be going off and the noise of traffic would resume. Her resolve from the night before was still strong within her. She would go and see Jackson's room one more time, allowing herself that most precious stolen moment from the past, but she wouldn't tell Mark. Instinctively she knew he would not want her to go.

Quietly, she dressed for the day in warm slacks and a pullover sweater. Fishing her keys out of her purse she checked them and was relieved to see that her old house key was still on the ring with the others. She only hoped the locks had not been changed. On the pad at the desk, she scribbled a quick note to Mark: *I'm taking a little time to see some familiar places. Don't worry about me — I'll call you later. — Kate.* She slipped the note under their connecting door and walked out. It was way too early for her to go the house. She knew Brent would not leave for work until at least seven thirty and she needed to make sure he was gone. She also needed to call a cab, but first she would take care of the hole in her stomach.

An I-HOP was just two blocks down from the inn, and she walked there. When her plate of pancakes arrived, she attacked them hungrily. As she ate, many thoughts came and went in her mind. First and foremost was her eagerness to just be in Jackson's space once again. To see his things, feel his blanket, and to pretend for just a moment that time had stood still, that she hadn't taken him to choir practice that night and that nothing awful had happened. She knew it was a crazy idea, that it wouldn't change a thing, but all the same, she couldn't resist it.

Being in Careytown after such a long time away was surreal. The businesses and streets were the same, the trees and parks unchanged, but she was the exception. Kate knew that because of what had happened here, she was forever changed.

She had left this small town a shattered person, all of her dreams of a happy marriage and the joys of motherhood left at the bottom of a lake. In their place had lain a barrenness she had never experienced before and the burden of new fears. Her heart had been cold, her reputation destroyed, and her future bleak. But she realized as she sipped her coffee that she had returned a stronger person.

For that, she knew she had to thank Beulah and Dee — both women of great insight who were at completely different places in their lives. Because of them, she knew she was able to have the courage to return. And because of them, she had the courage to walk back into her past and face it head-on with a strength she hadn't realized she possessed.

Kate checked her watch and found that it was already eight o'clock. Outside she noticed some people waiting for a bus, and that gave her an idea. Instead of calling a cab, she could take a bus. She wasn't pressed for time anyway, and she didn't mind changing buses in mid-town. It would give her a chance to see more of the place. She paid her bill and walked out to join the group at the bus stop.

When Dave Davenport finished with the morning staff briefing, he walked back to his desk and sat down. He had been putting off this phone call since he arrived at work, but it was time. He picked up the phone and dialed the New Eden Community Church. When Amy answered, he asked for Pastor Reed.

"Pastor Reed here."

"Hi, Brent, this is Dave," he said and then paused a bit awkwardly. "I uh, we need for you to come in and chat for a bit."

"What about?" There was an edge to his voice.

"Well, it involves Angie," he said. "She's filed a complaint against you for assault."

"That's ridiculous, Dave! She fell down the back steps! I was there, I saw it. She was mad at me for working such long hours, and she flew out the back door in a rage. I guess she's just trying to get back at me or something."

"Well, that's what we need to talk about. So why don't you come on down to the station."

"Look, I've got a lot going on here, Dave. I can't leave work just because Angie's got some wild hair. She'll simmer down. I'm beginning to realize I don't have the best track record when it comes to choosing women. I had no idea Angie was so unstable until we were married. Suddenly she was getting riled at the smallest of things. I've tried to deal with it, but lately she's been really hard to manage." His voice dropped to a quieter tone, as if he was trying to not be overheard, "Dave, I recently had to let her go from her job here because she was so difficult. I let everyone around here think she quit, but that wasn't how it was. And that really made her angry. Now what's it going to look like for me if I get dragged down to the police department? You've got to help me out here, Dave. You understand how women can be."

"I'm sorry, Brent, but we've got procedures to follow. A complaint has been filed and I can't just toss it in the wastebasket like it doesn't exist. You're going to have to deal with this."

"Where is she, Dave?" he asked, the hard edge back in his voice.

"I don't know," he answered. There was silence on the line for a bit.

"What happens if I don't come right now?"

"Look, Brent, I called you as a courtesy. I'm giving you the opportunity to come down here on your own," Dave answered. "I didn't have to do that."

"Isn't there something you can do, Dave?" Brent pleaded. "You realize what could happen if anyone believes Angie? I could lose my position. I'll never be able to repair the damage this could do to my reputation. You've got to make her understand what she's done here."

"Brent, are you coming or not?" Dave asked, allowing some irritation to seep into his voice.

Finally Brent responded, "I've got to go back to the house and pick up something, then I'll be there."

"Good, see you then." Dave hung up the phone with a heavy sigh. He took out his cell phone, selected a number and hit the Send button. "Charlie? It's Dave. How's it going with the retrieval?" He smiled, "Good, it won't be long now. Call me when you've got it out. Thanks." He put the phone in his pocket.

As Kate got off the second bus, she had a block to walk before she reached her house. The neighborhood hadn't changed at all. The same modest homes with their roomy porches were lined up along the streets just as before. The trees were bare of their leaves which allowed her to have a better view of the homes and she suddenly realized that the people in the homes would have a better view of her, so she quickly drew her scarf closer to her face.

The bus had driven past the church on its way to her old neighborhood, and she had been relieved to see Brent's car parked out front. She was glad not to have to abort her mission. Kate had a feeling of anticipation as she neared the back door, almost as if she expected to see Jackson but she chided herself for her momentary lapse into pure make-believe. There was no one about, and she slipped her key into the back door lock. She was relieved to see that it still worked. Upon entering, she noticed that her cheery blue and white curtains had been taken down and not replaced. There was a cup of cold coffee sitting on the counter next to a plate with a small piece of what was once a bagel, obviously the remains of Brent's breakfast.

Although this was a house that she had lived in for a number of years, she felt out of place here now. A small shiver ran through her as she remembered the tension of living in these rooms, remembered the icy silence that was her life with Brent, and the unexpected bouts of violence that left her feeling so helpless and afraid. It was as if the walls themselves were speaking those memories back into existence. She kept her coat on and walked down the hall, eager to enter Jackson's room.

She opened the door and stepped inside. Unlike the rest of the house, this room looked exactly as it had the night she had taken Jackson to choir practice. Even the sheets hadn't been changed. She went around the room and touched every surface as if trying to connect with some other time. She was surprised to see there was no dust on anything. On his bed was the red, furry Elmo that always made him laugh. She picked it up and held it to her face. As she set it back down she wondered how many times she had bent over this bed and picked up her little son, his outstretched arms raised to her. How many times had she stroked his back as she tried to get him to sleep? Her eyes glistened with tears as she stood in his little timeless world, absorbing and reliving her times with him.

So absorbed was she that Kate did not hear the sound of a car door shutting. It was not until she heard the sound of the back door opening that she was abruptly shaken from her reminiscences. A burst of adrenalin shot through her, giving her the signal to flee, but she had nowhere to go. Who was it? Could it be Brent? But why would he be here this time of the morning? Maybe it was Angie, coming back for some things. Oh, how she hoped that was it.

Kate had left the door to Jackson's room open and now she knew she couldn't walk over and close it without making noise. The house was just too small. She had no choice but to hug the wall and hope that whoever was here would not notice the open door. Her heart pounded. She heard footsteps and realized they were too heavy to belong to a woman. Her heart sank.

Chapter 39

After finding Kate's note, Mark headed down to the front desk at the inn to pick up a package that was waiting for him there. On his way down, he struggled with the fact that he didn't know Kate's whereabouts. He hadn't had a chance to tell her what he had learned from Archie the night before, and he now believed that if Brent discovered she was in town, she could very well be in danger. He had tried to call her cell phone, and it had gone straight to voicemail. He doubted that she had simply forgotten to turn it on. More than likely, whatever she was up to, she wanted to be alone.

A manila packet was waiting for him, and Mark was glad to see it was from Kevin Hughes, a friend of his in law enforcement. Kevin owed him a favor, and Mark had called it in, asking him to do some in-depth background investigation on Brent Reed. It had taken some time, but he was thankful it had finally arrived just when things were heating up.

Taking a seat in the small café at the inn, Mark ordered breakfast and then opened the packet. He carefully read through all the material Kevin had compiled. There was a significant amount of material to wade through. When he was done, he realized that the New Eden Community Church had not done their homework when they hired Brent to be the pastor of their small church. He wasn't surprised, however. He had sat in that same church and listened to the man as he had charmed the congregation. It was easy to see how they would have accepted him immediately. His striking good looks and charisma, coupled with his keen knack for manipulation, could have easily influenced the committee to forego normal screening procedures.

Among the facts gathered together by Kevin was the proof that Brent had never actually received the degree in theology that he claimed to have been awarded. In fact, there was never any record of him having been a student at that university or any university, for that matter. In addition to that, there were charges of physical abuse by a former girlfriend which were later dropped. Going farther back, it was noted that Brent had spent several years in foster care before he was adopted at the age of ten by the Reeds, a childless, church-going couple of modest means. There were reports of the Reeds having great difficulty with him when he reached adolescence, coming close to returning him to foster care at one point.

Mark finished the last of his breakfast and put the papers back into the manila envelope. He knew one thing for sure — he had to find Kate and let her know what he had learned. And he had to share this latest information with Dave Davenport. Mark paid his check and walked out to his car. Just as he got in, his cell phone rang.

"Matson here," he responded.

"Hi, Mark, this is Angie," the caller said.

"Good morning," he answered. "I hope you're feeling better today."

"Yes, I decided to go in to work. I do most of my work sitting at a desk anyway, so I might as well sit here and get paid instead of sitting in some safe house."

"Makes sense," Mark said.

"Anyway, Mark, when I got to work this morning, I remembered something that my boss told me the day I interviewed. He said he knew Brent because he had taken out a life insurance policy on his wife the very day that Jackson drowned. I thought that was odd since Brent told me he was planning on divorcing her soon. Why would he have done that?"

"Good question, Angie. Thanks for calling me with that. Do you think you can find out how much the policy was for?"

"Sure, I'll look it up and get back to you."

"Thanks," Mark said. He put his phone back into his pocket. In the ten minutes it took him to get to the police station his phone rang again. It was Angie.

"It was $250,000 dollars," she said, aghast.

"Thanks Angie," he said. "I've got to go." He hurried into the building. He found Dave Davenport at his desk.

"Good morning, Dave," he said, as he took a seat in the chair facing the desk. "Have you talked to Brent Reed yet this morning?"

"Morning, Mark. Yes, I'm afraid he tried everything to get out of coming down here. According to him, Angie fell down the back stairs after showing indications of unstable behavior since their marriage."

Mark rolled his eyes. "Sound familiar to you?" he asked.

"Unfortunately, yes."

"I've got something you'll find interesting," Mark said as he placed the manila envelope down in front of Dave. As he began to look over the pages, Mark filled him in on some of the highlights. Dave skimmed the documents as if he couldn't believe what Mark was telling him. Finally, he put the papers down and said, "I'll be damned."

"There's something else too. Angie just called me and told me that Brent took out a life insurance policy on Kate for $250,000 on the day of her so-called accident."

Dave looked like he'd seen a ghost. "Who is this guy?" he said, running both hands through his hair, a look of disbelief on his face. "None of this seems to fit with him. How could I have gotten it so wrong?"

"He's just very good at it, Dave," Brent said. With a note of urgency in his voice he continued, "Kate left a note under my door this morning that she'd gone off by herself to look around town. She doesn't know any of this stuff, and I think we need to find her fast." Mark's voice was filled with concern. "Is Brent coming in?"

"An hour ago he said he was coming in. He said he had to get something from his house first. In light of what I've just learned, I'm wondering if he's coming in at all. To get to his house from the church, he had to cross that bridge. He couldn't help but see the retrieval operation that's been going on out there. I don't like the smell of this." Dave reached for the phone and dialed the New Eden Community Church. "This is Sgt. Dave Davenport. Is Brent Reed, still there?"

Amy Woodhouse replied, "Pastor Reed is not in."

"When did he leave?"

"Can I take a message?" she asked, avoiding the question.

"Look, Amy, this is police business. You need to tell me what time he left and you need to tell me now."

"Oh," she said, startled. "He left an hour ago. What's this all about? What's happened?"

"Thank you, Amy," he said, hanging up. He looked at Mark. "I was afraid of this. We need to go out and find him. If he's still at his house we'll be lucky. I have a hunch he's planning on running now that he's seen that we're going after that car."

Mark dialed Kate's cell phone number and again it went to voicemail. He hoped desperately that she was nowhere near Brent Reed. He left a message, detailing that Brent was considered dangerous and she should call him right away when she received the message. Dave grabbed his coat and the two of them headed out in his cruiser.

"Are you armed?" Dave asked.

"Yep," Mark answered.

"Good. No telling what'll happen today." They didn't waste any time getting in the car and pulling out of the lot. They headed in the direction of Brent's house.

Chapter 40

Kate held her breath as the footsteps became louder. Just outside the door to Jackson's room, they stopped for a moment. Then they continued on toward the master bedroom. She heard a drawer open and close, then the footsteps coming closer again. She was across the room from the closet and there was nowhere to hide. She could feel the panic rising within her, and she fought it desperately. She needed to keep her wits about her.

Brent slowly peeked around the edge of the door. Immediately he saw Kate standing against the wall. A look of total surprise came upon his face but he quickly recovered. "What are you doing in here?" he asked, his voice hard.

Kate left her place at the wall and faced him from across the room. "I..I wanted to see Jackson's room one more time," she said, trying not to sound as frightened as she felt.

"And what made you think it was going to look the same as it did?" he asked. "Maybe you've been talking to Angie? You two are alike you know — you're both crazy and nothing but trouble." There was something different about Brent today that she couldn't put her finger on — a new level of intensity that she did not recognize.

He took a few steps closer to her, his eyes more menacing than she'd ever seen them. He was wearing a red button down shirt and black slacks. Kate watched him carefully. She had a fleeting feeling that she might pass out, and she took a deep breath to steady herself. Her mind was whirling, trying to think of some way to get out of there, and she could see she had no options. Brent stood between her and the door.

In the frenzy of thoughts that raced through her brain, she suddenly saw something flash through her mind. It was the red of his shirt below that menacing glare that must have awakened that missing piece of her memory from the night of the accident. She saw it all unfolding in her mind with total clarity. As she had approached the bridge, a red car had suddenly darted out from the left side of the road, from a place where there was no road, and blocked her path. She had tried slamming on the brakes, but nothing happened to slow her down. Frantically pumping the brakes, she was almost upon it when for just an instant, she had seen Brent's face glaring at her from within the red car. In a panic, she had swerved to the right to avoid hitting him, and she had almost made it. At the last second, the front left of her car had hit the red car, and her head had hit something. The next thing she remembered was waking up in the water. The blood drained from her face as her mind, running at warp speed, grasped the full import of this revelation. She was standing before the very man who had tried to end her life, and no one knew she was there. How could she have been so stupid to have come without telling Mark?

"You look like you've seen a ghost, Kate. It's only me," he said as if he was trying to get her to drop her guard. But Kate would never be fooled by his wiles again. She knew very well that she was in grave danger.

"I've accomplished what I've come for," she said as evenly as she could manage. She kept her hands firmly on her purse so that he couldn't see how she was trembling. "I'll leave now, Brent, and you'll never see me again."

"Not so fast, Kate. I don't think I can let you go this time." He came a few steps closer again, as a cat would that was toying with a mouse. "I noticed they're bringing your car up out of the lake this morning. I guess you weren't satisfied that you killed my son. You had to come back and make more trouble, didn't you?"

Any hope Kate had of feigning ignorance was now gone. It didn't matter anymore what she remembered. The car would tell the tale and Brent knew it. She tried again to appease him. "I mean no harm to you, Brent. I only wanted to touch Jackson's things one more time. Please, let me pass." She started forward but he stood his ground. From behind his back he brought forth a handgun and aimed it directly at her. She caught her breath in an audible gasp. "Brent, please. You don't want to do anything crazy. Think about what is happening here. Just let me go out the door and this will be over once and for all."

Brent came forward and grabbed her by the arm. With his other hand he shoved the muzzle of the gun into her ribs and forced her to walk with him to the kitchen. "Lie face down!" he ordered. He shoved her to the floor. Her purse went skidding under the table. "Don't even try to make a sound." She obeyed. Fear gripped her in an iron vise, and she found it hard to draw anything but a shallow breath. While she was down, her cheek pressed against the cold linoleum floor. Brent pulled a drawer open and withdrew a roll of duct tape. First he taped her hands behind her back, and then he taped her mouth. He then grabbed her arm and pulled her up. With the gun still in her ribs, he forced her to walk back to the bedroom. Again, he pushed her to the floor. While she watched in panic, he pulled a suitcase out from under the bed and began to fill it with clothes. When he had finished, he pulled her up once more and led her to the back door. He taped her ankles so that she couldn't walk, and then he left her there, taking his suitcase with him.

As she lay there, she hoped and prayed that he would just leave, but soon she heard the sound of his car engine and realized he was bringing the car close to the back door. He came in again and picked her up. She struggled violently, but he had an iron grip on her. Quickly, he walked down the steps and threw her body into the trunk, slamming the lid. As she winced with pain, she heard his car door open and close, and then she felt the car moving. He was going to finish the job this time, she thought with despair. And no one would ever find her. Brent would make sure of that.

In the total blackness of the trunk compartment, Kate prayed for the first time since Jackson had died. "Oh, please, God. I need you! Help me! I was so angry at you, but I know that you didn't take Jackson — Brent did. Please, please help me!" Tears flowed freely down her face. She could feel their wetness in the darkness. She grieved for Jackson, for her mother and dad, and for the future she wasn't going to have. She thought also of Mark, and right now she ached for his calming presence and his strength. She would never have a chance to tell him how she truly felt about him, or thank him for finding the truth for her. But she would see Jackson soon, and that soothed her heart.

CHAPTER 41

As they passed the approach to the bridge, both Dave and Mark were happy to see that Kate's car had already been brought up and was being loaded onto a flatbed trailer for transport. "If Brent passed by here, which he would have had to do if he went to his house, then he certainly saw what was going on," Mark said.

"Are you thinking what I'm thinking?" asked Dave.

"Yeah, he's a definite flight risk." Mark took out his cell phone and tried again to reach Kate but still had no luck. They continued on across the bridge and into the neighborhood where Brent's house was. Mark was quiet, consumed with concern for Kate.

When they arrived at the house, they found no car in the driveway. Both officers got out, and Dave approached the front door while Mark went around to the back. There was no answer to Dave's knock. The back of the house was in the shade of some tall trees, and there were still large patches of snow on the ground. Mark noticed right away that there were tire marks in the snow directly behind the back porch steps, as if someone had backed a car onto the lawn just recently. He noticed also two sets of footprints. They both led from the driveway on the side of the house to the back steps. One set was small, most probably a woman's. The other set belonged to a man, probably a size eleven or so.

Dave walked up to Mark. "There was no response at the front door. It looks pretty quiet in there."

Mark studied the ground. "He was just here. Look at these." He motioned toward the tire tracks. "Something's not right," Mark continued. "The woman's prints go in, but they don't come back out. Yet we have his prints going in and out a couple of times, and from the pattern, it appears that he stopped at the back of the car."

Dave squatted down to get a closer look. "Do you think they're Kate's?" he asked.

"Hard to say," said Mark. "She does have a pair of running shoes like this, but so do a lot of women." He was trying hard to make himself believe it wasn't Kate, but his gut was telling him something different. Dave avoided the snow by jumping onto the back steps. He tried the door. "Hey, it's not locked!" he said.

What they saw when they entered the kitchen sent chills down their spines. A typical "junk" drawer stood open and a roll of duct tape lay on the counter. They silently drew their guns and went room to room, hoping desperately that they would find a woman alive and taped, waiting to be rescued. But that did not happen. The closet in the master bedroom was open and it was obvious that clothes had been removed. A drawer in the nightstand was hanging open.

They retraced their steps back to the kitchen. Something under the table caught Mark's eye. It was a purse — not just any purse; it was Kate's. All of his attempts to convince himself that Kate had not been here this morning had just ended. He felt a knot of fear in his stomach. He checked the contents. There didn't appear to be anything missing but her cell phone. He knew that she often carried it in her pocket and he hoped she could find a way to use it. If she was still alive.

"He's got her, Dave," Mark said with finality. "We've got to find him. He can't have gone too far yet."

Mark had barely finished his sentence when Dave started for the door. The two got back into the cruiser, and Dave got on his radio immediately as he pulled out of the driveway. Once he got the plate number, he asked for an APB to go out with the information on a suspected kidnapping. He also asked for a team to go to the house for the collection of evidence.

"You know this place, Dave. Where do you think he's headed?"

"Well, he was in Baltimore before he came here, so my guess is he might head back to some place familiar." He paused for a moment and then said quietly, "We don't know what his immediate plans are for Kate, but we can safely assume that he's not intending to let her talk to anyone ever again."

Mark lay his head back against the head rest and closed his eyes. This was not routine police work any longer. All the stakes had changed for him when he found Kate's purse. The thought that she was in the hands of that man right at this moment, and he was helpless to change that, was almost more than he could bear. That he had brought her back to Careytown was something for which he would never be able to forgive himself.

Dave looked over at him. He said softly, "I don't mean to get personal, but I take it Kate might be more than just a friend?"

Mark opened his eyes and sat up. "I've been trying to pretend she's just a friend for quite some time as I've worked this case. I don't believe in mixing my business and my personal life." He looked away as he continued, "But I can't pretend any longer. Dave, we've got to find her!"

Dave was silent for a while and then he said, "I'm thinking Brent's first instinct was to put a lot of distance between himself and Careytown. That will buy Kate some time."

"You're probably right," said Mark, a spark of hope igniting in his eyes. "It only makes sense." With all his might, he forced himself to push his emotions aside as much as possible, knowing he wouldn't be much help to Kate or Dave otherwise. He pulled out his cell phone again and tried Kate's number. Again, it went to voicemail. He would not give up, he decided.

Chapter 42

It was pitch black in Kate's mobile prison. She tried hard not to let panic take hold of her as she struggled to accept the fact that she was going to die very soon. She wondered how he would do it. She wondered if anyone would ever find her, and she wondered if it would be quick, or if he would make her suffer. These were strange new thoughts, and they seemed almost other-worldly, yet she knew that the gravity of her situation was all too real.

As she lay there in the blackness, she suddenly heard a voice in her head say, "Think, Kate. Don't give up!" She wondered if her mind was playing tricks on her because of the stress. She tried to keep calm. The voice spoke again, clearly, "Think, Kate. Don't give up!" In an instant she realized this was a voice of truth; there was hope in it, and she needed to listen. While she had been lying there alternately paralyzed by fear and trying to figure out how she would meet her end, she had been losing valuable time in considering what, if any, options she might have to try and save her life. She would obey.

The very next second she remembered her cell phone. She had put it in her pocket right after she had gotten dressed. With her hands bound behind her back she found that if she twisted her body just right she could reach into her side pocket. Carefully, she used her fingertips to slide the phone out. She had just gotten the new phone a few weeks ago, and she was thankful that she had taken the time to learn the features. Kate found that she could accomplish a lot just by feel. First she rolled onto her back and kept it beneath her as she turned it on, muffling the tell-tale chime that sounded. She couldn't dial 911 she realized. There was no way for her to find the right numbers on the new screen. But she hoped that there might be an incoming call. It was a small hope, but it was a hope.

It seemed like miles and miles of road had passed beneath her. She was doing her best to think of anything that she might be able to do to help herself. When thoughts of death came at her, she refused to entertain them. If it came, it would come soon enough. She didn't need to live it ahead of time.

She couldn't tell how many minutes had gone by since she had turned on her phone, but she felt she was probably on an interstate now because there had been a steady rate of speed for quite some time. In her mind, she continued her fervent prayers, the only thing she was able to do. Suddenly she was startled as her phone began to vibrate in her hand! Quickly, she opened the connection and just as quickly realized that she had no way to acknowledge that she was on the line. Tears of frustration and despair came to her eyes and then she heard the command again run through her mind, "Think!"

Kate had no idea who was calling her. She hoped with all that was within her that it was Mark. With her fingernail she tapped on the voice intake portion of the phone: three quick taps, three long taps, and three quick taps again. She waited a few seconds and then she repeated it. She kept her phone line open. Over and over she repeated the sequence.

Chapter 43

Mark listened intently to what he was hearing on his cell phone. After a moment it was unmistakable. "Kate's alive," he said. "She's tapping out an SOS!" Dave smiled broadly. This was good news indeed. Mark continued excitedly, "She's got one of those new phones. I think it has GPS in it."

When Dave heard that, he wasted no time getting on his radio and getting the tracking set up. Mark kept his end of the line open, and Kate continued to send her coded plea every few seconds. It didn't take long to locate her. The radio dispatcher announced, "Subject is headed north on I-95, about thirty minutes south of Baltimore."

"Get a chopper in the air right away!" Dave told her. "Alert all ground units in the vicinity!" Dave put his siren on and picked up his speed considerably.

"Your hunch was right," Mark said. "And they aren't more than ten minutes ahead of us!"

"Not for long!" Dave replied with fresh excitement in his voice.

Chapter 44

Kate continued to tap her message. Like a robot she focused on this simple message, hoping it would make a difference, hoping there was still a line open. Above the road noise she thought she heard a faint sound of a siren. She strained to hear and it got louder. Suddenly, she felt the speed of the car increase and the driving was no longer smooth and straight. She felt the car swerve first one way, then the other. Her heart pounded as she realized Brent was being pursued. The siren was louder now, and it sounded like there was more than one. A new fear crept into her mind — would she end up in a fiery crash on an interstate?

Her hopes for a quick rescue began to dim as the car continued to increase its speed. She felt her body slide wildly inside the trunk, as much as was possible in the cramped space. Kate pictured Brent weaving in and out of traffic. She knew how desperate he must be at this point. His entire house of cards was falling down around him.

It wasn't long before Kate heard the unmistakable sounds of a helicopter overhead. She felt the car begin to slow a bit and then felt it turn. He must be getting off the interstate. The car slowed almost to a stop and then sped up again. There was a lot more weaving, some horns honking, and the sounds of screeching brakes. Still he kept going. The helicopter stayed overhead. She felt lots of turns, and once she was jolted as the car must have jumped a curb. She was relieved to still hear the sirens.

The wild ride continued, and Kate felt the longer it went on the more desperate Brent would become. She knew him very well. He was not a man who liked to lose — at anything. She curled up in a fetal position. It was the only thing she could think of to do. Her terror was real. This was like the worst ride she could ever imagine in an amusement park, only this was far from amusing. It was life or death.

Just as she was thinking that she couldn't take it anymore, she heard a sudden screech of tires and felt a tremendous impact that sent her body slamming against the side of the trunk interior. The sound of ripping and tearing metal, at first so loud, grew quickly dim as a sharp pain coursed through her body sending her into the silence of an inky blackness.

Chapter 45

Kate remembered only bits and pieces of her journey to the hospital. Bright lights, strange sounds, concerned voices, and sirens all blended together into an unpleasant hodgepodge as she had drifted in and out of consciousness. X-rays, scans, and busy people in multi-colored scrubs became part of the blur of activity that surrounded her.

It wasn't until late that afternoon that the pain in her head abated somewhat, and she was able to think with any kind of clarity and make sense of what had happened to her. As she was wheeled in and out of an elevator and along the corridor toward her own hospital room, she tried to piece together the events of the morning. The more she thought about it, the more she understood that the violent car crash she had endured had probably saved her life.

When her bed was wheeled into position in her room, she recognized immediately the tall, handsome man standing against the wall waiting for her, a wonderful smile spread across his face. Mark — what a wonderful sight! Immediately she was infused with a sense of great relief, and she could feel the tension in her body diminish. As soon as the orderly departed, Mark came to her side and took her hand warmly and held it between both of his.

"Kate," he said, "I'm so thankful that you are going to be all right!" She could see the depth of concern in his eyes.

"I am?" she asked, not sure of anything at this point.

"You've got a concussion, some cuts, and a dislocated shoulder, and you've got a lot of bruising, but nothing life-threatening. They're only keeping you overnight because of the concussion."

"I feel like I've been run over by a truck!" she said, feeling aches from all parts of her body at once.

"Well, almost," Mark said. "Brent ran a light and one of those big muscle trucks T-boned him. If you had been sitting in the car, you would've been gravely injured. As it was, the impact was far enough forward of the trunk compartment that your injuries are largely from being tossed against the walls of the trunk. Because it was such a small space, it kept you from being hurt worse than you are."

"What happened to the truck driver?" Kate asked.

"He was pretty shook up and he's got two broken legs, but his air bag saved him from a much worse fate. He's a young guy. He'd just driven his brand new truck off the lot not twenty minutes before impact. Talk about rapid depreciation!" Mark grinned.

There was a silence as the question that was unspoken hung in the air between them. Finally, Mark said, "Brent's in very bad shape, Kate. He's in the ICU. He has internal injuries, a broken shoulder, arm, and leg, several broken ribs, and no movement or feeling below the waist. They aren't sure if he is going to make it through the night."

A bag of mixed emotions spilled through Kate all at once — relief, anger, and sorrow to name just a few. Mark waited while she sorted through them. Finally, she spoke, her voice low, "I can't believe he wanted me dead, Mark. I tried to be what he wanted me to be for such a long time. Whatever my shortcomings were — they can't have been so huge that I deserved to die!" Tears came spilling from her eyes as the tumult of emotions from the day began to converge upon her. She couldn't stop them. As her shoulders shook from her sobs, she felt fresh pain and her head throbbed.

With a strong but gentle hand, Mark stroked her brow. With his other hand, he held her hand firmly, as if trying to send his strength into her. "You're going to be okay, Kate. It's over now. He will never be able to hurt you again. Everyone in Careytown is going to know that you were a victim of a heinous crime. I will see to that." He leaned over and kissed her brow softly. Slowly, her sobs subsided and she felt spent, as if all her strength had spilled out of her through her tears.

"I don't know how to thank you, Mark," she said as she looked up at him with raw emotion. "If it weren't for you, he would have gone on hurting people, and I would have gone to my grave carrying the responsibility of Jackson's death."

"I can think of something," he said, lightening the mood with a playful smile.

"What?" she asked, "I'll do anything. Just name it."

"Marry me," he said, his expression earnest and ardent.

Kate was stunned and more than a little confused. "You shouldn't joke about a thing like that, Mark."

"I can see how you would think that," he answered thoughtfully. "I've been trying to keep my emotions at bay for quite a while. I just didn't want them to interfere with what I was trying to accomplish on this case." He looked down for a minute and then continued, "But more than likely, that was just an excuse not to fall in love and risk getting hurt again. This morning, when I realized that Brent had taken you and that your life was in danger, it all became crystal clear for me. When I thought I might not ever see you again, I couldn't ignore the fact that I am in love with you, Kate, and I have been for a long time. And I don't want to waste another minute of our lives running away from what is going to be the best part of our lives. I promise you a real courtship — one without the burden of all that we've been dealing with. Take all the time you need. I'm not going anywhere, at least not without you!"

There were tears at the corners of his eyes, and Kate knew he had never been more truthful to her than he was at that moment. Her heart was flooded with warmth and the feeling of a hope fulfilled. Her tears ran freely once again, but they were tears of pure joy. Kate reached up and pulled him toward her. It hurt but she didn't care. As he leaned in close to her, she whispered in his ear, "I love you, too, Mark. And yes, I will marry you." Softly and tenderly, so as not to hurt her, he kissed her on her lips — a gentle but unmistakable kiss that carried with it a heart full of love and promises of good things to come.

Chapter 46

The following morning, Angie stood outside Kate's hospital room and deliberated about whether or not she should go in. Ever since she had received Mark's call the day before about what had happened, she had been shaken to the core. By rights she knew that she was probably the last person Kate wanted to see, and yet she felt that the two of them would somehow be forever connected by their association with the man that lay so grievously injured just one floor below.

A nurse came out of Kate's room. When she saw Angie standing outside, she smiled and said, "Are you here to see Ms. Reed?"

Angie was startled at first to hear her own last name, a name that had been hers for such a short time. "Uh, yes," she said.

"Well, she's awake. You can go on in."

Angie took a few tentative steps inside the room and stopped. She saw that Kate was sitting up in bed, and she was relieved to see that she was smiling. A breakfast tray was on the rolling table positioned over her lap, and she was buttering a piece of toast. A look of surprise flashed momentarily across her face. "Hello, Angie. Come on in," she said as if the two of them saw each other every day.

"I — I didn't know if I should show my face here or not, Kate," she gestured toward her black and blue bruises and continued, "and I mean that in more ways than one."

Kate laughed. "Well, I'd say that right now we are the only two members of a very exclusive and not very popular club."

"You're right, Kate, and that's why I'm here. I just had to see you before you left town. When Mark filled me in on what happened, I guess I was in shock for a while. I kept going back over the night that your car went into the lake, and everything just fell into place."

"What do you mean?" asked Kate.

"Brent was just so different that night. It was like he was restless or something. He couldn't relax. And then he wanted to go fill my car up with gas, which he'd never offered to do before. I thought it was nice, but it still seemed strange. And then when he came back and said there was a scrape on the front fender and someone had run into him, he was really agitated. I thought at the time that he was upset because of what had happened to my car, but now I know the real reason. Oh Kate, when I think of what he tried to do to you, it sends chills down my spine."

"I'm still grappling with it, too, Angie. I didn't remember what really happened that night until yesterday when Brent came in and surprised me at the house. Seeing him in that red shirt triggered my memory of his face looking right at me as he sat in that red car blocking my path. Of course he'd seen to it that I had no brakes and had no choice but to swerve, sending me onto that downhill path into the lake. If only I could have remembered that right away. Things might have been so different."

"Kate, the reason I came here was to tell you how sorry I am for creating this whole mess. I've had a lot of time to think about things in the last twenty-four hours. I didn't sleep hardly at all last night." Angie looked down, struggling to find the right words. There were tears at the corners of her eyes. "If it hadn't been for me, none of this would have happened to you. Your little boy would still be alive now. I don't know how I can live with the knowledge of what my actions have done."

"Angie, don't — ," Kate began, but Angie interrupted her.

"No Kate. Let me say what I came here to say. I knew it was wrong — the whole time. And still I kept on with it. I told myself that because he was a pastor it must be okay — that you really were a miserable wife, and he needed me to help him deal with all that. Can you believe I was actually proud of myself that I had found a good man? Not a man like my father was, but a pastor! I wasn't going to repeat the mistakes that my mother had made." She shook her head with scorn as she continued, "Instead I made an even bigger mess with far more at stake. An innocent little boy is dead, and you're lying here in a hospital bed. You will always have to live with your loss, and I will always have to live with the fact that it's my fault." She dug in the pocket of her coat for a tissue and wiped her eyes. "I'll go now." Her voice quavered as emotions took hold of her, "I'm so very sorry — that's what I need for you to know." She turned and began to walk away.

"Wait! Don't go," Kate called after her. Angie stopped and turned, her eyes two dark pools of misery, lost in the bruises that surrounded them. "Please, Angie, come sit down."

Hesitantly, Angie walked back and sat on the chair next to Kate's bed. She kept her head down, wearing her feelings of shame like a heavy cloak. Kate pushed her tray table away from her and said, "Thank you for coming here. I know it wasn't easy. So much has happened to both of us at the hands of this man, but we can't let him steal any more from either of us. There's something you need to know, Angie, and I've never told anyone this before." Angie looked up as Kate continued, "The morning of that fateful day, Brent and I had been arguing again. I finally told him something that I had not had the courage to say before. I told him that I didn't think I could stay with him much longer if things didn't change. I was afraid of what he might do, but I had made up my mind."

"What did he do?"

"He just looked at me with a very strange look. I think he understood that I was really serious. He told me that leaving was not an option."

"But that doesn't make sense," Angie blurted. "He kept telling me he wanted out of the marriage."

"What Brent really wanted, Angie, was to keep the power of his position intact. I can see that now. The New Eden Community Church was his little kingdom, and he didn't want to lose his status. He loved the way people looked up to him. He put a lot of energy into making sure that they did. But in reality, he was a fraud because he couldn't apply the things he preached from the pulpit in his own life. He certainly didn't understand what love is."

"So he never did intend to end your marriage?"

"I don't think so. I think he always believed that he needed to be married, but the marriage itself was not that important to him. The idea of me leaving him and letting the congregation see he wasn't the perfect man he had created in their minds was something he wasn't about to let happen."

Angie sat back in her chair, absorbing what she had just heard. "He's sicker than I thought. How could I have been so blind?"

"Some people are very adept at knowing how to manipulate others. Brent was a master at it. I watched him over a long period of time until it made me sick — so sick that I felt that if I didn't leave I would end up sick, too. But most of all, I was afraid for Jackson, afraid that he would somehow learn those things from him." Kate paused for a moment as she thought of her son.

"Kate, that must have been so hard for you, to be carrying that knowledge for so long while everyone thought he was so wonderful. How did you manage it?"

"Not very well, I'm afraid. I was pretty miserable. I threw all my energy into being Jackson's mom. That's where I found my joy."

The two women sat silently for a moment, lost in their individual attempts to process their parallel experiences. Finally, Angie spoke, "If you hadn't come back here, I know I would have been in a great deal more danger than I ever thought possible. I'll always be grateful for your courage, Kate."

Kate laughed. "If I had known what was in store for me, I wouldn't have come!"

Angie laughed, too, and felt the tension leave her. "Every time I start to feel sorry for myself, Kate, I'm going to remember what you went through."

"Remember something else, too, Angie. Remember that just because you made some bad choices, it doesn't mean that you can't learn from them and make good choices from now on."

"It's funny you should say that. The lady at the shelter said the same thing to me. They have some counseling sessions for the women there, and they're free. I'm going to go. It's time to try and figure out why I let myself do what I did. They told me that once I understood why I was in this mess, I wouldn't have to worry about falling into the same situation again."

"Sounds like you're in the right place." Kate paused before she asked the question that had been lingering in her mind since Angie had come. Finally she said, "Have you seen Brent?"

"No. I started to go to the ICU and then I stopped. It's like he's a different person to me now that I know what he's done. I realize that I never really knew him at all. I thought I was in love with him, but maybe I was just in love with the idea of being in love. I don't know that man who is lying in that hospital bed downstairs. I doubt very much if anyone does."

"I think you're right about that," Kate said. "Have you heard any more about his condition?"

"I talked to the doctor this morning. He said that it looks like he's going to make it. But he's going to have to learn how to do almost everything all over again; everything except walk — he won't ever be able to do that again. He'll have a lot of time to reflect on what he's done, sitting in a wheelchair the rest of his life."

"What are you going to do now? Will you stay in Careytown?"

"I wasn't going to, but I had a talk with my boss yesterday after everything happened. I knew it was going to be all over town in no time and he probably should have a head's up. He was amazing — no, more than amazing. He told me that he and his wife had a little house on their property just outside of town. They live on about five acres. He offered it to me as a place to live. He said the company didn't want to lose me and he thought I was doing a great job."

"See, Angie? That's a good start on the future right there."

"You're right. I'm so glad that I went out and got that job." She stood up. "Speaking of my job, I told him I would be in shortly. I warned him what I looked like, but he said to come in anyway."

"Angie?" Kate said, "Thanks for coming. It was a good choice. See? You're already making them!"

Angie smiled. "You're a good person, Kate. I hope you find happiness."

"I already have," she answered.

Chapter 47

Three days later, Mark and Kate were on I-95 heading north toward Lake Pendant, having completed their long flight from Maryland. As the beautiful northern Idaho scenery flowed past her window, she couldn't help but compare this day with the one just a few months ago when she had been on her way to start a new life. She never would have dreamed that in that span of time, which in some ways was so short and yet had seemed to encapsulate a life time, she could have arrived at such a sense of well-being.

As they approached the Long Bridge, Mark reached over and took her hand in his. Lake Pendant stretched out before them in both directions in quiet splendor, a view unparalleled in Kate's estimation. She breathed deeply and took in the magnificent view, all too aware of the fears that had accompanied her first foray across. She had come a long way, she realized, and she was finally "home."

"Gram and Mom can't wait to see you!" Mark said.

"I feel the same way," Kate said. "I've really missed Beulah."

In no time they were coming in the front door of Beulah's large, friendly home. There were greetings all around and careful hugs as everyone watched out for Kate's shoulder. When they had hung their coats, they sat in the living room.

"Well, I guess I warned you about Mark," Beulah said, with a twinkle in her eye. "When he gets a hold of a case, he won't let it go until it's solved!" She looked with pride at her grandson. Mark smiled at her in return.

"I have a lot to be thankful for," Kate said. "Most of all I'm thankful that this whole family saw a woman in need and went out of their way to make a difference."

"Well, we're thankful to you, too, Kate." Laura looked over at Beulah and the two shared a conspiratorial smile. "In fact, Mom has a little surprise for you," she said.

Beulah sat there like the cat that had swallowed the canary as all eyes turned toward her. With a great deal of determination and effort, she placed both hands on the arms of her wheelchair and raised herself up to a standing position. She took one step forward and then another and stood straight before them, a look of pride on her face as Kate's and Mark's jaws dropped in surprise. They both leaped to their feet. "Gram, that's great!" Mark exclaimed.

All Kate could say was, "Wow," as she stared at this unbelievable sight before her. She had never seen Beulah standing upright without assistance before.

"All your tenacity about those exercises made the difference," she said to Kate. "I know I was a rascal about them, but you wouldn't let me quit, and now look at me. I'm not trapped in that chair anymore!" She was beaming. "I've got a ways to go, but I can feel it coming back more and more every day."

Kate could see the gratitude on Laura's face as she said, "Mom worked extra hard while you were away. She really wanted to surprise you, Kate."

"Well, she surely did," Kate said, a look of pure joy on her face. "After all of your fussing about how those exercises weren't doing any good! Now it looks like I'll soon be out of a job!"

Beulah took a couple of steps back and settled back into her chair. "It's high time you went from employee to granddaughter-in-law anyway," she said. "Congratulations to both of you. I couldn't be happier."

"I second that," Laura said.

"I hate to bring up a sore subject, but I'm dying to know how things ended up for Brent," said Beulah in her characteristically forthright manner.

"Not too well," Kate said. "He's a paraplegic and he's got serious internal injuries. He will remain a prisoner in his broken body for possibly a long time."

"Will he go to trial?" Beulah asked.

Mark answered, "The court has already appointed legal counsel for him, but with the sworn statements of Kate, Angie, and Archie, coupled with the evidence of the cut brake lines they found on Kate's car, not to mention the subsequent kidnapping, it's pretty clear that his days of freedom are over. If he's smart, he'll plead guilty and not go through a trial. I don't think a jury will look kindly on a man who is responsible for the death of an innocent little boy, even if he is in a wheelchair."

"What happened to those poor people at the church?" Laura asked.

"According to Dave, the leadership committee took the news pretty hard. No one enjoys being duped," Mark said. He turned and smiled at Kate. She nodded knowingly in return as he continued, "They're starting the process to find a new pastor right away, and you can bet they're going to be a lot more careful this time around."

"And Angie?" Beulah asked.

Kate chimed in, "She actually came to see me at the hospital. She looked almost as bad as I did. I could tell she was so relieved when she mentioned that Brent couldn't come after her anymore. She's decided to stay in Careytown after all. She loves her new job, and she says she's learned some pretty important things that she doesn't intend to forget, but she is looking for a new church," Kate said with a chuckle.

"Speaking of the church," Mark added, "Dave told me they're giving Archie a small bonus and a raise for his willingness to make things right. He was overdue anyway, but it made him feel great, just the same."

"Well, what an ordeal, is all I can say," Beulah offered. "It makes me exhausted just hearing about it. I'm glad it's all behind you." She was thoughtful for a moment, and then she looked at Kate in that special way she had when she wanted to probe deeper. "And what about you, Kate? How are you really? That must have been such a horrible experience to have been locked up in that car trunk thinking it was your last few minutes on this earth."

Kate smiled at Mark as she squeezed his hand. "It's not anything I would ever want to do again, that's for sure," she said,

"But at the same time, I will always be grateful for it. It brought into focus for both Mark and me what the really important things are in our lives. And Beulah, you'll be happy to know that I found my faith again in the trunk of that car."

Beulah smiled. "That's all I need to know," she said.

Epilogue

Kate sat on the deck at Beulah's home, gazing out over the water. Lake Pendant was enjoying the tail end of an unusually mild Indian summer. It was her thirty-fifth birthday and there was to be a party there for her that afternoon. Mark, her husband of four years, had planned it as a surprise but hadn't quite been able to pull it off thanks to their daughter, Jackie, who never had been able to keep a secret since she had learned to talk. Just three years old, she was inside napping while her Grandma Laura got things ready for the party.

Beulah sat at Kate's side as together they enjoyed the view. "I was just thinking about the first day you came here, almost five years ago to the day," she said. "You took one look at that lake, and your whole body just flinched."

"I remember that," Kate answered. "I almost turned right around and left, except I really needed that job."

"I'm sure glad you didn't leave," Beulah said. "It would have been our loss in more ways than one."

Kate reached over and patted her hand. "More mine than yours, I'm afraid," she said with a smile. "When I think about what you did for me, I still get choked up."

"How about what you did for me?" she answered, a twinkle in her eye. "I probably would never have gotten out of that wheelchair if you hadn't been so patient with this old lady!"

"That's nice of you to say, but we both know that you have enough spunk to have managed it either way."

"Well, thank the Lord, we never had to find out 'what if'!"

Kate shifted in her chair, trying to find a comfortable position. She was just a few days from her due date, and comfortable seemed to be something unattainable these past couple of weeks. "When I came to Lake Pendant, Beulah, I wanted to start a new life, but I never believed it could be as good as this. Mark and I have enjoyed such happiness, and I feel that I've been given a whole new family. None of that would have happened without your challenging me to face some of my fears, and without Mark's efforts, I would probably still be believing that I had been responsible for Jackson's death. No one will ever know what that has meant to me."

"And to think he started that whole investigation just to prove to me that you were a dangerous person who might poison my lunch!" Beulah chuckled.

"I'm thankful that the truly dangerous person is behind bars," Kate said. "It wasn't easy going back for that trial and having to live through those painful memories, but it did provide some closure for me."

"It would seem that Brent lives in two kinds of prisons," Beulah answered. "He's got the rest of his life to sit in that wheelchair and think about what he did. Having sat in one of those chairs for a time, I can tell you that it gives you a lot of time to think, and that man doesn't have too many good things to think about."

When Kate thought of Brent, all she saw in her mind now was a troubled soul living with the consequences of his actions. She had long ago let go of her bitterness toward him. She had realized, with Beulah's help, that not relinquishing that bitterness would have put her into a different type of prison — one of her own making. She had to admit that having a husband like Mark had made it a lot easier to do that.

"Did I tell you that Mark ran into Dave Davenport at a conference a couple of weeks ago?"

"No," Beulah answered with a grin, "But you could have, and I can't promise that I would have remembered."

"He ran into him in Dallas. Dave told Mark that Brent is making little wooden toys in prison. He's kind of like that Birdman of Alcatraz, I guess. They call him the Toy Man and he spends all of his time making those things, and he doesn't talk to hardly anyone. He's gotten really quiet for one who was such a charmer. Dave said he was a model prisoner, which I guess isn't too hard to be when you can't walk." Kate chuckled at the irony of it. She was quiet for a minute and then continued, "You know, I really do believe that Brent truly loved our little boy. I think those toys he makes are all for Jackson in some crazy way."

"You're probably right," Beulah said with a sigh. "No one is entirely good or entirely bad, but we're all made up of parts of each at any given time. Brent's love for Jackson was probably the best part of him."

"I shudder when I think of all the things that were revealed at the trial about Brent when he was growing up in those years before he was adopted. It's no wonder he was so messed up. I think he saw in our little boy a chance to somehow redo his own childhood. When Jackson died, that hope died with him."

The two women were quiet for a time, both of them looking out at the sparkling blue lake reflecting like diamonds in the early October sun. Kate turned to Beulah, "You've taught me so much," she said. "It's kind of sad that so many young people think older people have nothing to contribute. You have a lifetime of wisdom, and thankfully, you were generous enough to share some of it with me."

"Thankfully you were open to receiving it," she answered, "And someday you'll be passing it on to someone else. That's how it works." She looked up to the sky and added, "Actually, that's how He works!"

The screen door slammed, and Dee appeared with Kevin and four-year-old Katie. "Hi, Beulah! And hello, birthday girl!" she exclaimed, then put her hands up in protest as Kate tried to sit up. "Don't get up!"

"As if I could," Kate groaned.

"Happy Birthday!" Kevin said. "We got you a double stroller!"

"Kevin!" admonished Dee, "You're not supposed to tell her! You're supposed to wait until she opens it!" Katie, always shy, clung to her mother's leg and just smiled.

"Well, thank you — all of you!" Kate said. "I can really use one of those!"

"When is the baby coming?" asked Kevin.

"Just a few more days," Kate said. No sooner were the words out of her mouth than a very sharp pain hit her. She clutched at her expanded body with both hands. She had been experiencing discomfort all morning but this was a serious pain, and it definitely got her attention. As it gradually subsided, she understood what was happening.

"What is it?" asked Beulah.

"Are you okay?" asked Dee.

"I think this little party is going to turn out to be for someone else's birthday," she said, trying to catch her breath. She knew from experience that her babies came quickly. "I think I'd better get ready to go to the hospital."

Dee drove and Kate called Mark on the way. The children had stayed behind at Beulah's. "He'll meet us at the hospital; he's on his way," she told Dee.

By the time Kate was admitted and settled in a labor room, Mark had arrived. He held her hand as each pain escalated in intensity. With his other hand, he held a cool wash cloth to her forehead. For an hour he sat with her as Dee kept him supplied with fresh damp cloths. Kate's body continued with its all-important task. When she was wheeled into the delivery room he remained with her. Finally, with a great and final push, their son made his entrance into the world and took his first breath, followed by a healthy cry. As Mark cut the cord, Kate thanked God for the best birthday present anyone could ask for.

Later that afternoon, as Kate lay in her bed, the small sweet bundle in the blue blanket nestled safely in her arm, the door opened and Mark and Jackie came in. Jackie ran to her mother's bedside, her eyes wide with excitement. "Let me see my baby!" she cried, "Let me see!" As Mark held her up she reached for the tiny little hand, curled against his cheek. "Oh, Mommy! My baby is so pretty!" she said. Kate smiled at Jackie's sense of ownership of her new little brother.

"Jackie, meet your brother, Michael," she said. "His name means 'resembling God'."

"What's 'resemble' mean?" she asked with a curious frown.

"It means to be like or to look like," Kate answered.

"He doesn't look like God!" said Jackie. "God's not that little!"

Mark and Kate laughed, and Mark leaned over and kissed Kate and then kissed his son on the forehead. "Happy Birthday, Kate and Michael," he said.

The following afternoon, with Michael secure in his car seat and Kate settled in the passenger seat, they left the hospital for the trip home. Before they had gone two blocks, Kate realized they weren't headed for home. "Where are you going, Mark?"

"Gram wanted us to come by and have a piece of your birthday cake since you missed your party," he said. "I know you probably don't feel like it, but I was hoping that you wouldn't mind giving her a little peek at Michael."

"Sure, why not? I can sit down there as well as I can at home."

Beulah was beside herself with delight at seeing her newest great-grandson for the first time. "Oh my! This little fellow looks just like you, Mark," she exclaimed. "I can't believe how strong the resemblance is."

"Mommy says no, he looks just like God," Jackie offered. "So which is it?" She held up both her hands, palms up with her shoulders shrugged, clearly perplexed.

"You'll understand one day, child," Beulah said with a smile and a wink.

When they were settled in the living room, Beulah brought out cake for everyone. "Well, yesterday was the first time I ever gave a birthday party for someone who didn't stick around for cake and presents," she said. "When you feel up to it, there's a nice little pile right there waiting for you." She gestured to the little table where she usually had a puzzle going. It was piled with brightly wrapped presents and gift bags.

"Open them, Mommy! Please?" Jackie said as she ran to the pile and grabbed one.

"I'm a little tired right now, Jackie; maybe tomorrow." The little girl was clearly disappointed as she put the present down.

"How about just one, Kate?" asked Beulah. She walked over to the mantle and reached for an envelope. It had a piece of curled crinkle ribbon and a bow taped to it. She walked over and handed it to Kate.

Kate recognized Beulah's handwriting. It had gotten a little weaker in the past few years.

She opened it to find a card that was blank inside except for a personal handwritten note. Jackie was peering over her shoulder while Mark held little Michael. "What's it say, Mommy?" she asked.

In her spidery hand Beulah had written:

My birthday gift to you this year has been well thought out and I pray you will accept it. I want you to have my lake house as your own home. It is meant for the noise and laughter of children and has gone too long without those things. It is time for me to have a smaller place. Nothing would make me happier than to know the love of a family with growing children would once again fill these rooms, especially if they are my own great-grandchildren!

Happy Birthday to my friend and granddaughter. With all my love, Beulah.

Kate looked up, her eyes moist. She knew it wasn't just her fluctuating post-natal hormones that were making her cry. "Did you know about this?" she asked Mark.

He grinned. "Yes, but I was sworn to secrecy," he admitted.

Kate got up and walked over to Beulah. She didn't say a word for a minute but instead enfolded that very special lady into her embrace. Tears slipped down her cheeks.

"What's wrong, Mommy? What happened?" Jackie asked, alarmed.

"Nothing's wrong, Sweetie. These are happy tears. Great Grandma has just given us her home." She knew how much Jackie loved this lake house.

"You mean we can live here for our very own?" she asked, her eyes full of excitement.

"Yes, we can." Kate wiped her eyes and looked at Beulah. "But you said you were never going to leave here."

"Well, I know what I said, but one day I just woke up and realized that this place, as much as I have loved it, doesn't fit me right any more. It is way too big for a ninety-one-year-old lady to rattle around in."

"But you don't have to leave! You can stay here with us," Kate said. "We'd love that."

"I appreciate that Kate, but you have your own busy lives to lead. And besides, I like my quiet time. It tends to mean more as you get older, and I won't have people tip-toeing around me. That wouldn't make me happy."

"Well, what are your plans?" Kate asked.

"There's a brand new little development that the church is building over by the river, just for old folks like me. It's going to be perfect, and a lot of people I know from church are moving in there. They're small, one bedroom apartments, and there's even a central dining room where I can eat if I don't want to cook for myself. And they've got activities, too."

"Are you sure this is what you want?" Kate asked.

"As I said, I took my time thinking on it and my mind's made up."

"I don't know how we can ever thank you," Kate said softly.

"Gram, this is so generous of you," Mark added. Right then, Michael began to stir. His eyes opened and he made little newborn sounds as he stretched in his daddy's arms. "I wonder if this little fellow knows that he's home already?"

The sound of gentle laughter filled the room bringing with it the promise of much more to follow in the years to come. Kate looked around the room with its beautiful woodwork on the shelves and the mantle and its large window that let the outside in even in the coldest part of winter. Already she was picturing how she would arrange her own things in here, at the same time wondering how it could be possible that she would soon be able to call this grand old house her home. When she had crossed the Long Bridge for the first time five years ago, how could she have known that instead of running away she was actually coming home?

Carol AuClair

www.carolauclair.com